rh

PERFECT TOGETHER

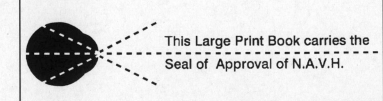

This Large Print Book carries the
Seal of Approval of N.A.V.H.

PERFECT TOGETHER

CARLY PHILLIPS

WHEELER PUBLISHING
A part of Gale, Cengage Learning

GALE
CENGAGE Learning·

Farmington Hills, Mich • San Francisco • New York • Waterville, Maine
Meriden, Conn • Mason, Ohio • Chicago

GALE
CENGAGE Learning

LIBRARY OF CONGRESS CATALOGING-IN-PUBLICATION DATA

Phillips, Carly.
    Perfect together / by Carly Phillips. — Large Print edition.
        pages cm. — (Serendipity's Finest series) (Wheeler Publishing Large Print
    Hardcover)
    ISBN-13: 978-1-4104-6399-9 (hardcover)
    ISBN-10: 1-4104-6399-0 (hardcover)
    1. New York—Fiction. 2. Large type books. I. Title.
PS3616.H454P467 2014
813'.6—dc23   2013050596

Published in 2014 by arrangement with The Berkley Publishing Group,
a member of Penguin Group (USA) LLC, a Penguin Random House
Company

Printed in Mexico
2 3 4 5 6 7 18 17 16 15 14

PERFECT TOGETHER

ONE

There was something about being a Marsden that made people think if they asked him for a favor, Sam — the younger brother and the *good* cop — would be nice and accommodating. Take how his sister-in-law, Cara, was looking at him with big, pleading eyes, fully expecting him to agree to her beyond-unreasonable request.

"There is no way in hell I'm going on a date with Margie Simpson." Sam Marsden glared at Cara, a woman he usually also called his best friend, from across their respective desks at the Serendipity police station.

"Her last name is Stinson, not Simpson, and you know it." Cara frowned back at him. "Come on, Sam. Her parents are the biggest donors for the Women's Heart Health fund-raiser, and the Serendipity Police Department is a co-sponsor. Do you want to be the one to tell the hospital, who will be the recipient of that shiny new medical equipment, that the Stinsons pulled their donation because one of our finest wouldn't escort their daughter?"

"She's more like a pit bull," Sam muttered. "And isn't there another single cop you can get to take her? What about Hendler?"

"He's too old."

"Martini?"

She shook her head. "Too young. Besides, Margie wants to go with you."

He shuddered. "All the more reason for me to say no. I don't want to give her the wrong idea." Margie was one of those women who assumed that just a look implied male interest. Sam didn't want to go there. No way, nohow.

"Are you giving my wife a hard time?" Sam's brother, Mike, strode over to Cara's desk and placed a possessive hand on her shoulder.

"More like she's giving me one. Call her off, will you?" Sam asked.

Mike laughed and shook his head. "I like my life just the way it is. Sorry, bro. You're on your own."

Sam rolled his eyes. Ever since his bachelor brother had fallen — hard — for Sam's sometime partner, Cara, he was now

8

wrapped around his wife's cute little cowboy boots — when she wasn't in uniform, that is. Where she went, Mike followed. Sam was happy for him. Problem was, Sam's single friends were dwindling fast. First Dare Barron, then Mike, and even their sister, Erin, had fallen.

Sam wasn't jealous, but he could admit that his life and the routines he'd always enjoyed were growing stale around him. But that didn't mean he was open to marriage, let alone escorting the female from hell, even for a good cause.

Cara rolled a pencil between her palms. "Do you already have a date?" she asked.

"Hell, no," Mike said, before Sam could answer. "He hasn't dated anyone in longer than I can remember. In fact, the last woman who remotely interested him —"

No, he would not let his brother go *there.* "Don't you have an office to get back to?" Sam pointed to the police chief's workroom at the back of the stationhouse.

Mike grinned. "Not when this is so much more fun."

Cara elbowed him in the stomach. "Go. I'll have more luck if you aren't here poking fun at him and making this worse."

Mike shrugged. "Hey, it's not my fault he's such an easy target."

"Now that you're happily married, you're an even bigger pain in the ass," Sam muttered.

Mike smirked and kissed his wife on the lips, lingering way too long before he finally walked — make that swaggered — away.

"Get a room."

"You too could find true love," Cara said, leaning closer. "We all want that for you."

But Sam didn't want that for himself. He'd tried, come close, and failed in the biggest possible way. As a cop, he trusted his instincts, but when it came to women? To relationships? To personal choices? Not so much.

His so-called gut instinct had hurt one good friend, and his gullibility had led to him being betrayed by his fiancée and best friend. His family knew only some of the reasons he remained wary of trusting his personal instincts, and with his siblings settled down, Erin with a husband and a baby, they'd all turned up the pressure on him.

Cara leveled him with a serious stare. "I'm not asking you to marry Margie, just accompany her to the benefit. Make nice and go home. Can you do that for me? For Mike and the police station? Please?" Cara batted her eyelashes over her big blue eyes.

She'd been his best friend long before she became involved with Mike, and he'd have thought he was immune — except now she was also his family and he didn't like turning her down. Besides, as she'd pointed out, the fund-raiser was for a good cause and he'd be representing the police force.

He blew out a disgusted breath. "You're only doing this because I can't say no to you," Sam muttered, shuddering at the thought of accompanying the one woman in town who sent fear into any single man's heart.

"Is that a yes?" Cara tapped her pencil against the blotter on the desk, her expression almost gleeful.

"Yeah," he muttered, knowing he would absolutely live to regret the decision.

"Yay!" She jumped up and hugged him tight before resettling herself into the chair behind her desk. "This is *perfect*! One huge problem taken care of. I knew I could count on you."

Yeah, perfect, Sam thought, hating that word even more than usual.

"Hey, I promise Mike and I will stick by you all night. I won't leave you alone with that leech."

Sam narrowed his gaze. "So now you admit she's a leech."

Cara didn't look up or meet his gaze, but the red flush in her cheeks gave her away. Yeah, he was a patsy for his sister-in-law and a good cause.

"You know," Cara said, peering out from beneath her long fringe of lashes, "you could avoid this whole kind of thing if you'd just —"

Find a woman of his own. "Let it go," he said in response to her unspoken words.

"Okay, but Mike's right. The last woman who interested you was —"

"Let. It. Go." Sam set his jaw.

"Fine. I won't say her name." Cara buried herself in work at her desk, but she'd accomplished her mission.

She'd brought up the one female in more than a decade who'd made Sam want to drop his guard and rethink his vow not to get emotionally involved with any woman ever again. But Nicole Farnsworth, the raven-haired beauty who'd triggered his current state of discontent, had left town months ago and she wasn't coming back.

Nicole Farnsworth packed up her clothing and the last of her things, trying to convince herself she was moving, not running away. In fact, she'd planned to leave Manhattan since deciding to end her engagement, but now instead of just the excitement of beginning a new life, she felt the dual need to flee. She closed her eyes and drew a deep breath. Nothing she could do but go — get away — and do some soul-searching, during which she hoped to find clarity. But what clarity was there when she knew she held people's livelihoods and even freedom in her hands?

The doorbell rang and she looked into the peephole, unwilling to take chances by just opening her door. She stared into the familiar if unwelcome face of her mother, who, as usual, was perfectly dressed in a Chanel jacket and wool slacks.

Suppressing a groan, she opened the door and let Marian Farnsworth inside.

Before Nicole could say hello, her mother launched into one of her typical tirades. "No sane woman breaks off her engagement to a handsome, extremely wealthy man. One you grew up with, might I remind you? He and his family are in business with your father. What were you thinking?"

Nicole walked into the family room and leaned against the nearest wall, knowing not to give her mother an edge by sitting down. "I was thinking that I shouldn't marry a man I don't love."

Her mother joined her in the room filled

with the remaining boxes waiting to be loaded into her car. She folded her arms across her chest and pinned Nicole with her disappointed stare. "What does love have to do with anything?"

Nicole did not want an explanation for that bit of insanity. It meant she'd have to look more deeply than she cared to into her parents' marriage. Instead she drew a deep breath and promised herself she'd be on her way soon.

"Nicole, it's insane to think someone like you needs to worry about a love match."

She shrugged. "You know as well as I do, sanity doesn't run in our family."

"Don't talk that way about your sister," her mother chided, always looking to hide Victoria's mental instability, as if being bipolar carried a stigma Marian couldn't bear to admit to in her family.

The irony was Nicole hadn't been talking about Victoria, merely making a not-so-subtle joke.

"Darling, you need to call Tyler and beg him to forgive you."

This, Nicole had heard before. "No." And she had more important things to worry about than her mother's reaction to her breaking her engagement. Like the illegal activities Nicole had overheard her ex-fiancé's father and his accountant discussing — and what she was going to do about them. Considering, as her mother reminded her, that the partnership of Farnsworth and Stanton Financial Investments affected both families, Nicole needed distance to study all the angles.

Such as, did Nicole's father know that his partner was accepting money from mob-connected companies and funneling that money into investments from which they all made millions? Did her ex-fiancé Tyler know?

"Nicole," her mother said, snapping her fingers in front of her face. "You're not listening to me."

"Because I have things on my mind. Like moving." Not just so she could get away and think, but so she could forge a new life where people would get to know and like Nicole for herself, not her family's connections.

Her mother's face flushed red at the reminder. It was amazing how the woman could ignore the evidence in front of her: the boxes, packing tape, and clothing covered by heavy-duty bags. "You have to reconsider. This whole situation is humiliating in the extreme. Not to mention, you have a job. Tyler's mother is running for borough president and you're her number one fund-raiser. She needs you."

"I gave her notice. My assistant is capable and ready to take over. She'll be fine."

"You'll cause a rift between the families," her mother pushed on.

Nicole stiffened, not missing the irony. Growing up, she'd sought her parents' approval and attention by being good and kind and perfect — without success. But now, when she no longer cared what her family thought of her choices, she'd accomplished her goal. Her mother was here, paying attention to her life, begging her to help them.

"The Stantons won't hold my choices against you."

"Nicole!"

"No. Stop it. I told you before. I am not going back to Tyler. I don't love him. I should have realized it long before now." And the reasons why she hadn't were glaringly obvious in light of her mother's callous disregard of her daughter's feelings.

She'd desperately wanted someone to love and approve of her, and Tyler, unlike her parents, had been kind and caring. He paid attention to her and he'd given her everything she'd yearned for in her emotionally deprived life. Unfortunately, Nicole had mistaken her gratitude toward him for love,

16

and she'd hurt Tyler in the process.

It had taken her sister's downward spiral and Nicole's resulting meeting with a sexy small-town cop to point out to her exactly what she didn't feel for her then-fiancé. Desire, excitement, the pounding of her heart every time he was near. She'd settled for less every minute of her childhood. She couldn't bring herself to do it in marriage.

Nicole realized her mother was still staring at her with frustration and disappointment in her expression.

"It's better I made the decision now than after the wedding," Nicole told her.

Marian huffed. "Just when did I teach you that fairy tales come true?" she asked in disgust.

Nicole met her mother's gaze. "You never did."

Without so much as a word, not *good luck* or even *good-bye,* her mother turned and stormed out the door.

Nicole swallowed the lump in her throat. Her mother hadn't changed in all of Nicole's twenty-eight years. But Nicole had. With this move, she wasn't looking for some improbable happy ending. All she wanted — no, craved — was a life of her own that fulfilled *her* dreams and desires, not those of her impossible-to-please family.

So she was heading to the one place where she'd found a sense of peace despite the insanity — no pun intended — that had brought her to the sleepy upstate town. She hoped that once there, she'd figure out the right thing to do about the information she'd stumbled over.

Nicole was ready for Serendipity. She just hoped the people in Serendipity were ready for her.

One of the things Nicole liked about Serendipity was its old-fashioned charm. Where else could you find a diner-slash-restaurant named The Family Restaurant? After spending the morning moving into her new apartment over Joe's Bar, she decided to eat dinner out and go food shopping tomorrow.

She sat at the counter, happy to just soak in the atmosphere, and had just finished a delicious plate of meat loaf and mashed potatoes when a dark-haired woman approached her from behind the counter.

"Wait. I know you," the woman said, her gaze narrowing.

Nicole met the other woman's concerned stare, well aware of the reason for the worry in her eyes. The one thing that had concerned Nicole about moving here was being mistaken for her twin. But the pull of the small town had been strong, and despite Victoria's actions, people here hadn't judged Nicole, at least not once she'd tried desperately to help them find her twin.

Nicole wanted to give them the same benefit of the doubt. "I don't believe we've met."

"I'm Macy Donovan. Occasional hostess, waitress, you name it. My family owns the restaurant. Aren't you —"

"Nicole Farnsworth," she chimed in quickly.

"So you're not Victoria? The psychopath who —"

"No," Nicole said, cutting her off before she could elaborate on Victoria's crimes. When her sister went off her medication, anything could happen — and had. "She's my twin."

Macy's cheeks turned red in embarrassment. "Sorry, but she hurt a friend of mine and . . . Never mind."

Nicole winced. "I expected to deal with the fallout if I moved here."

Macy raised her eyebrows. "And yet you decided to settle in Serendipity?"

"Yes, I did." She squared her shoulders, intending to communicate to Macy Donovan that not only was she sure of her decision but she wasn't about to be bullied

19

because of her sister's illness. Her twin was in a criminal mental health facility, living with the consequences of her actions.

"Listen, I'm blunt but I'm not judging you," the woman said. "Erin Marsden's my best friend, and your sister stalked her for months."

Nicole grimaced at the reminder.

"But Erin told me you helped them find where your sister was hiding out, and she said you came to town in the first place to warn her and Cole. So . . . truce?" Macy held out her hand.

Letting out a deep breath, Nicole accepted the other woman's peace offering. "Thanks." From inside her purse, her cell phone chimed, calling for her attention.

"I'm going to do a few things in the back. I'll come out again in a few minutes," Macy said, leaving her alone to take the call.

A quick look told her it was her ex-fiancé, so she blew out a breath and hit Decline. She'd explained everything in person and there was no reason to rehash things over the phone. His call only reminded her of what she still needed to deal with, but she wasn't any closer to a decision. Should she confront her father and ask what he knew of his partner's accounts? Should she ask Tyler?

She'd stood outside the office of her own father — a man she didn't know all that well, as he certainly never made an effort to spend time with her as a child — and as she raised her hand to knock on the open door, she'd *heard.* There'd been no question that she'd mistaken the spoken words.

Robert Stanton and the firm accountant had specifically said they were laundering money from the Romanovs, a father and son who were known art dealers in Los Angeles. The Russian mob, she thought, her stomach churning. Their entire business could crumble, not to mention they could all end up in prison. Her stomach in knots, she'd turned to run, but Nicole's father strode up to her at that very moment. He'd called out her name, which in turn brought Robert and Andre, the accountant, out into the hall to greet them.

The look Andre had given her chilled her even now. She told herself he couldn't possibly know she'd heard anything. But she had. Which meant she didn't need to worry just about her family and the business, but also about the men on the other side. Dangerous men.

Should she go to her father with the truth? If he already knew about his partner's illegal dealings, she wouldn't accomplish anything except to out herself. If Paul Farnsworth was in the dark, he probably wouldn't believe his daughter's word over his longtime partner's. Nicole's own mother would remain in useless denial even if confronted, and Tyler's mother's main source of campaign funds was her husband. No way would she risk using dirty money. So she ruled out her being aware. Which left the police — and she wasn't ready for that yet.

And what about Tyler? She knew he was honest to a fault. She couldn't imagine him allowing illegal dealings to go on, any more than she could envision his father involving him. He'd grown up as heir to the proverbial throne — entitled, privileged — and to his credit he rarely acted the role they'd bestowed on him. She had to assume they'd keep him squeaky clean.

But again, she couldn't rely on assumption. The unknown players were just too dangerous.

Macy picked up a towel and wiped down the counter. "So what brings you to Serendipity?"

Easy answer, Nicole thought. "A fresh start."

Macy grinned. "Because you liked it so much your first time around?"

Nicole laughed, grateful for this chatty woman and the distraction she provided. "That too. Seriously. Considering the reason I was here, the place and the people made an impact."

Macy leaned on the counter. "It just so happens that there's a fund-raiser this weekend to raise money for women's heart health. I'm selling tickets and you should come!"

Nicole hesitated; the thought of walking into a big event all alone was not something she was ready to face. "I don't know. I mean, I'm new in town —"

"All the more reason to go where you can meet people! Dates aren't required. I'm not going with anyone, so we can hang out. What do you say?"

Nicole figured Macy was right, as far as it being a good way to get to know people, and now that Macy had invited her to join her, she felt more comfortable.

Before Nicole could answer, her new friend chimed in once more. "It's for a good cause. The police department is co-sponsoring the event, and since this place is basically like a doughnut shop for Serendipity's Finest, I agreed to pimp tickets for them. Please?" Macy was nothing if not persistent, and her enthusiasm was infectious.

So was the fact that the police sponsorship guaranteed Sam Marsden would be at the event. And she'd like to see him again . . . "Okay."

"Yay!" Macy's smile dimmed. "But it's expensive since it's a fund-raiser."

"How much?"

"Seventy-five dollars."

Nicole nodded. She had a plan for her life that included opening her own bake shop, but not right away. She needed to research the area, see if it could sustain what she had in mind. Which meant she needed a job while she plotted her future. In the meantime, she had the trust fund her grandparents had left her, something that irked her parents to no end, since it meant they couldn't control what she or Victoria did.

Nicole didn't plan to blow through the money frivolously, and she'd need it for her business venture, but it did enable her to rent the apartment and cover the cost of living until she got on her feet. As far as she was concerned, getting to know people in her new town and supporting a worthwhile cause certainly fell under that heading.

"No problem." She met Macy's gaze, and the other woman smiled wide.

"Great! Oh. Another thing."

Nicole leaned forward on her arms and waited. Clearly she'd met someone in the know.

"Cocktail attire."

"Also not a problem." She'd packed up everything she owned, which, thanks to Tyler and his mother's world, included formal and cocktail dresses, but she'd kept out a few favorites.

"That was easy," Macy said.

Nicole grinned. "I try."

"So are you interested in a primer on your new hometown?"

"I'm all ears."

Macy propped a hip on the counter, relaxed and happy to chat. "Wednesday night is Ladies' Night at Joe's. You should join us — the *us* depends on who is free because there's been way too many marriages and babies lately, so the ladies and the men are dwindling. But not for you because you're new to all the men and they'll all be new to you. So you'll come to that too?"

Nicole nodded, pleased to have plans. "Absolutely."

"Great." Macy looked toward the front door and the family who'd entered. "I have to go seat people. If I don't have time to

25

talk more today, I'll see you Wednesday? Seven P.M."

Nicole smiled as the other woman headed off to do her job.

She liked Macy Donovan, and it seemed like Macy had already accepted Nicole. She hoped everyone else in Serendipity felt the same way.

As on a typical Wednesday night, Sam met up with some guys from the station at Joe's Bar. Josh Mercer had bought the current round and the jokes were flowing freely. Mike and Cara walked in, followed by his sister, Erin, and her husband, Cole.

"Looks like it's family night," Sam said, calling them over. "How did you two get away?"

Erin had had a baby six months ago and rarely left her daughter's side.

His sister greeted him with a kiss on the cheek. "Mom showed up and practically shoved us out the door. She said we needed a break and she needed time with Angel." The hazel eyes she shared with Sam lit up when she mentioned her baby daughter.

Cole slipped an arm around Erin's waist, greeting Sam with a nod. "She's already called home twice to remind your mother about the time of her next bottle and what to do if she cries."

"Like she didn't raise three of us?" Sam teased his sister.

"Funny," Erin said to her brother. "And *he*" — she poked her husband with her elbow — "already called Mom to make sure she had our cell phones on speed dial."

Sam still couldn't believe they'd gone from his sister getting pregnant after a one-night stand with Cole Sanders, undercover cop with no intention of remaining in town, to being a happily married couple and overly concerned parents.

"All my favorite people are here!" Sam turned at the sound of Macy's voice.

Erin spun and gave her best friend a hug.

"How is that adorable goddaughter of mine?" Macy asked.

"Cute as ever." Erin beamed.

"Hon, want to go get a drink?" Cole asked her.

Erin nodded.

"Anyone else want anything?" Cole asked.

"I'm good," Macy said.

"Me too," Sam added.

Erin and Cole walked toward the bar, leaving Sam alone with Macy. She was his sister's best friend, so he was used to her being around.

"Hi, Macy. How are you?"

"Hi yourself." Her smile, as usual, was infectious. "I'm good. Busy as usual. You?"

He shrugged. "Same old."

She shook her head, her long dark hair falling over one shoulder, and sighed. "You so need to get laid."

Sam rolled his eyes, not surprised by her outgoing ways. In addition to her blunt manner, she was beautiful, sort of exotic, her Italian heritage showing through. If she hadn't been like family, he might have looked twice — until she started busting his balls, that is. She wasn't for him, but no doubt she'd give some guy a run for his money.

She glanced around, a frown furrowing her eyebrows. "Where's Nicole?"

Sam whipped his head around to meet her gaze. "Who?" He had to have heard wrong. That or it could be another Nicole. It was a common enough name.

Macy scanned the crowds before refocusing on Sam. "You probably know her? Nicole Farnsworth, the stalker's sister? She's new in town and renting the room over Joe's. I invited her to meet me here tonight." Macy glanced at her watch, and her concerned expression turned to a frown. "She's late. You haven't seen her, have you?"

Sam expelled a harsh breath. Nicole had

moved here? Months of thinking about her and she was now as close as upstairs?

"Maybe she's uncomfortable, not knowing anyone . . . and considering I mistook her for her crazy sister at first . . . I should go check on her." She shoved her glass at Sam. "Hold this for me?"

Sam shook his head. "I'll go."

Macy narrowed her gaze and stepped into Sam's direct path. "So you do know her."

He nodded, his heart racing at the thought of seeing her again. No woman had ever made him feel so many things in such a short time. Protective, aroused, attracted . . .

"And you're interested," Macy concluded in the wake of his silence.

"No comment. I'm going upstairs. You can hold down the fort here." This time he handed her his beer bottle.

Macy watched him, her stare too perceptive for his liking.

"And do not give my sister or brother the wrong impression. I just want to say hi and welcome her to town. Make sure she feels comfortable enough to come down and join us."

"If you say so, Detective," she said, using his brand-new moniker.

He still wasn't used to the title or the promotion, but he'd worked hard for it, and nepotism — his brother being chief — had nothing to do with his new position.

He turned and headed for the back entrance of the bar and slipped out the exit. As soon as he hit the top of the stairs and stood outside the apartment door, he paused. Everyone he knew had lived here at one time or another, from Faith and Kelly Barron, to his brother, Mike, and then Erin's husband, Cole. The place was a revolving door, a pit stop before people settled down for good.

Now Nicole.

He'd known her for a short time, when she'd been in Serendipity tracking her missing sister, who it turned out had been stalking Erin. Sam had arrested her lurking outside Erin's condo, assuming she was her psychotic twin. But there was nothing unstable about Nicole . . . and she'd made a profound impact on Sam. From her dark hair to her big beautiful blue eyes, he felt like he could see inside her soul.

On first meeting, she'd been scared, then defiant, but ultimately he came to admire how she'd handled herself while in that small interrogation room. But the real turning point between them had come when Cole barged in. She'd immediately turned to Sam, as if assuming she could trust him to look after her. She hadn't been wrong. And not just because he had a reputation for being the *good cop* in any scenario. With Nicole, the protective surge he'd experienced surpassed the normal doing of his job. It made no damned sense to him then, and it still didn't now. Hell, her draw scared him as much as it pulled him toward her.

Once her sister had been arrested, Nicole had gone back to the city where she belonged before Sam could act on any stupid sexual or deeper impulse he might have. He hadn't had an emotional connection with any female since Jenna's betrayal, and he wouldn't allow himself to be hurt that way again. But none of that seemed to matter now that *she* was back in town.

Sam couldn't imagine why Nicole had opted to move to Serendipity — but there was one way to find out. Raising his hand, he knocked on her door.

TWO

Nicole had spent the last couple of years — oh hell, why not admit it? She'd spent her entire life wearing, saying, and doing what was appropriate and expected of her. Not wanting to disappoint her parents, she'd always taken the path of least resistance, at least until she'd broken her engagement.

Tonight was the first time she could wear exactly what she wanted and be true to herself. Yet instead of being downstairs meeting new friends, she stood in front of her closet, unsure of . . . everything.

The good news was, although she'd spent her time in skirts and silk blouses, Chanel-style jackets, and pearls like her mother, that hadn't stopped her from buying the kind of items she wished she could wear. On her way out of town, she'd dropped off all her Nicole Farnsworth, dutiful-daughter-appropriate items at the Manhattan branch of Dress for Success, where disadvantaged women would now have interview suits and clothing to start over.

Now it was Nicole's turn to live for herself. She was just about to reach into her closet and pick something when someone knocked on her door. She figured it was Macy, wondering what had happened to her since she was already twenty minutes late.

She cinched the tie on her bathrobe. Used to being extra careful in Manhattan, she glanced into the peephole of her door.

The unexpected visitor standing on the other side made her breath catch in her throat and her heart begin a steady gallop.

"Sam," she whispered, shocked right down to her toes.

He knocked again, and she fumbled with the lock before opening the door.

He braced one muscular arm on the door frame and grinned. "Hi."

"Hi," she managed in return, her gaze steady on his.

His smile deepened, revealing dimpled grooves in the sides of his mouth. "Welcome back."

"Thanks," she said as his husky voice rippled through her.

He hadn't shaved, and with stubble and sexy messed hair, he looked even more delicious than she remembered. Her mouth ran dry and she ran her tongue over her lips in a desperate attempt to find moisture.

"I wasn't expecting you," she said, wincing as the words came out not at all like she'd intended.

"Disappointed?"

Lord no, she thought, and shook her head. "Of course not. Just surprised."

His heavy-lidded gaze met hers. "So was I when I heard you'd moved here."

"I bet."

"Are you going to invite me in?" he asked.

She clutched her bathrobe lapels together, torn between doing just that and doing the proper thing. "Umm, I'm not exactly dressed."

A grin lifted the corners of his mouth. "I don't mind." Those gorgeous eyes, green mixed with brown and rimmed by gold, traveled over her, from her bare legs to the short hem of the silk robe, up again to meet her gaze.

Sweet heaven, this man was potent. Unable to resist him, she stepped aside. "I haven't had a chance to do much with the apartment yet." Though she'd unpacked her clothes, she still needed the accessories and personal touches that would make the place feel like home.

He shrugged, obviously unconcerned.

"I'm used to it. My brother lived here before you and he did nothing to it at all."

She raised an eyebrow, surprised. "I didn't know that."

"Yep. Then he married Cara, bought himself a big house by the lake, and settled down."

"Do you like his wife?" she asked, because he didn't sound happy about the settling-down part. His voice had turned grumbly over the words.

"She's great. You remember her, Cara Hartley? The police officer who arrested your . . ." His voice trailed off awkwardly.

Nothing like the memory of Victoria to bring an abrupt end to any conversation, Nicole thought. "I remember Cara. She was decent to me."

Sam openly studied her. "She had no reason not to be. You weren't your sister."

Nicole drew a deep breath and nodded. "That's why I decided Serendipity would be a good place to start over. Nice town, people willing to give you a chance to prove yourself, not jump to conclusions or put you in a little box where they think you ought to be."

Sam, being as perceptive as she remembered, narrowed his gaze at that.

She bit the inside of her cheek, realizing

she was getting too deep. "I should get dressed and meet you downstairs."

"I'll wait." He headed for the small dining set in the corner that came with the apartment, hooked one foot around the leg of a chair, and settled his very fine rear end into the seat.

He relaxed comfortably, as if he'd been here many times before and belonged. He had said his brother lived here before, which explained his familiarity — but not the sense of rightness she felt on seeing him in her personal space.

Uh-oh. She shook her head to dispel that wayward thought. No matter how strong the attraction between them, Nicole had just ended one engagement. She was not interested in anything other than getting her life together and on track. No emotional or sexual entanglements needed or wanted. No matter that her raging hormones and completely wired body said otherwise.

She quickly grabbed a pair of soft, faded jeans, a hot-pink fitted V neck, and a belt, and closed herself in the bathroom to change.

She dressed quickly. A glance in the mirror showed that her cheeks were flushed — *thank you, Sam* — so no need for more blush. She swiped on a light peach lip gloss, spritzed on some of her favorite perfume, fluffed her hair, drew a deep breath, and walked back out to face him.

His gaze raked over her and his mouth curled in a genuine smile of approval.

At his reaction, pleasure of every variety rushed over strategic body parts, and given the thin texture of her top and the darkening of those sexy hazel eyes, he noticed.

Oh yes, she was in definite trouble.

No sooner had Sam followed Nicole back down to the bar than Macy took over, hooking her arm through Nicole's and stealing her away. Macy maneuvered her through the crowd, introducing Nicole to people as she went.

Sam told himself he was happy for the separation. It gave him a chance to catch his breath — because Nicole's impact was even more potent the second time around. He'd barely taken in the fact that she was here and they'd come face-to-face, forcing him to call on a cool he didn't feel.

He'd have liked to blame his over-the-top reaction on the silk robe she'd worn and clutched to her chest like armor. Still, he'd been unable to stop wondering if her skin would be as soft as the satiny material looked. If she'd feel soft and supple beneath him.

He groaned, knowing it wasn't just the robe or the long bare legs beneath that captivated him. After the surprise of seeing him, it was the pleasure in those beautiful blue eyes that had floored him. Of course, she'd quickly composed herself and tried to hide her reaction. They had that in common, at least — a wariness of their combustible chemistry. He took heart in knowing she was uncertain too.

And when she'd returned from getting dressed? Gone were the ladylike slacks and silk shirts she'd worn her first time in town, replaced by jeans that hugged her shapely ass and a top that accentuated her sweet curves. Curves he wanted to trace with his hands and taste with his mouth, exploring her thoroughly. He wanted that with a desperation he'd never felt before.

But more than sexual attraction intrigued him. When she'd mentioned coming to Serendipity to start over, to prove herself and not have people jump to conclusions or put her in a little box — well, then he'd realized there was much more to Nicole's move here than met the eye, making him wonder just what she had left behind.

And why did he care? He wished the

answer were as simple as him being a cop and it being second nature to question and to wonder. He knew better. He cared and wondered because it was Nicole.

Everything about her aroused his curiosity — among other things. The heat between them was mutual. The way her nipples tightened beneath his stare affirmed the same shocks tripping him up even now, when she was on the other side of the damned room.

"That's interesting." Mike eased up alongside him, standing shoulder to shoulder as they looked over the crowd.

"What is?" Sam asked.

"Victoria's sister's back in town." And Mike didn't sound pleased.

"It's a free country," Sam reminded him.

"Just seems odd she'd come back here after what her sister pulled." Mike took a long drag of his beer.

"She's not her sister and she helped ours. She came here to warn Erin and she gave up her sister's hideout, remember?"

"Don't get yourself worked up. I'm just pointing out the truth. Macy says she's moved here and I think it's an odd choice. Unless she found something here she liked." Mike's low chuckle was meant to annoy Sam.

He refused to take his brother's bait. "She said she found the people here accepting."

"You've spoken with her already?"

Shit. "Yeah." He didn't elaborate.

"Be careful. Her sister's got mental issues," Mike warned him.

"And she's getting treatment while awaiting the disposition of her case." *Even so,* Sam thought. "What do Victoria's problems have to do with Nicole?" Sam asked, his gaze never leaving the woman in question.

"Depends on what, if anything, *you* have to do with Nicole," Mike replied.

Sam's gaze narrowed both at Mike's words, as well as at the scene before him. Macy had moved on from the women and was now introducing Nicole to some of the cops who frequented her restaurant. When Rob Burnett, a known player, looked her over, a predatory gleam in his eyes, Sam tensed and pushed himself off the wall.

"Hey."

Sam turned back to his brother. "What?" *And make it quick,* he thought.

"I meant it when I said be careful. You don't know anything about her except for —"

"Her crazy sister? I heard you loud and clear." But Sam wasn't listening. He was more concerned with not allowing the single

40

guys at Joe's to take in the new girl without him staking some kind of claim first.

He made his way to where Macy had finished her introductions and the men were eyeing Nicole with interest.

"Hey, Sam," Macy said with a welcoming smile.

"Macy." He greeted her with a grin before turning to Nicole. "Good to see you again."

Her gaze warmed and his entire body sizzled in reaction. "What's up?" he asked.

"Just meeting the new girl in town," Rob said, immediately making himself a part of the conversation. "Isn't that right, honey?" He lifted Nicole's hand and kissed her smooth skin.

Sam's fingers curled into a fist, itching to hit his friend. Rob was always too smooth with the ladies, and the result went one of two ways. Either they were desperate and fell for his fake charm, or they found him over-the-top ridiculous.

Nicole pulled her hand back quickly and Sam relaxed.

"Everyone has been very welcoming," she said, not singling out Rob or acknowledging his interest.

"Some more than others," Sam muttered, noticing that his other cop buddies were engaged in a conversation with each other.

"Want to go get a drink?" Sam asked Nicole, eager for time to get reacquainted.

"Why don't you go get this round and one of us will grab the next one," Rob not so smoothly suggested.

Sam forced a smile. "Since I can't remember the last time you actually put your hand in your pocket to cover any of us, why don't *you* get this round for the guys? I've got Macy and Nicole covered."

Macy raised her eyebrows and an amused smirk lifted her lips.

"I'll go hang with the boys. Go on, Rob. Fetch our drinks," she said with such a silken laugh that no man in his right mind would deny her.

Flirting and teasing were part of Macy's charm, but no man ever got past her walls, which didn't stop even those who knew her best from wanting to please her.

Burnett scowled but realized he'd been caught in his own noose. "Beer for everyone?" he bit out.

Even the other two guys nodded at that.

"Works for me," Macy said, placing her hand on the other man's shoulder. "Thanks."

"Yeah," he muttered, and stalked off.

Sam shook his head and laughed. "Subtle, Mace."

"You're no better."

He did his best not to flush. He knew damn well he'd been proprietary, knew how out of character his behavior had been. And he couldn't control it worth a damn.

Nicole watched his byplay with Macy but remained silent. Sam wasn't sure if she'd caught on to his intent or if she thought he was just giving Burnett a hard time.

"I got rid of Rob," Macy said, leaning close so she could whisper for Sam's ears only. Obviously *she* hadn't missed a thing. "Now go take my new friend and show her a good time."

No sooner had Macy spoken than Joe grabbed a microphone and announced the start of karaoke night. He hadn't had the theme in a while and obviously thought with the bar full of regulars, it was a good time to start.

"Karaoke isn't my thing," Sam muttered.

Nicole met his gaze. "Mine either."

That made up his mind. "Want to get out of here?"

She appeared startled at the suggestion but nodded, much to his relief.

A few minutes later, they were outside Joe's.

"Where are we going?" Nicole asked.

"With a little luck? Some place quiet." His

fingers itched to take her hand, but the maxim *too much, too soon* ran through his head, and he refrained.

Nicole fell into step alongside him and they walked across the street to the center median, which was covered with a multitude of colorful flowers.

"These are incredible," she murmured and went on to name a variety of flowers she obviously recognized.

He blinked at her knowledge. "Are you a florist?" he asked, realizing he'd never found out what she did for a living.

She shook her head. "No. But my mother was always very specific about flower orders when she planned her dinner parties. Many, many dinner parties." Her voice droned with the memory.

"Sounds painful."

"Very." Her smile packed a punch. "Still, these are beautiful." She swept her hand through the air to indicate the panorama of flowers and color spread out before them.

"*Beautiful* is an appropriate word in more ways than one," he said, speaking more of her than the flowers.

Her jet-black hair and Mediterranean coloring must come from her mother, he figured, since Farnsworth wasn't an ethnic name. Those blue eyes stood out against

44

her olive skin, like two deep pools, beckoning to him, making it difficult for him to follow the thread of their conversation.

Somehow he pulled the subject from the back of his mind. "The town's beautification committee works hard on maintaining this area."

"I'm so used to the city, being able to see so much color and space is such a treat."

And her appreciation of something he passed by every day and took for granted touched him deeply, prompting him to explain more about their origins. "There's a yearly event to raise money to fund this area. It's a big, formal party at Faith Barron's house over Labor Day weekend."

"Who?"

Sam shook his head and laughed. "Right. You're not a local. Did you notice that big house on the hill when you drove into town?"

"How could I not? It resembles my childhood home."

He let out a whistle. "Nice." And way out of his league.

She laughed. "No, the mansion here is much grander. It just happens to remind me of my parents' home. The way it's set off from reality and obviously meant to impress, that sort of thing." She shifted from foot to foot. "But it's not who I am at all," she said, as if desperate for him to understand and still accept her.

He nodded in grateful understanding. He didn't want a spoiled princess in his life — and if he had his way, this understated woman would, at the very least, end up in his bed. Still, she was clearly the kind of girl he'd be taking his time with, and he appreciated that about her.

"So back to the house on the hill," he said. "Faith and Ethan Barron live there now, and they're nothing like Faith's parents, who were the previous owners."

"That's unusual," she murmured.

He nodded. "It is. And yet it's very right. You and Faith have a lot in common. She's down to earth and sweet." Nicole blushed, but Sam merely continued. "Now that you're living here, I'm sure you'll meet them at one point or another."

She smiled. "I'll look forward to it."

"Want to sit?" Sam pointed to the empty bench beneath the white gazebo.

She nodded and walked up the few steps, easing down on the wooden seat. He settled in beside her.

"This is the best part of the summer," she said, relaxing and leaning back.

"What is?"

"This time of day. The sun doesn't set until late. When I was younger, my sister and I would stay outside until it turned dark." Her lips lifted upward at the memory. "We'd play games and make up stories. Anything to avoid going back into that cold, empty house with people who . . . people like my parents." She shivered but clammed up, obviously realizing she'd said more than she wanted to.

As far as Sam was concerned, she hadn't said enough.

"Thanks for showing me this place." She stretched her legs out in front of her and let out a blissful sigh.

His groin responded to the sound. "My pleasure. So . . . you told me why you chose Serendipity, but why the move in the first place?" He asked the question dogging him since he'd discovered she was here.

She turned to face him, her gaze serious. "Because I was finished living my life for others."

He already knew that meant her parents.

"I liked the town . . . and the people from when I was in town before. Despite the horrible situation, I felt a connection here."

She didn't shift her gaze from his, warming him with her statement, which clearly included him.

47

"I'm here for me." She shrugged. "It was really that simple."

So much . . . and so little revealed, Sam thought, intrigued by her. "What are your plans?"

"Eventually I want to open up a specialty bake shop, but I'll start by seeing if there's someone here who'll hire me while I'm getting my bearings in town. I want to do some research on the area and make sure there's a need for what I'm offering before I invest."

"There was a bakery off Main Street that closed down a while back. Not because they couldn't sustain business, but it was too much for the couple who owned it."

"Hmm. I'll have to look into it."

"It's smart that you're not rushing into something. Taking your time to understand whether a business is viable is an intelligent move."

Again, her cheeks flushed a deep shade. "Thank you."

Unable to stop himself, he reached out and twirled a strand of her dark hair around his finger. "Would it bother you if I said I couldn't stop thinking about you after you left town?"

She gazed at him through her thick lashes. "Only if it doesn't bother you to know I felt the same way." Her husky voice tripped the

48

lever on his banked desire.

"Good to know." He tugged on her hair and she leaned in closer, their mouths inches apart.

God, he wanted to taste her, to explore this living, breathing desire that shimmered between them. And when her tongue swept out, moistening her lips, the unpracticed move broke his control. Covering the distance between them, he brushed his lips over hers and she welcomed him with a soft sigh of acceptance. But she held back, waiting for him to take the lead. His pulse pounded as hard as his groin had become.

His body wanted to go fast, but something about Nicole kept his baser impulses in check. Keeping the kiss under control, he tasted her lips, sliding his tongue back and forth until she parted and let him inside. His tongue brushed hers and the taste of her exploded inside him. Her flavor was better than he'd imagined, and her sweet scent went straight to his groin.

Without thinking, he twisted her hair tighter, tilting her head for deeper access, which she freely granted. His heart knocked against his chest, the connection between them deepening along with the kiss. Only his free hand, clenched into a tight fist, helped him keep a grasp on reality.

Her tongue tangled with his and the kiss went on, sweeping him along with her, until he was lost completely. Suddenly laughter and the rowdy sound of a group of kids broke into their intimate moment.

She jerked back, face flushed, lips damp and curved in a smile.

He grinned back just as a pack of teens strode up to the gazebo, talking loudly and ribbing each other with insults and innuendo.

"Oh, man. It's taken," one of them said.

Nicole quickly rose to her feet, straightening her shirt, shaking her hand over her jeans. "We were just leaving," she said to the boys.

Sam stood, grateful for the darkness that had begun to surround them, hiding the obvious evidence of his arousal. "I'll walk you back," he said, his voice unsteady.

"Okay." Her lips twitched in a knowing grin.

He placed his hand on the small of her back and she trembled. Good. At least he wasn't the only one still being pulled under by the desire they'd unleashed.

Sam couldn't remember the last time he'd made out with a woman in the middle of town, where anyone could see. Not that it mattered when all he could think about was this woman — and when he could see her again.

Nicole spent the next day getting her new apartment into shape. It helped once she unpacked some personal photos and knick-knacks. She liked knowing she was settled, that she could look around and feel like she was surrounded by her favorite things.

She had a mental to-do list, and with her personal space in order, she could turn her focus to her career. As for what to do about Tyler's father . . . she still didn't know. Each option turned her stomach. So she focused on Sam — which wasn't difficult since she couldn't concentrate on anything but that kiss. Her lips still tingled with pleasure.

When she'd first met him three months ago, after she'd gotten over the fact that he'd arrested her and dragged her down to the police station, their crazy chemistry had taken her by surprise. Although nothing happened between them, the sizzle she'd experienced was one of the things that had persuaded her to end her engagement. If just looking at Sam Marsden awoke parts of her that had been long dormant, she'd asked herself what the hell she was doing with Tyler Stanton, a man with whom sex was just . . . nice.

No matter how good and kind Tyler was, intimacy had been pleasant and occasional. It had never been a priority for either one of them. Maybe it was because they'd grown up together, the expectation of marriage always underlying things, and they were comfortable together, but his kisses were uninspired. And that was what she'd thought before Sam Marsden's lips touched hers and the earth shifted beneath her feet.

Yep, it had been that cliché. That awesome.

Which explained why she woke up this morning still off-kilter and jittery. She shook her head, trying to clear her mind. She started by reminding herself that she wasn't looking to start something new when she was still getting over something old. But she was getting ahead of herself with her worries. It wasn't like Sam had reached out in the time since she'd seen him at Joe's.

Pushing that thought aside, she showered and dressed, her plan being to drive over to The Family Restaurant. Macy said late mornings were slow and she could spend some time talking. Since her new friend was in the restaurant business, Nicole wanted to discuss her bakery ideas and get insight.

In desperate need of caffeine, she stopped at Cuppa Café, even before she got in her car and headed across town. She'd yet to fill her kitchen cabinets and refrigerator, but even if she had, Nicole liked to treat herself to a good, fresh cup in the morning.

The shop was nearly empty, with one woman who looked about Nicole's age, give or take a few years, working behind the counter.

"Hi," Nicole said.

"Hi, and welcome." The other woman greeted her with a friendly smile. "Are you new in town?"

Nicole laughed. "That obvious?"

"Only to someone who grew up here. I'm Trisha Lockhart. I own this place."

"Nicole Farnsworth. Are you related to Joe? He's my landlord."

"He's my brother. He pumps the good people in town full of alcohol and I sober them up or help their hangover the next day." Her words were light and teasing. "What can I get you?"

"Regular coffee with milk and sugar," Nicole said.

"Coming right up."

As Trisha poured her drink, Nicole stepped back to study the items behind the counter. There were prewrapped pastries and assorted other things like name-brand granola bars, but nothing that appeared freshly baked. She wrinkled her nose at the choices.

"Something wrong?" Trisha placed her cup on the counter.

"Not at all," Nicole rushed to assure her, embarrassed that she'd been caught turning her nose up at the other woman's offerings.

"You looked like you just ate a Sour Patch or something."

Nicole shook her head, mortified. "I'm sorry. I was just looking at your breakfast offerings —"

"Pitiful, I know." Trisha lifted her shoulders in a shrug. "It is what it is. I can't bake and I don't have the equipment even if I could."

"Hmm. Well, it just so happens . . ."

"Yes?"

Nicole braced her hands on the counter. "I can bake. And I want to bake; I moved here hoping to find a place to do that, or open my own business." She met Trisha's interested gaze. "I have the savings for it, but I'm not sure I'm ready to dive in alone."

Trisha eyed her speculatively. "I would be interested in bringing fresh items into the store. I'm certain it would only add business." She shrugged. "Why don't you drop off some baked goods for me to try?"

Heartened, Nicole nodded. "I will." She

placed money, enough to include a tip, on the counter and picked up her cup. "It was nice meeting you."

"Same here. I'd say don't be a stranger, but in this town, no one really is." Trisha grinned and turned to refresh the decaffeinated coffee.

Smiling, Nicole spun around and bumped into a hard male body. Her coffee sloshed over the lid, burning her hand. "Oh crap," she muttered.

Ignoring the sting, she backed up, then glanced up and into the same hazel eyes that had starred in her dreams. Sam stood in front of her, freshly shaved, wearing a dark sport jacket, and looking hotter than any man had a right to.

"Oh God. I'm sorry. Did I get any coffee on you?" she asked, embarrassed.

"No. I'm fine. Are you okay?" He lifted her burned hand in his for inspection.

Shocks that had nothing to do with the hot liquid tingled along her skin. A quick look up told her he'd experienced the sensation too.

"I'm okay," she murmured. At least her hand was. The rest of her was another story. "Where are you going all dressed up?" she asked.

"Work."

She narrowed her gaze. "No uniform?"

"I got a promotion since I saw you last," he explained. "Detectives get to ditch the uniform."

"Congratulations!" she said, impressed and happy for him.

"Thanks. So how about you? Where are you headed next?" he asked.

"The Family Restaurant. I was going to brainstorm some things with Macy, but I couldn't wait to get there to get some caffeine into me," she explained.

He laughed. "I hear you. If I don't stop here, I end up starting my day with the sludge at the station."

"Good to know where I can find you," she murmured.

They stared at each other for a few moments, the air between them crackling with intensity.

"I've been thinking about you," he admitted.

Her heart skipped a beat at that. "Same here."

"Are you free Friday night? We could go out to dinner."

She sighed. "I'm going to the movies with Macy." She paused before plowing ahead. "But Saturday night, Macy talked me into going to the women's heart health fund-raiser. Will you be there?" If she couldn't go on an official date with him this weekend, at least they could spend time together.

His brows drew close and he hesitated, his attitude going from outgoing and inviting to downright uncomfortable. "Never mind. I —"

"Listen, I —" They spoke at the same time.

His cell rang and he immediately glanced at the phone screen.

"Work call," he explained, shooting her a regretful look. He spoke to the person on the other end and met her gaze as he disconnected. "I have to go now, but I —" He shook his head. "No time," he muttered.

She nodded, understanding the urgency. She'd see him Saturday night, or not.

With a last lingering glance, he headed for the door.

She watched him go, her eyes devouring him from behind. The man was built in a way that spoke of working out to maintain his physique but not in a way that screamed gym god. No, he was a fine specimen all on his own.

She wished he'd had a chance to say whatever was on his mind about the fundraiser, but she wouldn't let herself worry about it. He had asked her out first, which indicated interest. And if he really wanted to go out with her, he knew where to find her. It was a small town, after all.

She might not be looking for a serious relationship right now, but she'd be crazy to deny she wanted something with this man.

Just what remained to be seen.

THREE

Sam found that work as a detective was feast or famine in a small town. Now, when he wanted to get in touch with Nicole, a string of burglaries on a residential street kept him busy. He didn't even have time to return his mother's call about their Sunday family dinner. She wanted to make sure he was coming. Of course he was. Not one of his siblings said no to Ella Marsden. Now that Mike and Erin were married, it was a bigger gathering than ever before. Add Erin's baby . . . and the pressure was *on* for Sam. But he could handle his mother, and he'd be there because he knew what was good for him. Besides, he loved his family no matter what.

He ended up spending that Friday night on a stakeout, watching for the teens who were breaking into parked cars and vandalizing them for the hell of it. Saturday consisted of viewing hours of video of the same street, courtesy of a paranoid home-owner who'd had cameras installed outside his home. Good thing, since they'd caught a glimpse of a lone car coming into the neighborhood after midnight a week ago when the vandalism had started.

Sam was exhausted and needed a good night's sleep that lasted a solid twelve hours. Unfortunately, he had just enough time to shower, change, and pick up his obligatory date for the fund-raiser. His stomach churned, for more reasons than why he'd argued with Cara about it in the first place. He hadn't had the chance to explain the situation to Nicole at Cuppa Café, he didn't have her cell phone number, he hadn't run into her again, and he had no time to stop by her place to talk before he picked up Margie Stinson.

He wasn't looking forward to running into Nicole tonight with another woman on his arm. His throat constricted at the thought and he shoved his fingers beneath the collar of his tuxedo shirt and tugged, needing air.

Though he and Nicole barely knew each other, that kiss changed everything for him, and he was sure she wanted to explore things further too. They might not have a commitment between them, but Sam wasn't a serial dater. Thanks to his mother's and sister's influence, he understood and respected women. As a result, he had a gnawing feeling that tonight was going to be memorable, and not in any way he would have wanted.

When Nicole moved to Serendipity, she hadn't thought she'd need a formal dress, but having been raised to always be prepared, she'd saved her favorite one and stored it in the back of her closet. She dressed in a sapphire-blue dress with silver shoes, not allowing herself to second-guess or change.

Macy had given her the address for the country club where the event was being held, and as she pulled up to the filled parking lot, nerves assailed her. She didn't know anyone here, not really. Despite the urge to turn around and go home, she continued on to the valet and gave them her car.

As a man took her small Mercedes and drove off, Nicole had no choice but to gather her courage and head inside. She walked in and the first thing she noticed was a table with beautiful red and white flowers — red for heart disease, she assumed — and picked up the heart-shaped card with her name on it. Table five. Which meant nothing to her, since other than

Macy, she had no friends here. Well, there was Sam, but she didn't know what to think about things between them. She put the place card in her silver clutch and made her way into the lobby area, looking for Macy.

The first familiar face wasn't Macy but Erin, Sam's sister, the woman Nicole's twin had stalked and nearly run down with her car. For someone who'd given birth a few months ago, she looked amazing in an emerald-green sheath dress. The green brought out her eyes, which were so much like her brother's.

Erin she could handle, but her now-husband Cole? He was another story. Nicole still vividly recalled him bursting into the small interrogation room at the police station, yelling at her and demanding answers. Only Sam's presence had reassured her, and though Cole had eventually come to believe that Nicole only wanted to help, he was still intimidating enough that she'd like to avoid him if she could.

She turned away from the couple and toward the bar, only to hear Erin call out her name.

Okay then. She'd have to deal with them after all.

Straightening her shoulders and tightening her grip on her purse, Nicole turned to find Erin walking up to her.

"I thought it was you," Erin said, her tone welcoming. "Sam and Macy said you'd moved to town. Somehow I missed seeing you at Joe's, but I heard you were there."

Nicole was unable to hold back a smile at Erin's warm rambling. It didn't seem like she held a grudge about her sister. "How have you been?" Nicole asked, still wary.

"Great. Motherhood is amazing. You have to meet my baby girl."

At that, Nicole relaxed her muscles and her guard. Erin had been pregnant last time Nicole had seen her. "Congratulations. What's your daughter's name?" she asked.

"Angel. And she is one. Unless she's crying." Erin laughed, but the love and maternal devotion in her eyes caused an unexpected lump of emotion to settle in Nicole's throat.

"I'm glad things are going well for you," Nicole said, meaning it.

"Thank you. I'm happier than I thought I could be. Marriage is amazing," she said with a wink.

"That I wouldn't know," Nicole murmured. She'd broken her engagement in Manhattan and had every intention of leaving both thoughts and discussion about it there. "But I'm happy for you. After everything you went through, you deserve smooth sailing."

Erin met her gaze. "So do you. I'm not sure I ever got the chance to thank you for coming here in the first place to warn me about your sister. That was . . . brave, and it couldn't have been easy."

Nicole sighed. The truth was she hadn't known Erin or anyone in Serendipity when she'd driven here to warn her. Her goals in doing so had been twofold, and she might as well be up front with Erin.

"All I wanted was for my sister to get the help she needed, and I didn't want anyone to get hurt." And she definitely hadn't wanted her twin to do anything she couldn't undo, or would have to live with for the rest of her life.

Erin nodded in understanding.

"I should thank you for advocating for Victoria's mental health," Nicole said to the woman who, at the time of the incident, had also been an assistant district attorney. As the victim, she hadn't been in charge of the case, but Nicole knew Erin had pushed hard for her sister to get help. "You could have just come down on the side of putting her in jail."

"It was the right thing to do," Erin said.

A low growl behind her told Nicole that

64

Erin's husband didn't agree.

"Cut it out," Erin said. "It's over and done with. Nicole's living here now, so let's all play nice."

Cole wrapped his arms around her waist and nodded at Nicole. "Welcome to town," he said, sounding as if he just might mean it.

"Thank you."

"Hi, all!" Macy brought her bubbly personality, taking the pressure off Nicole of dealing with Cole and talk of Victoria's illness.

"Hi," Erin and Nicole said at once.

"Everyone looks beautiful!" Macy hugged each of them. "Well, not Mr. Sullen, but you are looking handsome." She pulled the gruff man into a hug.

"I'll take that as my cue to mingle," Cole muttered, extricating himself from Macy's grip.

Erin rolled her eyes. He patted her cheek and walked away. "You scare him," she said to Macy.

The other woman laughed. "How's that sweet angel of yours?" Macy asked. "Get it? Her daughter's name is Angel," she explained to Nicole.

The new mother beamed and launched into a description of things only a new mother would appreciate. Any time Tyler had brought up babies, Nicole would lapse into panic mode. Now she understood why. She had only to look at Erin's beaming face when she looked at her husband to know — Tyler hadn't been the right man for Nicole to start a family with.

"What table are you sitting at?" Nicole asked, when they'd finished their conversation.

"We're at three. With my brothers and parents," Erin said.

"Five," Macy said, winking at Nicole. "Don't you worry, I took charge of the whole situation. I wouldn't leave you alone. We single women have to stick together."

Nicole smiled, finally understanding why Macy had been so quick to embrace a friendship with her. It wasn't just that Macy was warm and generous — she was — but there was more to the dynamic going on. The changes in Erin's life meant she and Macy didn't do as many things together anymore. Which meant Macy needed Nicole's friendship as much as Nicole needed Macy's. The knowledge eased a painful knot she'd had in her chest since walking in here feeling out of place.

"So, Nicole, what will you be doing here in town?" Erin asked.

"I'm looking into opening a specialty bakery, but not right away. I want to start small and see how things catch on," Nicole explained.

"Tell her the rest." Macy nudged her with her arm.

She'd had time to fill Macy in about her talk with Trisha the other morning.

"Well, I've spoken to Trisha at the coffee shop, and she said she would be interested in taking in my items and selling them, and Macy said she'd approach her father about doing the same at the restaurant."

"What kind of specialty items?" Erin asked.

"Cupcakes, cookies, pastries . . ."

"Aunt Lulu bakes pies and cakes, not pastries, so I think it would be fine," Macy immediately chimed in.

Erin narrowed her gaze. "Are you sure about that?"

Nicole blinked. "Is there a problem?"

Macy shook her head. "Nope. I think Aunt Lulu and Nicole will complement each other perfectly."

"Well, I love the idea! Where would you work? I hear you're living over Joe's, and that kitchen is tiny."

That was the issue Nicole had run up against, at least in her head, and maybe subconsciously that was the reason she hadn't filled up the place with food and baking necessities.

"I'm not sure . . . yet. I'm working on it." She tapped the side of her head. She was thinking it through, but so far she hadn't come up with any ideas.

"You'll figure something out." Macy's gaze drifted to a point beyond them, and her eyes widened. "Listen, I need to go check in with my aunt. She's looking a little lost, and when Aunt Lulu is at loose ends, trouble happens. I'll see you at the table," she said to Nicole, then waved at Erin and walked away.

Erin shook her head and laughed. "They're both characters, Macy and her aunt." She glanced over Nicole's shoulder, her eyes opening wide. "Sam!" She waved at her brother, indicating he should join them.

Nicole's stomach immediately spun like she was on a roller coaster. Not in a panicked, *get me off this ride* kind of way, but in a *this is awesome, I could stay on here for another loop* kind of way. She couldn't recall a time when she'd felt so excited about a man. Affected by hearing his name, psyched to see him, flushed, silly and girly. *This* was why she'd broken off her engagement, because if she and Tyler didn't share this in the beginning, what would be left when the newness wore off?

She pivoted to greet the man who starred in not just her dreams but her fantasies too, only to see he wasn't alone. She blinked but the fact remained, there was a woman by his side. A pretty blonde, her arm hooked through Sam's. Nicole had to admit, with their light hair and good looks, they made a striking couple, and more than a few heads turned as they made their way across the room.

Nicole's stomach, along with her hopes, plummeted at the sight, and she now knew what Sam had been about to tell her the other day. She drew her shoulders back, determined to get through this with grace and class. Her disappointment could come later, when she was alone.

Erin hugged her brother. "You two know each other, right?" Erin asked, oblivious to the undercurrent between them.

"Of course. It's good to see you again." Swallowing over her unreasonable hurt and disappointment, Nicole managed a politeness she didn't feel.

Sam's gaze remained steady on hers, but she didn't let herself make eye contact.

"Sam, aren't you going to introduce me?"

his date asked.

Nicole forced a smile and waited for the inevitable.

Sam physically felt Nicole's discomfort, and he wished she would at least look up and see him, understand he wasn't happy about this situation either.

"Margie, you know my sister, Erin, and this is Nicole Farnsworth. She's new in town. Nicole, this is Margie Stinson. Her parents are big donors for tonight's event," he said, hoping she'd have to look at him now.

"It's nice to meet you," Nicole said, her voice sweet, covering the obvious hurt Sam knew he'd inflicted. "That's wonderful of your parents. It's a very worthy cause. In fact, that's how Macy persuaded me to come tonight." She paused and glanced around. "Speaking of Macy, I need to go find her."

"Nicole —" Erin called her name, obviously sensing something was wrong.

Nicole had already walked away, but not before Sam caught the wounded look in her eyes, and he muttered a curse.

His sister glanced at him, clearly confused.

Sam didn't have time for Erin's curiosity or Margie's arm still entwined with his. With every step Nicole took away from him,

Sam felt opportunity and something more slipping away.

"I need to see to something," he said, tipping his head in the direction of where Nicole had gone, shooting his sister a pleading look.

Erin narrowed her eyes, suspicion in her expression.

"Honey? I would love a drink," Margie said, oblivious to anyone other than herself, as she'd been since he'd picked her up.

Honey?

Erin choked over a laugh.

"A white wine spritzer," she continued. "No, make that a vodka with a splash of cranberry juice. No, a mimosa."

Just as on the car ride over, Margie talked to fill up space. Earlier she'd discussed her dress, her shoes, and her shopping, leaving Sam unable to get a word in edgewise. Sam thought she talked just to hear her own voice. She didn't need much in the way of conversation, only an escort on her arm and an ear for her long-winded stories, which was fine with him. Her parents must have catered to each and every whim she'd ever had for her to be so self-absorbed.

"Sam, why don't you go get us all drinks," Erin said.

"I'll go with you —" Margie immediately said.

"No, Margie. The line looks long. Stay here and keep me company. I'm home with a baby, and I really could use adult conversation," his sister lied smoothly.

Sam shot her a look filled with gratitude. He didn't miss the mouthed *You owe me one.* He did and figured babysitting and diaper changing was in his future. Well worth it, he thought, as he took off after Nicole.

By now, the bar area as well as the ballroom had filled up and he focused on searching for a deep blue dress or glossy, long dark hair. He'd noticed her immediately when he'd walked into the room: her lush curves accentuated by the gown, her beautiful smile a draw, at least for him. He found her now, disappearing out the door into the area where the restrooms must be.

He caught up with her in the nearly empty hall. Just a few women were walking out of the ladies' room. Sam waited until they were alone and stepped up behind her.

"It's not what you think."

She flinched and turned, clearly startled, at the sound of his voice. "It doesn't matter what it is. You don't owe me an explanation." She pivoted toward the restroom.

"Don't. Give me a minute. Please." He heard the plea in his voice.

With a sigh, she stepped away from the door and led them to a quiet corner of the lobby. With people milling around, they weren't alone, but at least she was with him. And she was listening.

"Margie's parents are huge donors. Cara's in charge of selling tickets for the station, and she begged me to take Margie. Hell, she basically insinuated that the Stinsons would pull out if I didn't. You weren't living here yet when I agreed, and even then, I did it under duress."

Nicole had folded her arms across her chest in a protective manner earlier. She didn't uncross them now.

His gut churned and acid flowed in his chest.

"Like I said, you don't owe me an explanation." Her lips twitched a little. "But . . ." She drew out the word. "I'm glad you rushed over here to give me one."

He released the breath he'd damned well been aware he was holding. "I wanted to tell you at Cuppa Café when you asked me about tonight."

"But you got called away."

He nodded. "And I don't have your phone number." He pulled out his cell and held it out to her, determined to rectify that right now.

She accepted the phone and programmed her information into it before handing it back. "Sam . . ."

He looked into her eyes, the blue appearing darker tonight, which seemed to match her suddenly serious tone. "What is it?"

"This isn't easy to say."

He didn't like the sound of that.

She exhaled and his gaze was drawn to her pink, parted lips. He already knew what she tasted like. He knew how soft her mouth was beneath his, what kind of little sounds she made in the back of her throat when that kiss got out of control. No way was she about to walk away.

Was she?

"I moved here to start over, and I left a whole host of complications behind." Her eyes glazed with the memory of something that clearly wasn't good.

Sam narrowed his gaze, but before he could respond, she continued.

"What I'm trying to say is that I'm not looking for anything serious or complicated now," she said in a soft, apologetic voice. "But —"

He wasn't looking for serious or complicated either. Still, she had something more to say, and he leaned in close. "But?" he asked.

"I do want something with you."

He grinned at that, everything in him easing in ways he didn't completely understand. "Good. Because I definitely want something with you. And after tonight, there won't be any more obligations getting in the way."

Many painful hours later, Sam drove Margie home from the fund-raiser. Nicole left earlier, after dancing with more single men than Sam thought Serendipity possessed, and because he had a date, there was nothing he could say or do.

That would end after tonight.

Margie still lived in her parents' home, which shared a property line with Faith and Ethan's house on the hill, both far from Sam's family's home on the opposite side of town. But economics had nothing to do with why he'd been ducking her advances for years. There was nothing about her he found appealing, not her personality or her looks from what he could see — and hear — because she hadn't stopped talking since they left the country club. Luckily, the club was closer to her end of Serendipity, and soon he pulled into her driveway.

". . . and I think your sister likes me, don't you?" Margie asked.

Sam blinked, realizing he'd missed most of the one-sided conversation.

"Umm . . . I'm sure she does." Actually, he figured Erin had as little tolerance for Margie as he had.

"Why don't you come in for a drink?" She turned in the seat so she faced him, her ample cleavage plumping over her gown.

"I don't think that's a good idea."

She waved away his concern, treating him to a whiff of her strong perfume, which he'd already been informed was Givenchy. "If you're concerned about appearances, I have my own private entrance around back."

Of course she did. Along with her own stipend, which meant she didn't have to work. He wasn't in her social class and her interest in Sam was purely sexual, which was why he didn't feel bad turning her down. She certainly wouldn't get her feelings hurt, but that didn't mean he'd deliberately set out to be cruel.

He gripped the steering wheel in both hands. "That's not it."

"Oh, you're shy!" She reached out a perfectly manicured hand and stroked his arm. "Good thing I'm not," she whispered in what he supposed was meant to be a

76

seductive voice.

God. He did not want to hurt her feelings any more than he wanted to have this conversation, but the woman couldn't take a polite hint.

"Margie, I had a nice time tonight, but —"

"Oh, so did I! I always knew if I could persuade you to go out with me you'd see the potential." She ran her hand down his arm.

He closed his eyes. "I don't. I mean I just want to be friends."

"Well, of course, silly. I want that too. Very good friends." She dropped her hand to his thigh, and Sam jumped so high in his seat his head nearly hit the roof of the car. She made him want to grab for his gun, which he always had on him, he thought, laughing to himself. Though he really wasn't amused.

He grasped her wrist before she could touch him anywhere else. "I *only* want to be friends," he clarified. "I'm sorry, but —"

"I'm offering you everything . . ." She gestured from her cleavage on downward. "And you're turning me down?" she asked, her voice rising. "Oh my God, you must be gay."

He blinked in shock. "I'm not gay." Although gay was preferable to her. "I'm just not interested that way. You're a nice woman and I'm sure there's someone out there who can make you very happy. It's just not me."

"Screw happy. I have everything I want except sex with a hot guy. What's wrong with you that you don't want to give me that?"

Sam stared at her, recognizing that she had more than one screw loose. "Like I said, I'm sure there's someone out there for you."

"I've always wanted you," she said, composing herself again.

And clearly she wasn't used to not getting what she wanted. So when he'd agreed to this date, she'd assumed they could be together. "But I don't want you," he said, deciding her persistence called for extreme measures.

She narrowed her gaze.

"I'm sorry," he felt compelled to say again.

"Fine. I'm sure Rob Burnett will be interested since you aren't."

Sam couldn't think of a better fit than Margie and Rob, the player. He remained silent, and with a huff of annoyance she flung open the car door, not waiting for him to get out or even react, and flounced — there wasn't a better word for her gait — down the driveway and around back to her private entrance.

Sam shook his head and pulled out of the driveway, glad to have this night over and Margie Stinson out of his life so he could move on to what mattered.

Just the thought of Nicole, looking so damn beautiful in that blue dress that draped her curves, had all thoughts of any other women evaporating as if they'd never existed for him at all.

FOUR

The morning after the gala, Nicole walked into The Family Restaurant for breakfast. She asked for Macy, only to be told her friend wasn't working this morning, so she settled into a booth and ordered an egg-white omelet and a cup of coffee. A few minutes later, a woman who looked to be in her midsixties made herself at home in the seat across from Nicole.

"Hello," Nicole said, not recognizing the older strawberry blonde with teased hair and wrists covered with bracelets.

"Hi yourself." The woman set her arms on the table and stared at Nicole.

And continued to stare until Nicole became uncomfortable. "Can I help you?"

"Get off my turf."

Nicole blinked. "Excuse me?"

"You're a baker?"

Nicole nodded warily.

"Then what I said stands. Leave and

80

nobody will get hurt." The other woman slapped her hand on the table for emphasis, revealing extra-long, fluorescent orange nails.

Nicole didn't know what to make of this crazy lady. "Look, I don't know who you are, but I'm new in town. I don't know you. I don't even own a business —"

"So let's keep it that way," she said, pinning Nicole with a heated stare.

Nicole grabbed for her purse, tempted to run and to get far away from this lunatic, but ultimately decided to stand her ground.

"Hello, ladies." Macy's familiar voice was a welcome interruption.

Nicole looked up at her new friend. "This . . . this crazy woman was threatening me."

Macy frowned and plopped herself onto the cushioned bench next to the insane woman and forcibly shoved her farther into the seat to give herself more room. "Aunt Lulu, I warned you to behave. I told you Nicole was a friend and that you two would have a lot in common."

"This is your aunt?" Nicole pointed to the woman, who was now grinning at her.

"Yes, and you two have so much in common, I just know you'll get along. Like I told you last night, Aunt Lulu bakes pies and cakes, while Nicole said she bakes specialty items, like cupcakes, cookies, and pastries. Aunt Lulu, weren't you talking about opening up your own bake shop?"

Nicole's gaze shot to Macy. "You didn't think to mention this?"

She waved away Nicole's question. "Because I knew you'd make fantastic partners, but you two needed to meet first. Aunt Lulu's protective of her niche, but trust me, this is a match made in heaven." She nudged her aunt again. "Tell her you're not threatening her."

Aunt Lulu let out a loud laugh. "Of course not. I had to make sure she could handle me," she said, an apology in her voice. "I am sweet, I am sarcastic, I am woman."

Nicole shook her head in confusion.

Aunt Lulu patted her hand. "I was testing you, doll. You passed. You didn't hit me, you didn't shriek like a banshee, and you didn't run. We'll get along just fine." The other woman braced her arms back on the table. "Now, ready to talk turkey? Or cakes, pastries, and pies, as the case may be?"

Nicole glanced at Macy. "Are you sure she's not insane?"

Macy shrugged. "No more than anyone else in my family."

Nicole couldn't say she felt any better

about that. She thought she'd left true insanity behind.

A few minutes later, she reevaluated her feelings on the woman and her mental state. Aunt Lulu had pulled a fully thought-out proposal from her oversized purse. Not only did she have a location for a bake shop in mind, but she also had a business plan. Apparently, she'd been working on the idea ever since she received a settlement from an accident of sorts at a local supermarket. But at her age, she wasn't sure she wanted to go into business alone, so she'd been debating on what to do.

Nicole, she'd decided, was fate, or she would be once Macy tasted Nicole's baked goods. She'd promised to bring some items by as well.

They brainstormed for more than an hour. Nicole added her thoughts, and Aunt Lulu — she insisted Nicole call her that too — promised she'd incorporate everything they'd discussed into a more thorough plan. She'd already been scoping out the old bakery Sam had mentioned to her the other day. She suggested that they each put in the same amount of money and approach the bank for a startup loan to cover other costs, and get started.

Everything about Aunt Lulu's plan was

professional, and since the Donovan family had been in business for years, Nicole had even more confidence in Aunt Lulu and her abilities. Still, Nicole would ask around town about her reputation . . . just in case.

During their talk, Nicole's cell phone rang twice. Tyler's name showed up both times. She winced, knowing she'd have to call him later today and make it clear she wasn't going to change her mind about ending their engagement. She was not looking forward to the conversation.

After wrapping things up with Aunt Lulu, Nicole headed to the grocery store for a major food shopping excursion. Once she arrived back at the apartment and started to put away all her staples and other items, Nicole stepped back and eyed the place in dismay. The cabinets were full and she'd had to stack things on the counters, cutting into her working space, what little there'd been to start with.

As much as she liked her apartment over Joe's, loved that it was in the center of town and had a month-to-month lease, the tiny space was slowly driving her insane. And she hadn't been there long. Her old apartment in Manhattan hadn't been huge, but it did provide room when she dove into baking. Here she hadn't even been able to unpack her beloved mixer and other countertop appliances.

She'd thought she could make do until she came to a decision about whether she'd get a job or attempt to open her own bake shop, but she was wrong.

She'd need to make another move, and soon. She needed the newspaper to see what was available. Grabbing her bag, she opened the door — and came face-to-face with a vase full of flowers. "What the . . . ?"

"Umm . . . Surprise?" Sam moved the vase away from his face. "You didn't give me a chance to knock."

She looked him over, taking in his weekend appearance. A worn pair of jeans, a black T-shirt, and stubble gave him a scruffy, appealing look, and pleasure rushed through her at the sight of him.

"Hi." She smiled, and he grinned at her in return.

"I obviously caught you leaving."

She nodded. "I was going to pick up a newspaper and see what houses or condos are available to rent. I thought this place was cute when I first found it, but it's too small. I can't bake anything substantial here and I'm feeling claustrophobic."

"I can understand."

She glanced at his full hands, realizing

how rude she was being, and stepped aside. "I'm sorry. Come on in."

He held out the flowers, and she felt herself blush as she accepted them. "Thank you. They're beautiful."

His gaze met hers.

He didn't say *so are you,* but the way he looked at her, devouring her with his eyes, as if he could see her inside and out, made her feel all kinds of special.

She set the bouquet down on her counter, where she'd have a good view of them from wherever she sat in the apartment, looked at him, and grinned.

"What's that smile for?" he asked.

She glanced at the flowers once more. "They're daisies. I love daisies."

"I'm glad. I wanted to get you something different."

"Why?" she couldn't help but ask.

"Because *you're* different," he said in a deep voice, and her entire body flushed hot.

He glanced around the small apartment. So did she, viewing the one counter in the kitchen and the bed that remained in her peripheral vision. Yep, it was time.

"Want company on your hunt for a new place to live?" he asked.

She raised an eyebrow. "Really? You want to spend your day off helping me house or condo hunt?"

"I want to spend my day off with *you.*"

She did a happy dance, at least inside. "Okay, then. Let's go buy a newspaper and check out the ads." She grabbed her purse from the counter and swiped the keys off the hook on the wall.

Hours later, Nicole had discovered that for a small town, there were a variety of rentals available and not all offered the same things. From condos like the one Cara had lived in, to an apartment complex down-town, to rooms for rent in a freestanding home, Nicole had her choice and she and Sam had walked through every one.

Her legs ached; she was exhausted and ready to call it quits. "I don't mean to be so picky, but nothing we saw works for me."

She stretched her legs out in Sam's SUV. He'd insisted on driving since he knew his way around town, and now she was glad she'd agreed.

"It's not picky to want to like where you live." He rested his arm across the two front seats, his fingers grazing her shoulder.

She suppressed a delightful shiver. "At least you're not annoyed. Which I don't understand. Most men in their right minds would have no patience for a day like today."

"Are you saying I'm insane?"

She shook her head and laughed. "No, just special."

He grinned, revealing that dimple in his cheek. "Thank you."

"I guess it's time to head home," she said, discouraged.

"Not quite. There's one more place that isn't listed."

She turned toward him, hopes raised. "Really?"

He nodded. "It's in a nice neighborhood, has a backyard with a barbecue, and a really good-looking neighbor next door." He winked at her.

Her eyes opened wide at his implication. "Seriously?"

He nodded, and his devilish grin had her wanting to agree to move in sight unseen. "Why didn't you mention this place before?" Unless he didn't really want her living so close to him but was offering because she'd run out of options.

"Because I wanted you to see everything else out there. The sellers are an older couple who want to test the weather down south for a year. You'd be making a one-year commitment and —"

She leaned in closer. "And?" She urged him to continue.

"It's a whole house. I wasn't sure you'd

want such a big responsibility on top of the year lease." He shrugged.

"So it wasn't because you didn't want me as your neighbor? Because I can understand why you wouldn't. I mean, we could hang out and discover we're not interested in each other and then we'd be living almost in each other's backyard, and that would be awkward."

He shook his head, the easygoing grin never leaving his face. "Like I said, I wanted you to see everything else first. That's it. You didn't like the other options and I'd have shown you this last even if you had. Besides, I would love to have you as my neighbor." He paused. "If that's something you'd want."

As if she'd say no. "I'd love to see it."

"Good." He turned and focused on driving, turning the car and heading toward his home.

"I have to say, I'm surprised you live in a house," she said.

"Why is that?"

She shrugged. "I guess I expected you to live in a bachelor pad of some sort. An apartment or condo where you don't have to worry about taking care of things when an association or landlord could do it for you."

"I always knew I'd stay in Serendipity, so why throw my money away on a rental?"

Why indeed? The man had *hearth and home* written all over him, making Nicole wonder why he hadn't settled down with one woman long before now.

"So why haven't these people listed their home in the paper?"

"It's been up for rent for a while, and they live on a fixed income. They didn't want to spend any more money on advertising, so they put up signs around town. But they plan on leaving their furniture for whoever rents. They left me the key to show to potential buyers when they're gone."

He turned onto a treelined street with older but appealing-looking homes. The kind she'd always imagined living in when she was growing up in her parents' overly large, too coldly decorated mansion.

"Home sweet home," he said, pulling into a driveway that appeared to have freshly laid blacktop.

"This is your house?" she asked.

"Mine and the bank's," he said. "But I've been able to pay a little more on my mortgage each month, and I hope to own it outright sooner rather than later." He jumped out of the truck and came around to her side just as she'd picked up her bag and opened her car door.

"Let's go inside and I'll show you around. Then I'll call the Browns and ask if it's a good time for us to come over."

Excited, she scrambled out of the car, eager to see where and how Sam lived. She followed him to the front door.

As Sam led Nicole into his house, damned if he wasn't nervous to see her reaction. Not something he understood, but he realized her opinion of him was important.

"The good news is my mother and sister insisted on making this place livable, so you won't find that bachelor pad you mentioned."

He swung open the door and gestured for her to walk in ahead of him.

This, of course, gave him a good view of her delectable ass in white, fitted denim. Her pink flip-flops with flowers on top smacked against the floor as she entered.

"Sam, I love it," she said from the den immediately on the right, the room that overlooked the street.

He shut the front door and headed into his favorite space, the family room, which boasted a large television on the wall above the stone fireplace and plush oversized furniture in brown and cream. But there were touches that made the place a home, like photos of his family, and accent pieces, as Erin called them, that looked good but Sam didn't know anything about.

"Oh, look! A softball trophy." She bent down and read from the plaque. "Star pitcher." Straightening, she met his gaze with a full-on grin. "I'm impressed, Officer Marsden."

"Detective," he automatically reminded her.

"Right." A smile curved her beautiful lips.

"We play two nights a week during the summer," he said, keeping his brain on track.

Her eyes lit up. "I'd love to come watch you play."

"Next game's tomorrow night at the high school field." He watched her expression to see if she was serious or just being polite.

She clapped her hands, her excitement genuine. "I'll be there."

"Pizza after?"

She smiled. "It's a date . . . Detective."

Their gazes held for a long moment, before she broke the connection and continued her inspection of the room.

"I'll call about the house," he said, before he crossed the small space dividing them and did what he wanted, which was kiss her senseless, this time without interruption.

Luckily, Charlotte and Henry Brown were home and thrilled to have Sam bring over a potential renter. A few minutes later, Nicole had toured the house that was but a few short feet from Sam's, and she'd fallen in love. In fact, he'd had a difficult time dragging her out of the kitchen to see the rest of the house. Although the appliances weren't brand-new, they were clean and white, the countertops spacious, the layout perfect for someone who loved to cook. And once she did tour the other rooms, the expression on her face was pure bliss.

"I have to admit, I didn't think about renting an entire house, but this place is perfect. Quaint and homey . . . and me. The kitchen is perfect." She spun around, and Sam knew he was looking at his new neighbor.

His sexy new *neighbor* that he wanted in his bed as soon as possible.

Macy had just finished her shift and was ready to head home. The restaurant was quiet, the evening help had taken over, and she planned to enjoy the first night she'd been free for dinner in what felt like ages because she'd been covering for a sick waitress.

She hung up her apron and grabbed her purse from the back room. She stepped into the main part of the restaurant in time to see a stranger sit down at the counter. Blond hair, cut short and styled well; he wore a navy suit with a red tie, and he looked as tired as she felt. But despite the weariness in his expression, she couldn't tear her gaze from his handsome face. A face so chiseled and perfect, she would remember if she'd met him before.

Suddenly, her urge to rush out of the restaurant disappeared. She slipped back through the doors and stashed her bag behind the desk. And silly though it might be, she stopped in the employees' restroom to check the mirror and freshen her makeup a little before heading out front once more.

She intercepted Nell, the waitress who was about to take his order. "I've got this," Macy said.

Nell glanced over Macy's shoulder and sighed. "Young, hot, and sexy. Of course you're staying longer."

Macy grinned. "Don't sound so put out," she said to the older woman. "You'll go home to your husband tonight."

"Oh honey, my husband didn't look like that man even when we met. But I do love him, so go. Take your shot with the stranger." Nell winked at her and retreated to the kitchen.

Macy twirled the drink tray in her hand, drew a deep breath, and walked over to the man. "Hi," she said, placing fresh silverware in front of him on the counter.

"Good evening." Startling green eyes settled on hers.

"Hi," she said again.

An amused smile curled his lips. "Can I get a menu? I'm starving."

She shook her head out of the cloud she'd been lost in. "Of course." She handed him a large plastic menu. "I recommend the meat loaf. It's today's special."

He lay the menu down on the counter. "Meat loaf it is."

His smile lit up something inside her she didn't recognize. "I'll just go put in your order. Drink?" she asked.

"Cola's fine."

She nodded. "Okay."

"Come back? I have a couple of questions maybe you can answer."

Macy raised her eyebrow. Intrigued, she nodded. "Be right back."

She turned the order in to her uncle, the chef, then filled a glass with ice and soda and returned to find the man where she'd left him, staring out the window onto the street.

"Looking for someone?" She placed the

glass and a straw in front of him.

"As a matter of fact, I am." He swiveled back around to face her.

"It's a small town. Chances are I know whoever you're searching for."

He shrugged. "I'm looking for my fiancée."

Disappointment filled Macy, but she wasn't surprised a gorgeous man like this had a woman in his life.

He let out a sigh. "Actually she's my ex-fiancée."

Macy perked up at that.

"I drove here straight from work, over an hour from Manhattan with traffic. I'm looking for Nicole Farnsworth. Know her?"

Macy blinked, surprised. "I do." She came around the counter and settled onto the stool beside him.

"Where is she staying?" he asked.

She narrowed her gaze. She didn't know him, and Nicole hadn't mentioned a man in her life. "Did you say Nicole was your fiancée?"

"Ex." His eyes hardened at the word.

"Your idea or hers?" she asked boldly, having her reasons.

He pushed back from his seat, surprise in his eyes. "Hers. Now will you tell me where she is?"

Macy eyed him warily, wondering if the handsome devil was telling her the truth. Because if he was, that meant Nicole had dumped this perfect specimen of a man, and that made no sense to her. At. All.

"What's your name?" Macy asked him.

"Tyler Stanton. Yours?"

"Macy Donovan."

"I would normally say it's a pleasure, Ms. Donovan —"

"Macy," she interjected.

He frowned. "But you're not helping me out. And I thought small towns were friendly." His jaw was now working in frustration.

She leaned in close, inhaling the potent scent of his aftershave. Even after a full day, he smelled manly and delicious. God, what a traitor she was, lusting after her new friend's ex-fiancé.

But no matter how humiliating, she wouldn't allow her hormones to override her common sense.

"I'm very friendly. In this case I'm protecting my friend. If you leave me a number or hotel information where she can reach you, I'll give her the message."

"Ms. Donovan."

"Macy."

He worked that sexy jaw once more.

"Macy. Don't you think I've called her cell phone more than once before I drove all the way upstate?"

She couldn't contain her grin. "I think she's obviously not returning those calls, which means she doesn't want to talk to you." And here she thought Nicole was a smart woman.

He scowled at her.

"What? If she wanted to see you, she'd answer your calls. What kind of new friend would I be if I just turned her over to you without making sure that's what she wanted?"

He ran a hand through his hair, his frustration obvious. "Fine. Tell her I'm in town and I need to see her. Can you please tell me where I can find the nearest hotel?"

"Five-star, or is a bed-and-breakfast okay with you?" Macy couldn't help teasing him.

"I'm guessing there are no five-star hotels around here."

She shrugged. "Twenty minutes away. But you look exhausted, and I promise you the Serendipity Inn is clean and the food homemade." She pulled out her cell phone. "I'll even call ahead and make sure they have a room available. How's that for friendly?"

"Works for me." His grin warmed her inside and out.

She made the call and secured him a room. "Tell you what. Eat dinner, then go get a good night's sleep. Then come back in the morning, breakfast on me. In the meantime, I'll try to reach Nicole."

"Now that's mighty neighborly of you, Ms. Donovan." He winked, and if she were another type of woman, she might have swooned. "You've made me reassess my opinion. You're definitely friendly. In fact, if I were Nicole, I'd be damned glad you had my back."

"That might be the nicest compliment I ever received."

"Macy! Food's up!"

"Excuse me," she said to her customer. She walked back to the kitchen.

"Who's the hunk?" Aunt Lulu asked.

Macy narrowed her gaze. "What are you doing here? Isn't it bridge night?"

"I stopped by to pick up the pie I baked for after we play. Now spill."

Macy loved her aunt, trusted her business sense, and knew she had a big heart. But she also loved to gossip, which meant she wasn't giving the woman any information. Not until she knew what was going on with Tyler from Nicole herself.

"Just a customer." She picked up his order. "Thanks, Dad!" She waved to her father, the cook in the back. He shared shifts with her uncle.

He winked at her and went about his business. He hadn't inherited his sister's propensity for talking or gossip.

"Have fun tonight," she said to her aunt, and walked back into the restaurant with Tyler's food.

She set his meal in front of him, noting once more the utter perfection of his chiseled features, and did her best not to sigh. In a small town like Serendipity, Macy had seen all the available men and often despaired of meeting anyone new. Didn't it figure the one she found droolworthy was her new friend's ex. And true friends just didn't go there.

"Enjoy," she said, turning to go.

"Keep me company?" he asked, surprising her.

She wasn't technically scheduled to work anyway . . . "Let me just get myself something to eat and I'll be right back," she agreed, knowing that her attraction to this man was a bad thing.

But he hadn't shown any reciprocal interest and clearly he was here for Nicole. And if Nicole had really ended things with him, he wouldn't remain in town for long. So

Macy decided that keeping him company wouldn't hurt anyone at all.

FIVE

After viewing the absolutely perfect house next door to Sam's, Nicole immediately agreed to the rental. She and Henry Brown, a nice older man, had shaken hands, and with them moving out for good tomorrow, she could be in this coming weekend. In true small-town fashion, the couple wasn't worried about doing a background check because they were happy to take Sam the cop's word, and he'd vouched for Nicole. Promising to forward the lease information tomorrow, they said good-bye, excited to let their children know about the rental.

Nicole had a new home.

Suddenly overwhelmed, she tried not to panic. She had to make a list of things to do — talk to Joe, her landlord, and give notice; pack up her apartment; hire movers . . . or could she do the move in short car trips?

"Are you okay?" Sam asked as they walked back across the lawn.

She nodded. "I think I'm just in shock."

He laughed. "Good shock, I hope."

She thought about the kitchen and the space, the beautiful bedroom with a small chaise longue giving her a place to curl up and read. "Awesome shock," she assured him. "I'm going to love living in a house."

"I'm going to love having you next door," he said in a husky voice.

She shivered at the sexual innuendo inherent in his words and his tone.

She followed him inside his house and into the kitchen.

Without warning, a yawn hit. She covered her mouth but was unable to stifle the small noise that escaped, and she laughed.

"The day must be catching up with me. I'm exhausted." She turned to Sam. "Would you mind driving me back to town?"

"Yes, I think I would mind." He stepped closer, invading her personal space, not that she cared.

He smelled deliciously male and her exhaustion disappeared, replaced by something far more pleasurable.

"I spent the whole day apartment hunting and I worked up an appetite. I kept you company while you did your thing. The least you could do is stay and have dinner with me," he said in a teasing but self-assured tone.

She was simultaneously amused and pleased with his blatant attempt to keep her around. "Pizza?" she asked hopefully.

"You got it," he said, with a satisfied grin.

She guessed he hadn't been sure she'd stay. As if she'd want to be anywhere else. These uncertain, awkward moments were normal, but she knew for sure there was nothing questionable about what she felt for this man. As long as she kept things simple and uncomplicated, she'd be fine.

"Toppings?" he asked, picking up the phone.

"Your choice. I'm easy."

His eyes darkened at her accidental double entendre. He ordered a large everything pizza, requested delivery, pulled two beers from the fridge, and offered her one.

She nodded. "I've always had a weakness for cold beer. Ever since college, other girls liked wine, but I preferred beer. I still do." But her recent life hadn't been conducive to brew.

Tyler, his mother, her parents, and their friends all preferred expensive alcohol.

He grabbed the opener from the counter, and as he popped the tops, Nicole's gaze fell to his broad biceps and the muscles that flexed as he moved. She stifled an appreciative sigh that caught his attention.

His gaze held hers, a wealth of desire in that one look passing between them. He placed the bottles on the counter and extended his arm toward her.

Heart pounding, she placed her palm in his rougher hand.

He pulled her against him, aligning her body with his. She acted on instinct and wrapped her arms around his neck. It felt right. Good.

He felt right.

His hand came up to cup the back of her head and he sealed his delicious lips over hers. They'd been dancing around this moment, building the yearning since the last time. The Nicole she knew didn't have such fire and intensity of any emotions burning in her veins, needing to get out.

With Sam, she did.

So, apparently, did he.

There was no way she could not respond, and she kissed him back with more passion than she'd known she possessed — sliding her lips sensuously over his, opening and inviting him inside. He kissed her back like a starving man who was now devouring what he needed and taking more, storing up as if he'd never have enough. His hands moved from her head to her cheeks, his thumbs smoothing over her skin, causing small electric shocks all over. A heaviness throbbed in her breasts and a definite pulsing began down below.

Unable to stop herself, she inched closer, threading her fingers through his shaggy hair. His masculine groan of appreciation reverberated through her. Oh, yes, they were in this together, and she liked that as much as she liked him.

His lips swept down her cheek, her neck, and finally landed on the sweet spot near her throat, where he took his time, nuzzling and nipping at her skin. This time *she* moaned. While he licked and teased her there, his fingers slid up her shirt and soon he cupped her aching breasts in his hard, hot hands. She arched her back, pressing herself against him, and he squeezed her harder, eliciting another moan. Heat settled between her thighs, and she squirmed, needing his touch there now more than ever.

Sam couldn't mistake her desire, not when she smelled so sweet, and she was so pliant in his arms. Her breasts filled his palms, each just slightly larger than his hand, and when she arched into him, the pebbled points of her nipples pricked his skin. His cock throbbed against his jeans, but he ignored his own needs, right now content to test just how sensitive she was and enjoy fulfilling her wants.

He brushed his thumbs over the lace fabric of her bra, turning her nipples into even firmer darts, and she gripped his hair harder, a clear signal not to stop. He couldn't if he wanted to. He was lost in this woman, like nothing he'd ever experienced before. He didn't want to break the kiss. Hell, as much he wanted to thrust inside her hot, willing body, he could kiss her like this forever.

And he would have, had her cell phone not rung, interrupting the moment.

He groaned and stepped back, his forehead still touching hers.

"Go ahead. Get it," he said, silently cursing whoever was on the phone.

With a disappointed sigh, she headed for the other room where her phone was, leaving him feeling the loss. He shook his head, knowing how crazy that sounded. Still, he was enjoying everything about Nicole — and the fact that she was moving in next door meant all systems were go between them.

He heard her steps as she came back to the kitchen.

As she entered the room, he glanced at

her, noticing she was paler than before and a lot less relaxed.

"What's wrong?"

"I . . ."

Nerves pricked at his skin. "Just say it," he told her, recognizing that her hesitation meant nothing good.

"Macy called. I had a visitor at her restaurant. Someone looking for me here in Serendipity."

Sam narrowed his gaze. "Okay . . . I'm sure you told people at home where you were going, so why would a visitor be a surprise?"

"Umm, there's two parts to that answer," she said without meeting his gaze. "One, I told my parents where I was going, but there's a good chance they didn't actually *hear* me. They aren't interested in anything more than me staying home and not messing up their plans."

"What sort of plans?" he asked, suddenly edgy.

She bit down on her lower lip. The same lower lip he'd been suckling on minutes before. "I was engaged."

The word echoed around the room and slammed into his brain.

"I broke it off before I left Manhattan and moved here to start over," she said, her words coming out on a rush.

Only one word stood out in Sam's mind. "Engaged," he repeated.

"*Was* engaged."

"So there's an ex-fiancé out there," he said, and as he spoke, he realized just who was in town, causing her to panic. "And he's the one who's here."

She nodded, eyes wide. "But it's over between us. I've told him it's over. I haven't been taking his calls because I don't want to give him the wrong impression. So I have no idea why he'd come." She rubbed her hands together, her panic and nervousness obvious.

Which were weird reactions, if he thought about it, but beyond having to confess to an awkward omission, he couldn't understand why she'd be so flustered. Then again, what did he know about the relationship between her and her ex-fiancé? He'd learned long ago not to think he knew people — Sam had set up one of his best friends with what he thought was a stand-up guy, only to find out once they were married that he was nothing of the sort.

Sam rubbed a hand over his face, exhaustion and frustration suddenly claiming him. He couldn't believe this night had done such a one-eighty.

But he only had one focus, one part of this story that involved him. "If the guy was your fiancé, chances are he had good reason to have the impression that you loved him," he said with bite, because he'd been in that ex's shoes and he knew what it felt like to have a woman break things off.

In Sam's case, *left at the altar* was an accurate statement, so he understood being blindsided. He didn't want to feel bad for the guy, who was probably here to try to talk Nicole into coming back to him. But hadn't he done the same thing? Right after Jenna ended things, he'd tried to get her to remember the good times, the plans they'd made. He'd tried to understand when she'd changed her mind — and why he'd been too blind to see it. To this day, he didn't have a clue.

"I thought I loved him," Nicole said, interrupting Sam's mental trip into the past. "And then I realized I didn't," she continued.

He swallowed hard, wondering just how easily she'd walked away from her ex. And how fickle would she become with *him* after a while? He shifted uncomfortably, this whole situation too sudden and way too close to his past. It had him questioning his own judgment when it came to Nicole, and he needed time to think.

The doorbell rang, giving him a reprieve, and he went to accept the delivery. When he returned, Nicole was looking at him with wary eyes, a far cry from the heavy-lidded, desire-filled gaze of earlier.

"Are we okay?" she asked, running her hands up and down her bare arms.

"We're fine," he said, knowing he was lying.

He needed to sort through his tangled emotions, which were clearly confusing Nicole and bringing up a past he wanted to put behind him. He wasn't sure how to accomplish that feat.

So they ate in awkward silence, and eventually Sam drove Nicole back to her apartment over Joe's. When she got out of the car, he didn't mention their planned date tomorrow night after the softball game.

And neither did she.

Nicole paced her apartment, not easy considering how small an area she had to walk, but she couldn't sleep. Nerves, anxiousness and not a little bit of panic raced through her. Not only because she'd clearly messed things up with Sam, but also because Tyler was in town. And that made no sense at all.

She'd dumped him. Most men's egos

would prevent them from calling, texting, or begging for a reconciliation. Initially after the breakup, he'd gone silent, as she'd expected. It wasn't until she'd arrived in Serendipity that he'd begun to call her.

Now he was here. Which raised the question, why the shift? What was he doing here?

Unable to settle her stomach, she still had to try to sleep. She didn't. At least, she didn't think she did. She tossed and turned, awakening early the next morning.

After a quick shower, she dressed, her thoughts bouncing from having to deal with Tyler to Sam's unexpectedly harsh reaction to her past. She just didn't understand the extent of his withdrawal. It wasn't like she was still engaged to Tyler. She'd been nothing but up front and aboveboard with her ex as soon as she'd realized she didn't feel the way she should if she was going to marry him. But Sam acted like she'd left Tyler at the altar or something equally cruel.

She'd called Macy last night for more information, and Macy told her Tyler would be at the restaurant this morning. As much as Nicole wanted to get this meeting over with, she couldn't go anywhere until she had her scheduled phone call with her sister.

Her mind was on everything but Vicky, yet Nicole needed to give her twin one hundred percent of her attention. She'd never seen Vicky try so hard to control her disorder, work with therapists, take her meds, and truly want to make amends for her behavior.

At least the gravity of what she'd done had finally sunk in. The incidents with Erin had escalated until Victoria had tried to run her over with her car. Only once she'd been medicated and thinking clearly had Vicky's own behavior scared her, and Nicole was willing to do anything to help her sister overcome her past and try to live as close to a normal, healthy life as possible. Someone had to, as their parents considered both girls a lost cause when it came to representing their high standards.

At nine A.M. on the dot, Nicole's cell rang and she answered, settling in the middle of her bed for the conversation. "Hello?"

"Hi," Vicky said, sounding clear and present.

"Hi yourself." Nicole paused, always uncomfortable asking the usual *how are you* when her twin was in a mental hospital for the criminally insane. At least the institution where she was housed was filled with minimal-behavior-problem inmates. Hopefully, her stay would be temporary, contingent on good behavior and doctors' reports to the court.

"So tell me what's going on in your life," Vicky said, before Nicole had to fill in the silence.

Nicole paused, knowing her sister was still too fragile to confide in about her own troubles. Vicky's recent behavior meant Nicole couldn't yet trust her to stay on medication and keep a secret about what Tyler's father had done. And though Vicky knew Nicole had moved to Serendipity, Nicole was still hesitant to talk about the town and remind her sister of Cole and her behavior there.

"I recognize that silence . . . you're afraid to talk to me," Vicky correctly said. "But my therapist said I shouldn't avoid conversation or worry about triggers while I'm in here. That this is the best place for me to be while testing the waters, so to speak. So stop worrying so much and tell me about your life in Serendipity."

"The twin connection at work again?" Nicole asked, figuring that was how her sister knew what she'd been thinking.

"No, it's just obvious."

To Nicole's surprise, Vicky giggled, sounding like the little girl she'd once been. The warm sound helped her relax, and she leaned back against the pillows and the wall.

Freed up to talk about Sam, Nicole decided that was as far as she'd go with her own situation. "Okay, well — remember the cop who arrested me when he thought I was you? Sam Marsden?"

"The good-looking guy with the shaggy blond hair? How could I forget?"

"Maybe because you've always been drawn more to the dark-haired types," Nicole said, teasing.

"Are you seeing him?"

Nicole swallowed hard. "I was — I'm supposed to catch up with him after his softball game tonight, but something happened and now I'm not so sure."

She went on to tell her sister about the house she'd agreed to lease, her night with Sam, kisses included — because who else could she tell but her twin — and how things had imploded after Macy's phone call.

"So now I have to head over to the restaurant this morning to deal with Tyler." Nicole's stomach churned at the thought. "Why can't the man take no for an answer?" she asked out loud.

"Because you're special, that's why," Victoria said.

Nicole opened her mouth, then closed it again. She couldn't remember the last compliment her twin had given her.

Ever.

The older she got, the less Victoria had been interested in Nicole's life, too self-absorbed to think about anyone but herself. Over time, it had become hard not to resent her twin, but as an adult and with her sister's diagnosis, Nicole had worked hard at overcoming that feeling. Victoria hadn't chosen to be as she was.

"Thanks, but come on. I'm not that special."

Vicky snorted. "Really. You're a good person, Nic. You give of yourself even when others don't give back. Me included. Well, me especially. But in Tyler's case, he knows how good he had it with you."

Nicole hoped and prayed that was all Tyler thought. She was beginning to wonder if maybe he was involved in things with the firm and was here to persuade her to keep quiet.

Nicole forced her mind onto the conversation with her sister. "But I don't love him the way I should in order to marry him."

"And you'll just have to keep gently driving that point home. You wouldn't want to end up with him stalking you," Vicky said lightly.

"Don't do that."

"If I can joke about it, you should be able to as well."

Nicole managed a smile. "Who are you and what have you done with my twin?" She decided to take her sister at her word and not sidestep the issues she was working so hard to overcome. "You sound great. You're focused on things around you, me included. And you haven't once talked about yourself. So now I'm giving you permission. Tell me how things are really going."

Her sister's sigh gave away more than her perky voice had. "It's lonely here. But let's face it, I'm not in this place to make friends, and I don't want to. So I'm focused on getting better."

"That's a good thing. And I told you I'd come visit." The institution was two hours away, but Nicole was more than willing to make the drive.

"No! I don't want you to see me here." Vicky's voice rose in panic.

"Whatever you want," Nicole quickly assured her.

It would have to be enough that they were talking weekly on the phone. Early on, Victoria wasn't willing to even do that. Their more recent phone calls were proof that the medication-and-therapy combination were working.

"I have to get going," Vicky said, before Nicole could ask if she'd been in contact with their parents.

Nicole already guessed the answer was no. In their eyes, Victoria was now a public embarrassment, so her parents would ignore her completely. At least they were paying for her lawyer and other expenses, hoping their daughter's recovery would help their public perception, which was all they cared about.

"You make sure to fix things with the hot cop," Vicky said. "I'll talk to you next week."

"Looking forward to it already," Nicole said.

"Bye."

"Love you."

Vicky paused, then whispered "Good-bye" before disconnecting the call. She still found it hard to reach out, or to say things like *I love you* or *I miss you,* but today's phone call had been the best so far.

With little things changing, Nicole felt the return of the bond she and her sister had shared when they were young. It also felt like a missing piece of herself was being returned to her — filled up slowly, like sand in an hourglass. And Nicole was grateful for each minuscule bit she received. She was also afraid to trust that it would last, having seen Victoria regress more times than she wanted to recall. Still, she reminded herself she'd never seen her at the low point she'd been at after her arrest, nor had she ever watched her try so intently for recovery.

Hope, Nicole thought, was a scary, elusive thing — no matter what kind of relationship was involved. For someone who'd been consistently rejected and ignored by her parents, the very people she should trust to be there for her, the fear of being hurt or rejected — by Sam especially — remained.

Pushing off those thoughts, she refocused on her most pressing problem: Her ex-fiancé.

Sam had the day off, so he agreed to meet Cara at The Family Restaurant for breakfast. He was in a pissed-off mood and his sister-in-law noticed immediately.

"Well? Are you going to answer me? What, or should I say who, has you in such a foul mood?"

Sam shoveled a mouthful of scrambled eggs into his mouth, ignoring Cara's question for the second time.

"You're not getting laid? Is that it?"

"God damn, you're persistent. Would you talk about something else besides me?"

"Nope. You're so much fun to annoy." She

119

pushed her uneaten breakfast away. "But the real reason is I hate to see you so worked up, so talk to me."

"It's Nicole," Macy said, coming up from behind them and squeezing into the booth alongside Cara.

"Eavesdropping? Seriously, have you no shame?" Sam asked.

But knowing she'd met the ex last night, Sam was glad to have her here. Not that he'd give her the satisfaction of admitting as much.

Macy met Cara's amused gaze. "No, none." She glanced from Cara's plate in the center of the table to Cara herself. "What's wrong with the food?" she asked.

"Nothing. I'm just not hungry," Cara said.

Macy frowned. "Can I get you something else?"

Cara shook her head, and even Sam wondered what was wrong. She usually out-ate him without worrying about calories. She had a great body and metabolism, not that Sam noticed much because she was his good friend and his brother's wife.

"I'm fine. Talk to me about Nicole."

Sam rolled his eyes. "Her ex-fiancé is in town."

"I didn't know she had one of those," Cara said, eyes widening.

"Me neither." Sam ground his teeth.

"Same," Macy said. "Although I met him last night and I have to say, yum yum."

Sam shot her a nasty look.

"Not helping the cause," Cara reminded her.

Macy blushed. "Oops. But come on. I asked who ended things and he said Nicole did. So obviously you have nothing to worry about where she's concerned."

He ignored her and took a drink of his coffee.

"He's not speaking today. To anyone, apparently," Cara said.

"Well, he's listening, so I'll just mention that I told Tyler — that's his name — to come here this morning for breakfast. And Nicole called and asked me to save a table in the back so she could talk to him without being interrupted."

Sam's stomach twisted hard.

"She said she wanted to make sure he understood she was serious about breaking up." Macy stared hard at Sam. "Do you hear what I'm saying?"

"His head's still in the past, isn't it?" Cara asked. "Now that you know Nicole broke her engagement once, you're worried she's just like Jenna. That you can't trust her or your feelings for her. Am I right?"

Before he could react, Macy reached across the table and slapped the side of his head. "Hey! That's ridiculous."

"When you're the one left stranded the morning of your wedding, then talk to me about what's ridiculous." He retrieved his wallet and threw money on the table, enough to cover his and Cara's breakfast, and rose from his seat.

"You're leaving? Before you see Nicole? Before you offer your support? Before you remind her you're here for her?"

Sam glared at Macy, annoyed with her intrusiveness.

"Oh, I'm sorry. Go right ahead and leave the door open for Tyler Stanton, since Nicole already thinks you're disappointed in her for breaking her engagement." She waved a hand in dismissal.

With a grumble, Sam lowered himself back into the booth, unwilling to *say* Macy had a damn good point. He might not be happy about the situation or Nicole's past, but no way would he step aside. Which meant he'd have to get over himself and his history — at least enough to admit he still wanted Nicole. Which meant they'd have to have an open, honest conversation and make it clear they weren't talking about a serious relationship between them. Just some feel-good sex while it lasted. He thought they were in agreement, but he'd feel better knowing for sure.

All well and good, Sam thought, knowing that what *he* wanted didn't take into consideration her ex-fiancé.

Which left him the odd man out while they spoke this morning. Waiting. Wondering.

Hoping for the best.

Six

Drawing a deep breath, Nicole walked into the restaurant a few minutes ahead of schedule. She planned to get settled in a booth in the back before Tyler arrived. To help, she'd pulled all the armor around her that she could think of, including dressing like the woman she was in Serendipity. Make that the woman she was — period. From her low-rise white jeans to Converse sneakers and a loose, flowing tank top, she was far from the couture-wearing fiancée she'd once been.

She arrived at the restaurant, shocked to find Macy, Cara, and Sam together in one booth. Uncomfortable but not willing to duck and run, she forced herself to meet Sam's gaze. He acknowledged her with his searing stare, giving her no indication of what he was thinking or feeling.

Insides quivering, she knew she had no choice but to pass them on her way to the booth she'd reserved in the back. "Hi," she said, pausing at the head of their table.

"Hey," Cara said.

"Hi, hon." Macy raised a hand in a wave.

Sam's gaze merely latched and held on to hers.

"I should go wait in my booth," she murmured, when she couldn't take the awkward silence any longer.

She turned and made her way to the back of the restaurant, knowing Sam's silence had clearly made his point. He was still angry and upset.

She reached the private booth in the back just as he called her name.

She spun at the sound of Sam's deep voice, finding him so close his body bracketed hers against the wall, confusing her since his actions were at odds with the emotional distance he'd put between them. "Sam —"

"I'm sorry."

She lowered her jaw. "You're —"

"Sorry I was a jerk. You were honest with me about your past and I reacted based on my own."

She narrowed her gaze, as relieved as she was baffled. "Your past?" What didn't she know?

"Yeah." He ran a hand through his golden

hair. "Look, we need to talk. How about after the game tonight?"

Before she could reply, a shadow loomed over them. "Nicole." Tyler's voice held more than a hint of disapproval, no doubt over finding her in a near-clinch with Sam.

She waited for Sam to step back so she could make the awkward introductions, but Sam was in no rush and remained in place, his hard body bracketing hers.

"Nicole!" Tyler repeated, obviously upset.

She eyed Sam imploringly.

"I'm just waiting for an answer," he reminded her. "Tonight after the game?" He touched her cheek with one hand, obviously staking a claim.

Oh God. Her entire body trembled. "Yeah," she said softly. "Okay."

He grinned, obviously pleased he'd won this round, and eased away from her oh so slowly. By the time he'd removed himself from her personal space, she was surprised smoke and flames weren't shooting between them.

Tyler cleared his throat. "Aren't you going to introduce us?" he asked.

She shook her head, hoping to clear her mind. "Tyler Stanton, this is Detective Sam Marsden. Sam, Tyler." She gestured between the two men, refusing to give either one of them a designation like friend, boyfriend, or ex-anything.

They eyed one another warily, each assessing the competition. Which was ridiculous, since Sam had none and Tyler had driven all this way for no reason. But she didn't want to hurt him, and Sam's deliberate claim-staking hadn't helped toward that goal.

By the time Sam strode away, Nicole was shaking inside, and she hoped her nerves didn't show on the outside.

"Shall we sit?" Tyler asked.

She nodded, aware of her friends at the front of the diner, along with the other familiar faces who'd come in since she'd arrived. Serendipity was a small town and, like most, people here enjoyed good gossip. Nicole's ex-fiancé and her new relationship with Detective Sam Marsden would certainly provide this morning's talk and entertainment.

It took everything inside Sam not to turn around and watch Nicole and her well-dressed, clearly rich, everything-Sam-was-not ex-fiancé. It took even more fortitude for him not to sit back down with Cara and Macy and wait for Nicole to finish with her talk. Instead he strode straight out of the restaurant, headed for his car, and drove away, deciding he'd be better off doing work around the house. At least that way he'd be productive and not pathetic.

He hadn't planned to compare, but clearly Nicole had a type. Both he and this Tyler Stanton had light hair and light eyes, his hazel, the other guy's green, but where Sam was more of a guy's guy, Tyler was obviously more of the *GQ* variety. Khaki pants, polo shirt, short hair that wasn't barbershop cut. Which raised the question — what was the classy Nicole Farnsworth doing slumming with a Serendipity cop? And how long would her walk on the other side last?

Knowing he was in a precarious position, Sam asked himself what the hell he was doing. For a man who didn't want to invest emotions or his heart, he seemed to care too damned much.

He'd been blindsided by a woman once before. This time his eyes were wide open, so if and when Nicole walked away, Sam had known the possibility existed going in.

And he'd have nobody to blame but himself.

Nicole couldn't read her ex-fiancé because Tyler was still focused on what had gone down with Sam. So was Nicole. At least he wasn't angry, but he had alluded to interesting information about his past. She couldn't begin to imagine what had happened to him, nor did she have time to think about it when Tyler faced her across the table, his expression tight.

"Tyler, why are you here?" Nicole got right to the point. Better she know immediately what she was up against.

He folded his hands on the table, took a visible, relaxing breath, and said, "I came for you. I came to see what kind of hold this town has on you and why you felt you had to leave home — and me — to settle down here."

Nicole expelled the breath she'd been holding, hoping things were as simple as he claimed. This, she could deal with.

"I already explained why I broke up with you. I don't want to hurt you, so please don't make me say it again." She stared into his green eyes, hating that he was putting her in the position of having to rehash the breakup.

"You said we didn't have sizzle. Chemistry. Then I come here and find you with that cop."

"Detective," she replied, then realized she was echoing Sam and managed not to smile.

"That detective is the reason you left me."

"That's ridiculous. I barely knew him when I was here last." But he had been the catalyst that made her realize what she had with Tyler wasn't enough. Still, why tell him and dig at his pride?

Tyler ran his hand through his closely cropped hair. "I'm not going anywhere, you know. I'm staying until you come to your senses."

Nicole stiffened. Such extreme behavior was not Tyler's normal MO, and now she had to wonder — again — whether there was more to him being here. What did he know? Was he aware of his father's activities, and on what side of the illegality did he fall? She knew what her heart told her, but she couldn't risk her safety by mentioning she knew his firm was money laundering. What if he suddenly turned on her, or, worse, called in the Russian mob to handle her if he couldn't?

"I don't . . . You can't . . . What?! Why would you stick around?" Nicole finally sputtered.

Completely unruffled, he replied, "Because we belong together." He reached across the table in an attempt to place his hand over hers, but she was quick enough to shift her shaking hands to her lap.

His eyes flickered with disappointment.

"I'm happy here," she told him.

He raised an eyebrow in an arrogant expression she knew well. Tyler was many things — a gentleman, yes, but also occasionally entitled. "We'll see."

She shook her head. "I'm going to go about my life," she warned him. And that meant seeing Sam.

"You do that. And I'll be here to remind you of everything you left behind."

Why? Because he thought they were such a love match? This determined behavior in the face of her rejection was so unlike him, she believed to the depths of her soul there was more going on than he was saying.

"Go home," she tried once more.

He shook his head and pinned her with a steady, certain, *determined* glare. "I'm not going anywhere without you. There's too much at stake."

The morning crowd kept Macy busy after her friends left, but not so busy that she didn't notice that Tyler remained behind for a while, obviously thinking over what had transpired between him and Nicole. Nicole, she'd noticed, had looked for Sam when she left, and had been disappointed to find him already gone.

What a tangled mess, Macy thought.

Something the likes of which Serendipity hadn't seen since . . . well, since Jenna left Sam at the altar for Brett, his best friend. Sam had had a rough time then. He'd been so humiliated and embarrassed, and everyone in town had gossiped about it for months. She shook her head, glad Sam was on the winning side of things this time around.

The rest of the day passed quickly, but Macy was embarrassed to admit she'd thought of Tyler Stanton more than a few times. He wasn't her usual type, too buttoned up for Serendipity, but that didn't seem to matter when he was so darned sexy. She sighed, wondering how many boundaries she'd be crossing by flirting with him. Just a little. Nicole was happily involved with Sam — or wanted to be — so what could it hurt?

She was pondering that very question around five P.M., knowing she could leave soon to head home and change before the seven P.M. softball game.

Tonight the cops were playing the firemen. *Hot* didn't begin to describe the field, she thought with a wry grin. Too bad she'd known all these guys since they were boys, dated a few, and was interested in none. She lifted her gaze at the same moment *he* strode into the restaurant.

"Hello, Ms. Donovan."

"Macy," she reminded him. "And we've got to stop meeting like this."

He shook his head, obviously unsure what to make of her. Which was fine. Many had that initial reaction. She said what she thought, joked even if only she understood, and tried to enjoy life.

"I'd like a seat. Counter or a table is fine," he said.

"Take your pick." She gestured to the line of empty booths.

He chose the first table closest to the hostess stand, and she eyed him with pure female appreciation as he took the few steps to sit down. Wearing the same khaki pants as earlier, she took in his very fine ass that accented his lean form.

She handed him the menu.

"I have a feeling I won't be needing one after a while," he muttered to himself.

She raised an eyebrow at that. "Planning on sticking around?" she asked, unable to stop the hope rising in her at the possibility.

"Looks like it. I think Nicole's testing the waters, and I want to be here when she realizes everything she's left behind."

What did it say about her that Macy was pleased? Pathetic, that was what she was.

Dimples or no, the man was stuck on another woman.

"What if she's not just testing?" Macy asked.

He set his jaw. "She is."

Macy raised her eyebrows. "Are you always so sure of yourself?"

He met her gaze, suddenly looking at her, really studying her as if seeing her for the first time, and she shivered beneath his steady stare.

"Are you always so blunt?" he asked.

"Yes, and you didn't answer me."

"Yes, I'm always that sure. If I want something, I get it." And he obviously wanted Nicole.

But Macy had been the bystander to many people falling in love over the last few years, and when that particular emotion hit, it hit hard. It also started with dynamic chemistry, and she'd seen explosive heat between Sam and Nicole. Tyler didn't have a chance, but then . . . why did he want one? Why pursue a woman who'd made her lack of interest and intentions not to be with him so clear?

Macy liked a good puzzle, and Tyler was that. Especially since he didn't look all that hurt by his ex-fiancée's obvious feelings for Sam.

"So what is there to do in town?" he asked.

She shrugged. "Depends on the night."

"Okay, how about . . . say tonight?" An amused smile lifted his mouth, making him even more handsome.

She swallowed hard. She really shouldn't bring up the softball game. Sam was playing and he'd mentioned plans afterward with Nicole. But if Macy didn't say anything and he wandered around town or asked someone else, he'd find out anyway.

"There's a softball game at the high school, but you don't know anyone here, so I'm sure that would be boring for you."

"Are you going?" he asked.

She nodded.

"And do most people end up there?"

She inclined her head once more.

"So . . . say Nicole would be there?"

"Could be." Macy rocked on her heels, consoling herself that she hadn't been the one to offer up the information without him asking first.

"Then I guess I'll see you there."

She looked him over, caught the determination in his green eyes, and decided not to argue, just to be there beside him. As a buffer, she assured herself, not because she was determined to turn his focus away from Nicole and onto herself.

"But you really can't go so dressed up,"

she said.

His eyes opened wide. "These are my casual clothes."

She sighed dramatically. "Jeans are casual clothes. Cargo shorts are casual clothes. Khakis are dress clothes."

He shook his head. "Suits are dress clothes."

She bit the inside of her cheek and did her best not to laugh even if she did think he was cute, something she doubted he'd find amusing.

"If you're hanging around for a while, do you want to stand out? Or do you want to fit in?" she asked him.

He frowned. "Your tone tells me there's only one right answer to that question."

"Did you bring *more* casual clothes than those?" Assuming he owned the kind of wardrobe to which she'd referred, which she was beginning to doubt.

"I didn't plan on more than a day trip. I can drive home later today to pack up some things."

"More of these?" She gestured to his polo shirt, this one a pale green with a blue pony on his chest. "Never mind, don't answer that. The mall's just twenty minutes from here. We can get you a couple of pairs of shorts and jeans, maybe a T-shirt or two, and be back before the game."

He let out an exasperated sigh. "I'm sure I have a pair of jeans in my closet."

She clasped her hands behind her back. "Are they pressed?"

He opened his mouth in outrage, then closed it again. "Probably."

She burst out laughing, enjoying this man way more than she should. "Come on. Order dinner and then I'll take you shopping and show you how the other half lives."

Sam was pitching at tonight's game, which meant he had less time to focus on what was going on outside the baseline. But he wasn't blind, his peripheral vision was just fine, and he could see exactly what he shouldn't let distract him.

Erin and the baby sat on a blanket, a safe distance away from the game and fly balls, with a good view of the field. Nicole had joined them, which provided enough of a diversion that Sam was off his game. But by the third inning, when his arm was warmed up and Nicole settled in to watch *him,* he'd begun pitching better. Until Macy arrived with Tyler Stanton — and they didn't go to the bleachers. Instead, they pulled up folding chairs and joined Sam's sister — and Nicole.

Instead of letting the other man get to him, Sam gritted his teeth and put his anger and frustration into the game.

Nicole had run into Erin at Cuppa Café, where they'd both had the same idea to bring large iced teas with them to Sam's game. They talked while they waited, and soon they'd agreed to meet up again on the field and share a blanket. Erin, an old pro, knew exactly where to sit so the baby wasn't in any danger of being hit by a foul ball, and Nicole was happy to have someone to be with and talk to. She liked Sam's sister a lot, and her daughter was the sweetest-smelling, most adorable-looking baby Nicole had ever laid eyes on. Both helped take her mind off her troubles.

Those troubles revolved around Tyler. Thanks to a phone call from Macy, who had apparently appointed herself Tyler's escort around town and Nicole's go-between, Tyler had informed her he'd taken a room at the Serendipity Inn for an extended and undetermined period of time. And Nicole still had that awful feeling his presence here was tied to everything she'd left behind and still hadn't decided how to handle.

She pushed the thought out of her head and focused on the reason she was here tonight. Sam. The man filled out his softball uniform, his thighs tight, his ass spectacular. Her sex clenched just watching him, a new and exciting reaction to just watching a man.

Three innings into the game, Erin realized she'd forgotten diapers in the car and took Angel with her to go get them. Nicole didn't mind being left alone, as she was already invested in the game. The cops were up by two runs and she couldn't take her eyes off Sam, his muscular arms flexing as he pitched, and the intense concentration on his face holding her transfixed.

"Do you mind company?" a familiar masculine voice asked.

Tyler. Nicole stiffened. "Umm — I don't think that would be a good idea."

She looked up and was grateful to find Macy standing beside him. Her presence took much of the pressure off Nicole. She didn't feel bad turning him down.

"Come on. You've got the best seats in the house," Tyler said, coming up beside her.

Resigning herself to the unavoidable, she waved her hand. "Have a seat," she reluctantly said, but she refused to let their presence dampen her enthusiasm for the game.

She did her best to ignore Tyler and cheer Sam through an erratic pitching period, relaxing when he settled into a rhythm once more. Up at bat, he drove in two runs, and when he hit what looked to be a grand slam, Erin, Macy, and Nicole yelled their loudest as he rounded the bases for home plate.

Nicole was aware of Tyler sitting beside her, a scowl on his face.

"You don't have to be here," she reminded him, no longer keeping her tone gentle or worrying about hurting his feelings. She'd made herself clear. He was choosing to ignore her request for him to go home.

"Yes, I do. Until you come home with me, I'm staying."

"I *am* home." With each day that passed, she felt more and more sure of her decision to settle in Serendipity.

Tyler grunted in reply.

None too soon, the game ended, the cops won, and they all stood, folding their chairs and blankets. Erin, who had the baby hanging from a sling around her chest, managed well, but everyone insisted on helping her carry things to the car.

"Thanks," the auburn-haired woman said with a genuine smile. "I'm going home. Hopefully Cole's finished working by now. He had a conference call with a new client and said he'd be a while."

"Drive safe," Nicole said, as Erin buckled

the baby into the car seat in the back of her truck.

"Always. Precious cargo in here." She shut the door and turned to face them. "It was fun. Let's do it again next week," she said.

"I'm in," Macy said automatically.

"Same," Nicole added, hoping she wasn't beaming because Erin had extended such an easy invitation.

She thought about her friends at home and the posturing that usually accompanied each and every invitation, nothing ever being what it seemed. Either there was a fundraiser where someone wanted to one-up the other with clothing, a date, or amount donated, or there was behind-the-scenes bickering that turned Nicole's stomach.

So different from the genuinely simple life here. No wonder leaving had been so easy. Her friends hadn't been genuine, but she was finding out there were better people in the world. People she liked and who liked her. In Serendipity, she was discovering friends and filling empty holes. Except now Tyler had arrived, bringing Nicole's old life here to confront the new. She didn't know how to make him go away, and even if he left, she was all too aware that he wouldn't be taking her most pressing problem with her.

Maybe once she and Sam settled things, she could consider confiding in him. . . . She immediately shook her head. He was a police officer, sworn to uphold the law. If she told him her father's firm was laundering mob money, he'd be forced to report the information — and if that was the route she decided to take, she certainly wanted time to talk to Tyler and her father first. Assuming she felt comfortable enough to think they weren't involved. Which brought her full circle and had her insides cramping once more.

"Hey, I'm starving. Let's go get something to eat," Macy suggested.

Tyler nodded, his gaze briefly meeting Macy's before landing on Nicole's — and lingering.

"Ummm, you two go. I'm going to wait for Sam." They had a date, and Nicole didn't plan on making it a double.

Tyler ran a hand through his neat hair, and Nicole recognized the sign of frustration. She glanced at Macy. "Show him a good time?" The imploring *please* didn't need to be said out loud.

She knew she was imposing further on her new friend, but she needed this night with Sam and she'd make it up to Macy. Who, Nicole suddenly realized, was smiling and not looking all that put out by the request.

"I think I can manage to keep him busy," Macy said. "Come on, big boy. Let's go get dinner. And maybe dessert."

"Macy, let's see what everyone else is doing first."

"Why, when I know all the good places to eat in this burg?"

She hooked her arm through Tyler's and began pulling him toward the car.

And Tyler, though he grumbled, went along rather than jerk his arm back from Macy and be rude. The woman was a true dynamo, unique among people Nicole had met. In a good way, unlike some other pushy women she'd known.

Macy led Tyler to her car and soon they were gone, leaving Nicole alone. She was grateful Macy could help her out, but she'd have to make sure the other woman knew Tyler wasn't a simple guy to date — without revealing everything she knew and involving Macy in her problems. Even if Tyler was a free agent, he came with other baggage and expectations. And Macy didn't seem the type to bend to someone else's needs and desires.

Nicole caught a glimpse of Tyler's back and the stiff, obviously new denim. The Tyler she knew did not own faded light jeans, which meant Macy had prodded him into the change. Instead of jealousy, Nicole felt pure amusement and a sense of hope that Macy could help Tyler see reason. She already had him changing his way of dress, and he'd allowed her to drag him away from the sole reason he'd come to Serendipity.

Despite all the potential problems, Macy could be good for Tyler, Nicole thought. She just wished she knew if Tyler could be good for Macy. Or if he'd take his head out of his parents' expectations that he'd marry well and into a connected family long enough to look at the treasure that was Macy Donovan. They'd just met, which meant it was way too soon to even think that way, but Nicole liked the thought.

"Hey." Sam came up to her, looking sexy in his dirt-stained uniform caused by numerous slides around the field.

"Hey yourself. Great game." She smiled at him, happy he was here — and they were alone.

"Thanks. Where'd your friend go?" he asked, his tone turning dark.

"Macy took him out to eat."

Sam raised an eyebrow. "That bother you?"

"Should it?" she replied.

He blew out a long breath. "Not if you're

telling me the truth, no."

She set her jaw, determined not to get into an argument with him about her ex. But there was one thing they needed to get straight now. "Either you trust me or you don't. And if you don't, we call this off right here and now. But if you do? No more digs about truth and honesty, all right?"

He blew out a deep breath before answering. "Fair enough," he said, a surprising smile lifting his lips. "I have an important question."

"What?" she asked warily.

"Did you enjoy your pizza the other night?"

She let out a loud laugh. "No, I didn't. I was too upset."

"I thought so, and me neither. Pop's really does make the best pizza, so I thought we could head on over there and try again. There are some things I think we need to get clear between us."

She nodded, knowing he was right. "I'd like that."

He hefted a bag higher on his shoulder, and she realized he was hauling around a lot of weight.

"That looks heavy. Where's your truck?" she asked.

"There." He pointed at his SUV a few feet

away. They headed there and stored all his gear in the back. He turned to her, sweaty and dirty from the game in the night heat, and he'd never looked better to her. Hotter. More sexy.

"I didn't think this through . . . I'm filthy," he said. "How about we go to your place over Joe's so I can at least wash up. I keep a change of clothes in the trunk, and then we can walk to Pop's down the street."

She nodded, okay with whatever he suggested.

Less than an hour later — because who cleaned up faster than a man — they arrived at Pop's Pizza. They settled into a booth and Sam reached across the table for her hand, causing excited flutters in her belly.

"So we both like pepperoni."

She grinned. "Something in common."

"Look, since it's quiet and we can talk, I —"

Before he could finish, the restaurant door opened and Macy and Tyler walked in.

Nicole closed her eyes and groaned.

"What's wrong?" Sam turned in his seat and stiffened. "Son of a bitch."

Tyler pulled Macy right over to their table. "Funny running into you here."

"Not laughing," Sam said.

Nicole met Macy's apologetic gaze. This truly was a coincidence, she knew.

"Tyler, let's have Chinese next door," Macy suggested.

"Good idea," Sam muttered.

He shook his head. "I'm allergic to MSG."

Nicole would have rolled her eyes, except he was telling the truth.

"Then let's take a table in the back." Macy tugged on his arm.

Tyler met Sam's steely gaze. "We're all adults and clearly this is a small town, so we'll be running into each other. Might as well get friendly."

Before he could slide into the booth next to Nicole, Macy whipped around him and inserted herself there instead. Tyler eyed the long bench Sam sat in the middle of.

"Hell no," Sam muttered, and shoved himself out of the booth. "Macy, out."

Nicole stared at Sam, who was acting in a way she'd never seen before.

Obviously responding to the authority in Sam's voice, Macy immediately scooted out of the seat.

"Sam, we've already ordered, so let's just eat and then we'll go," Nicole said, not because she wanted to stay but because it was the polite thing to do.

"Did you order yet?" Sam asked Macy.

147

Obviously he wasn't speaking to Tyler.

She shook her head.

"Then enjoy." He held his hand out to Nicole.

Without thought, she placed her hand inside his larger one, savoring the feeling of skin against skin as he helped her out of the booth.

"You're being rather rude," Tyler said.

Macy glared at him. "Shut up." She glanced at Nicole. "I'll talk to him. I promise."

"Still here," Tyler muttered. But he didn't argue anymore about Nicole and Sam leaving.

Nicole blinked.

She'd never spoken to Tyler that way, and she doubted he'd take it well if she had. But this was Macy's personality and she'd decided to take charge . . . and he'd allowed it. Still, she'd done it as if she and Tyler had known each other longer than twenty-four hours.

"Amazing how quickly you two became close," Nicole said, curious about this new relationship.

Macy chuckled. "I wouldn't call us close, but I'm the only almost-friend he's got in this town."

"Quit talking about me like I'm not here,"

Tyler said, more insistent this time. "I'm not an idiot. I just believe Nicole and I have too much in common to let things go so easily."

Nicole narrowed her gaze. Too much at stake. Too much in common, and he didn't sound like he meant pepperoni pizza. What was going on?

Sam tugged on her arm.

"I already told you where I stand," Nicole reminded Tyler. "We're leaving." She nodded to Macy, turned, and let Sam pull her out of the pizza parlor and onto the street.

SEVEN

Anger and annoyance beat through Sam until he reached the sidewalk and fresh air, putting Nicole's ex behind them. "What the hell?" he asked her.

She stared at him with wide eyes. "I honestly wish I knew. He was never that possessive when we were together. All I can think of is that maybe his family is putting pressure on him to fix things with me," she said, her eye twitching as she spoke.

Sam studied her. "Why?"

"Can we go somewhere and talk? Instead of doing this here?"

He nodded. Her hand was still in his, so he merely tightened his hold and led her back toward Main Street and the gazebo where they'd shared their first kiss.

She waited until they were settled in the seats there before speaking. "My father and Tyler's are partners in an investment firm in Manhattan. Our families have known each other forever. In fact, Tyler and I practically grew up together, so when we started dating, it seemed . . . meant to be."

He nodded, processing the fact that they'd had such a long-standing relationship. That they shared a bond. He fucking hated it. A sentiment way out of bounds when he didn't want more than a casual relationship with her, no matter how strong the desire.

"So they'd naturally want you two together," he said, pushing down the emotions that rose with her story. Jealousy was okay. Annoyance that her family thought her destined for someone else was not.

She bit down on her lower lip. "That's part of it," she murmured.

"There's more?"

She looked down at her hands, which now ran up and down her thighs. "I'm not sure."

"But you think so. Why?"

"It's complicated," she said, still not meeting his gaze.

He'd seen her in an interrogation room, and she'd been at turns feisty and scared but she'd always looked him in the eye. He shook his head, beyond confused by her words and demeanor. To the cop in him, she was hiding and avoiding, yet he couldn't deny there was truth in much of what she said. She just hadn't said everything.

"Can I ask you something?" Now she met his gaze head-on.

"Sure."

"What did you mean when you said you overreacted when you found out about Tyler because of your past?"

He blinked, startled by the change in subject. He wanted more information about her ex but sensed she'd told him the truth when she said she didn't know why Tyler was pushing so hard to get her back. Oh, he didn't doubt she knew more, but that more wouldn't change things between them, and he had enough faith in his skills to know he'd get the information eventually. And since Jenna, at least this time he knew better than to invest his heart in any woman, but especially one with secrets. And Nicole had plenty.

They didn't need full disclosure to have phenomenal sex and a great time together. They just needed enough of an exchange for there to be trust and a sense of comfort, and they could give each other that.

"I was engaged once too," he told her.

She sucked in a surprised breath.

"What? You can't imagine someone wanting to marry me?" he joked, because when discussing this part of his life, which he *never* did, he had to deflect somehow.

"Sam —"

"I'm kidding. But I was engaged. To my high school girlfriend. We stayed together through college, and honest to God I thought my future was set."

"What happened?" Her blue eyes remained steady on his, full of compassion and curiosity.

Pity, he didn't want, but so far she seemed far from that emotion. "She dumped me for my best friend," he said bluntly. "The morning of the wedding."

Nicole winced.

"And that's why I reacted so harshly to the news that you broke it off with Tyler. It's also why I understand where the guy's coming from, even if he's a complete pain in the ass," Sam muttered.

She straightened her shoulders defensively. "Tyler and I hadn't set a date yet, and I did not and would not cheat."

"I didn't say you would."

"You painted me with that same brush."

"For a little while," he allowed. "And I apologized."

She nodded. "You did. But I sense you're still holding it against me."

He shook his head. "No. It's just that you need to understand what that did to me and my ability to trust —"

"Anyone. You won't let yourself fully trust anyone."

He inserted his hands into his pockets, letting her words speak for him.

She sighed. "Okay, now I know. Is there anything else?" she asked.

Sam groaned, knowing he was screwing this up badly. "Just that I don't want any unrealistic expectations between us."

Her full lower lip came out in a pout. "What was it I said at the fund-raiser? I'm not looking for complicated or serious myself. So . . . tell me your problem again?"

Put like that, he didn't have one. Although he was surprised by how much he disliked her easy acceptance of his demands. And for the first time with a woman, after making sure they were on the same page, he wasn't comfortable suggesting they head home for sex. She deserved more respect from him than that, also a new thought for him. Usually if a woman was willing to go to bed, so was he.

She cocked her head to one side. "Sam? Are you still thinking about things?" she asked, her voice a husky purr as she stepped closer. "Because I'm thinking we're talked out, thought out, and in agreement about what we want to come next."

It wasn't like Nicole to be forward or

brazen, but she forced herself now, sensing that any step they took next hinged on her convincing Sam they were on the same page. Not having him was unacceptable. Especially when she knew, from how angrily he'd dragged her away from Tyler, he desired her as much as she did him.

True, her experience with men was limited to Tyler and one other, but her realm of flirting was much broader. She knew how to schmooze a man in order to get him to loosen his wallet for a good cause. How different could it be to get Sam to relax and trust that she wouldn't push for more than he wanted to give?

She braced a hand against his T-shirt, feeling his heart beat through the thin cotton fabric. "Don't you want to pick up where we left off the other night?"

He grasped her wrist with a low growl. Next thing she knew, he'd pulled her against him and sealed his lips over hers. So much simpler than she'd anticipated, Nicole thought, before his tongue darted out, swiping over her lips, and she stopped thinking at all.

She already knew Sam was a master kisser and he didn't disappoint now, taking control of both her and the situation. And she gladly ceded power. He devoured her with his mouth, ravished her with his tongue. Their bodies came together and he rolled his hips against hers, slowly, methodically, over and over until flames lit her up from the inside out.

Together they created a raging inferno — there were no other words for the heated passion flaring between them. When he lifted his head and she looked into his eyes, they sizzled with the same urgency thrumming through her.

"Home?" he asked.

She managed a nod, thrilled with the knowledge that she'd broken through the last of his reserves. Now she hoped she didn't get crushed in the dust when he was through.

Nicole had been packing for her move, and once they were at her apartment, boxes surrounded them but the atmosphere didn't matter. She and Sam had been building to this moment since they'd laid eyes on each other months ago.

She shut the door behind them and Sam spun her around, her back coming up against the wall. She didn't know who was more desperate. Her hands went to the hem on his shirt, his to the bottom of her tank. Clothes ended up in piles on the floor.

He cupped her breasts and she fit perfectly in his palms. She arched her back, pressing her nipples against his flesh, seeking pressure. He gave it to her, brushing his thumbs over the turgid peaks. She moaned and he tweaked them harder between his fingers, working both breasts at the same time. Sensation spiked from her nipples to her core.

"You are so much more beautiful than I imagined," he muttered. "I need to see more."

With a fast rip, he tore the flimsy bra from her body, baring her to his hot gaze.

"Oh, man."

She trembled beneath his yearning stare, so sinful and hot, she could almost come from that look alone.

"This is why I ended things with Tyler," she said.

Sam froze.

Her limbs felt heavy, her body already his. "I knew, if I felt like this just meeting you, I couldn't marry someone who didn't give me one tenth of this feeling."

With a low growl, he bent down and swung her into his arms, carrying her the few paces across the apartment to her bed.

In her entire life, she'd never felt so desired. She'd never wanted anyone as much as she did Sam. She stared up at his handsome face, his hazel eyes glittering, his jaw set. He stripped off his jeans, taking his boxer briefs off along with them. Freed, his erection stood proudly against his stomach and she swallowed at the sheer size and beauty of him.

Her mouth watered and her clit pulsed with desire, her insides clenching with need. As if in a daze, she reached for him, wrapping her fingers around his rigid length, sliding her fingertip over the head and the drop of come there.

He groaned, his hips jerking forward into her waiting hand.

Her hips bucked upward of their own accord. "Sam —"

"I've got you." He eased her jeans down her hips, then her legs, tossing them on the floor. Keeping his promise, he cupped her mound, his thumb brushing over the thin fabric of her damp panties.

He had her all right, in more ways than one.

She jerked beneath his touch, sensation shooting through her, pleasure just out of reach — but he wasn't. She pushed up on her elbows and cupped his firm erection in her hands once more. Silk and steel, she thought, the need for his hard shaft inside her building like the rising tide.

He shook his head and jerked away. "If you want me to last, no more touching beforehand."

She laughed. "Then get on with it, Detective," she said, her voice huskier than she'd ever heard it.

Her underwear went the way of her bra earlier and as he stared at her body, she found herself oddly unembarrassed. He slid one finger through her wet folds and a keening sound escaped her throat. She would have been mortified, but he immediately followed by inserting the same finger inside her and beginning a steady pumping rhythm that built her need. In and out, in and out, pausing only to make sure she was with him. And oh, she was. She so was, and when he pressed inside her, on a spot no one had found before, she cried out. He followed up with his other hand on her clit and the crescendo had built to epidemic proportions.

"Is this working for you?" he asked.

"Oh yes." Her entire lower body was on fire, but the slow pressure he exerted wasn't enough. "And no. More, please." Her hips gyrated with unanswered need.

"Like this?" His fingers worked magic inside and out. He rotated his thumb over her clit, harder and harder, then pressed upward with the single finger inside her.

She cried out, her body spasming. "Oh God. More. Harder."

He replaced his thumb with the heel of one hand and her climax took hold and from a distance, she heard herself chanting. "Oh God, oh God, Sam, yes. Yes."

Her womb contracted, his finger kept up a delicious pulsing inside her, his whole hand worked her sex, and wave after wave of pure pleasure crashed against her body.

It was the most amazing orgasm she'd ever experienced. On and on the sensation went until she collapsed, spent, against the mattress.

She heard the crinkling of a condom wrapper, thanked her lucky stars he was prepared, and then the head of his erection pressed against her wet heat.

She forced her eyelids open and met his gaze just as he thrust deep and filled her, thick and hard, pausing to give her time to adjust. Time in which she felt him completely, and to her shock, her arousal rose again from the sensation of him throbbing inside her.

Her eyes opened wide in amazement. She was barely a mini-one-orgasm girl. From the aftershocks still rocking her body to the new sensations building again, Sam was surpassing anything in her admittedly limited experience.

He braced his hands on either side of her head and began to move, sliding in and out, his hot gaze never leaving hers. Another thing that was different — by looking at her as if he could see into her soul, he increased the heat, the urgency, the intimacy of their joining.

"Wrap your legs around my waist," he ordered.

Knowing her eyes were still wide with wonder, she did as he asked, and suddenly he was harder, rooted further in her body. Even better, the position provided more friction to her clit and she began the slow, steady climb once more.

When he pulled out and pushed back in deep, he hit that place inside only he'd ever found. She moaned and clenched around him.

"Damn, you feel so good," he said. "So warm, wet, and tight." With those words, he picked up the perfect movement that synchronized their bodies and drove her higher.

Her hands gripped his shoulders, her nails digging into skin. He groaned his approval and pumped his hips faster until she saw stars behind and in front of her eyes, the pleasure so beyond anything in her world that once again, her orgasm hit without warning.

"That's it, come for me," he said, and the ripples and waves of pleasure continued, finally cresting.

"Sam!"

His name on her lips triggered his release and he pumped into her once, twice, and on the third time, his groan vibrated through her body, which was just beginning to come down from her climax.

She held on to him as he came, aware that this wasn't the tepid sex she'd had before. This was explosive. It could get addicting. What scared her most of all? So, she feared, could he.

Tyler paced the small room he was renting at the Serendipity Inn, which in reality was a large Colonial that the owners had remodeled into a bed-and-breakfast. The floral décor and the warm colors were soothing at a time he felt anything but. Macy had been right when she said he'd be comfortable here.

Hell, she'd been right about a lot of things, including the fact that Nicole meant what she said and wasn't coming home to him anytime soon. The thought should bother him more than it did, but instead of focusing on Nicole, he couldn't stop thinking about Macy.

There was something appealing about the dark-haired woman, and it wasn't that she looked a little like Nicole. Macy Donovan was a force of nature, a gorgeous woman who wasn't intimidated by anyone, who said what she thought and did what she wanted. He admired her a lot.

Unfortunately, he was also extremely attracted to her. But he didn't have the luxury of acting on it. Indulging in anything beyond friendship with Macy was something he could not afford. Even if he had gone to bed thinking of her instead of Nicole, the woman he was trying to win back as his fiancée.

He'd been shocked to feel the stirrings of desire for Macy when he'd been so convinced he and Nicole were meant to be. But meeting Macy had forced him to reevaluate Nicole's breakup words — maybe she had a point about there being no fireworks after all. With Macy, her quick wit, and her ability to force him to do what she wanted, there were sparks aplenty.

How had his life gotten so out of control? Tyler ran a hand through his short hair. Not long ago, he'd thought everything was perfect. Family investment firm doing well, him due to take over when his father and Nicole's retired. And Tyler had been engaged to the woman he'd been in love with for what felt like forever. Turned out he'd been living in complete denial.

First Nicole had informed him that what she felt for him wasn't love, it was comfort and expectation born of being used to each other. There were no sparks between them, she'd said. Tyler convinced himself his fiancée was just getting cold feet. He figured she'd come to her senses.

Then she up and moved to Serendipity, and he realized she was serious about starting her life over without him. If that wasn't humiliating and life-altering enough, his father informed him that Nicole had come into possession of information that could bring down the entire business and put them all in jail, Tyler included. Then Robert Stanton admitted he'd added mob money to help their coffers when the market was bad, and now he was in too deep to ever stop.

He'd ordered Tyler to get himself to Serendipity and return with his obedient fiancée in tow — or he'd have no choice but to tell his *clients* that there was a chance Nicole had overheard a conversation and knew about the money laundering. And those *clients* weren't the type to leave any loose ends no matter how uncertain. They would put out a hit on Nicole, and Tyler would be responsible. He wanted to believe his father was bluffing but couldn't take that chance.

Nausea and panic threatened to engulf him — still did — but he ruthlessly pushed those feelings away. He couldn't afford to give in to weakness in the huge mess he called his life. Tyler was in deep trouble and so was Nicole. So he had no choice but to remain here and try to persuade her to reconcile and pick up where they left off — with her running his mother's campaign for borough president, him heir to the family financial firm, their marriage set.

And he had to persuade her without letting on that he knew about his father's illegal dealings. Though it would be damned easier to get her to come home with him out of fear and loyalty, there was still a chance Nicole didn't know the truth, and his admission would be filling her in. The more people who knew, the greater the risk of someone going to the police. Especially Nicole, who was now involved with a cop.

Of course, Tyler was considering turning his father in himself. But he needed time to insulate himself, his mother, whose campaign accepted funds from the firm, and Nicole. Tyler also needed Nicole to cooperate. But from the way she looked at Sam Marsden, he didn't see them separating anytime soon.

But that didn't mean he wouldn't do everything in his power to try. Even if guilt rode him the entire time and he couldn't stop thinking about a woman other than his ex-fiancée.

Sam woke in a strange bed, with a warm body wrapped around his. Since he didn't normally spend the night anywhere but his own place, he came awake immediately and realized where he was and who he was with. Instead of relaxing, he tensed even more because no sooner had he realized he was with Nicole than he instinctively pulled her deeper into him, wrapping his arms tighter around her smaller body. She fit him perfectly.

Sex last night hadn't been good, it'd been incredible. And that was what put his radar on high alert. The last time he'd felt anything remotely like this, he'd been a naïve younger man, being duped by his fiancée and best friend. And he was enough of an adult now to be able to look back and see that what he'd felt for Jenna paled in comparison to the beginnings of what he felt for Nicole. Young love had been just that, he realized now. And if Jenna was able to hurt him, what kind of havoc could Nicole wreak on his heart if he let her?

He wondered if he could extricate himself without waking her. He was just about to roll over when she stirred, easing onto her back and looking up at him with big blue eyes.

"Hi there," she said in a sexy morning voice.

"Morning."

"A good one, I hope?" she asked, vulnerability shining in her expression.

Obviously she wasn't used to mornings after, and no way would he hurt her just because he was running scared. "After last night, how could it be anything but?"

The tension in her body fled fast and her smile sent awareness shooting straight to his groin, which apparently hadn't gotten the memo about keeping a safe distance.

Now to work on his tension. As long as he took things slow, guarded his emotions and his heart, he'd be fine. Just because they'd had great sex didn't mean their agreement of nothing serious didn't still hold. Leaving now would be his best bet.

"Breakfast?" she asked. "I packed up the big stuff for the move later today, but I have enough to whip up an omelet or pancakes."

His stomach rumbled, answering before his brain kicked in.

She laughed, the happy sound making him feel like an ass for his darker thoughts. "So which will it be?"

"Pancakes, if it's not too much trouble." And then, because he couldn't resist, he leaned over and settled his lips over hers, kissing her until the churning in his stomach and the bout of nerves became a distant memory.

"Mmm," she said when he broke the kiss. "Better than food."

He grinned.

"But I need to get up and shower . . . Joe said he'd help me move boxes to the car around ten this morning."

"I have to work, or I'd help. But I'll carry some down before I head out." He'd have to stop home and change clothes before going to work.

"Thanks." She eased out from beneath the covers. Before he could get a look at her incredible body, she swiped her robe from a nearby chair and wrapped it around herself. "I'd ask you to join me but we'd never get moving today." Her eyes twinkled, and he knew he'd accomplished his goal of not making her panic along with him.

She showered, and he jumped in after her while she made breakfast. While he was drying off, the doorbell rang.

He wondered who it could be. Pulling on his jeans, he stiffened as he heard Tyler Stanton's voice.

"Morning, sunshine," he said loudly.

Sam shook his head. Did the man have no shame? He never gave up. Well, Sam had every intention of giving him a reason to walk away with or without his dignity intact.

"Tyler, you shouldn't have," Nicole said.

Sam narrowed his gaze.

"I know they're your favorite," he said. "I know a lot about you, remember? We shared a lot of things before —"

Sam had had it. Without bothering with his shirt, his hair still damp, he stepped out of the bathroom, well aware of what this looked like, wanting to give Tyler the right impression. "What are you doing here, Stanton?" Sam asked.

Nicole's gaze lingered appreciatively on Sam before darting to Tyler, whose cheeks flushed dark in embarrassment.

"I'm giving Nicole an early-morning delivery." To his credit, he didn't ask Sam the same question.

"Thank you." Nicole accepted the vase of yellow roses.

"She prefers daisies," Sam muttered. Or did she?

"Tyler, this really isn't appropriate. I already told you —"

Sam swallowed back a curse and pushed down on the jealousy. It wasn't like Nicole was leading the man on.

"I know. And I see things between you two are . . . serious."

Sam immediately stepped up and wrapped an arm around Nicole. "You're damn right. Which means you bringing her flowers isn't cool."

Nicole sucked in a startled breath. Yes, she knew the two men were adversaries, and of course it made sense that Sam would be jealous of Tyler. She'd feel the same way about any woman showing him attention, especially the morning after. But they'd agreed on an affair, nothing serious, they'd both said. Which meant he didn't have the right to tell Tyler what he could or couldn't do. Yet he stood here, his arm around her, telling her ex just that.

Sweet pleasure rushed through her at his warm touch, hugging her close, and his possessive words. Much as she hated to admit it, she'd woken up in Sam's arms, wishing for this very thing. Of course she'd immediately chastised herself, since she'd been a willing party to their agreement last night. And she had a new, independent life to lead here in Serendipity. No strings, no ties.

"I think it's up to Nicole whether she wants the flowers or not," Tyler said to Sam.

She shook her head. In all the years she'd known him, he'd never been so obtuse or dense. "The roses are beautiful, but Sam's right. We're involved, and that means you can't come around here bringing me flowers." Yet she held the vase in her hand, unable to return them because that would be rude.

"How involved?" Tyler pressed on.

Nicole opened her eyes in shock. "That's none of your business," she said, at the same time Sam said, "Very," causing Nicole's heart to skip a beat.

Damn her weak self for liking his words that much. Wanting more could only lead to heartache . . . and yet she sensed that more was exactly what she wanted from him after last night.

Sam stepped forward, prodding Tyler out the door. To Nicole's relief, he went without an argument, and Sam shut the door behind him.

Leaning against the frame, Sam turned to

171

face her. "Well, I hope that little show persuaded him to back off," Sam muttered.

Show?

Disappointment welled in Nicole's chest. She drew a deep, calming breath, refusing to let Sam see that *she'd* nearly bought into his *act* right along with her ex-fiancé.

"Nicole? You okay?" he asked.

She forced a smile. "Just fine."

"Can I help with breakfast?"

"Sure. Just let me straighten up first." She swung away from him, needing a minute that wasn't beneath his scrutiny.

She headed for the bed and began fluffing pillows and drawing up the comforter, cleaning up after them without meeting his gaze. And she didn't return to the kitchen area to make breakfast until she was certain she had her emotions under control. After growing up in her parents' household, she'd thought her protective shell was impenetrable. One look at Sam's handsome face, dismissing any notion of a serious relationship, and she knew she'd been wrong.

But the last thing she needed was for Sam to think she couldn't handle the affair she'd so willingly gone into last night. If he saw the signs of a clinging female, he'd take off running for sure. Which meant she'd just have to buck up — and grow up. Oh. And

172

develop a thicker skin.

Sam and the also newly promoted Cara worked a case that took them into the weekend. His mood was foul and since Cara didn't seem to be feeling well, she left him alone, not pressing him for information. Which meant they were both lost in their own thoughts and that of the case, and the weekend passed slowly. Aware that Nicole was moving into her place, Sam stopped by whenever he could to help. He wasn't the only one. For a woman new to town, she'd already made friends.

Whenever Sam found time to drive over, a different group of people were there, from Macy and her aunt Lulu, to Erin and Joe and Annie. And of course, to Sam's frustration, Tyler had shown up and planted himself in her house.

Tyler was doing his best to make himself indispensable, moving boxes, unpacking, and just . . . existing. Sam was disgusted. Tyler clearly didn't want her staying in Serendipity, but he made damned sure to help her settle in, something Sam hadn't the time to really do. And it drove him insane, how much Tyler's presence bothered him.

At least Macy was there, keeping Tyler

busy and as far from Nicole as possible, something Sam appreciated even if her reasons appeared more self-serving. There was a clear attraction between Tyler and Macy, and if Tyler wasn't still pushing for a reconciliation with Nicole, Sam would say they were destined to hook up. Tyler and Macy as a couple would only help Sam's cause.

Of course it would be better if Sam helped his own. As a cop and now a detective, he'd been trained to notice the little things, the twitches in someone's face, the shift in their expression. And the other morning, he'd caught the disappointment in Nicole's face when he expressed his relief that Tyler had bought the show Sam had put on for his benefit. Though Sam wanted nothing more than to draw her into his arms and reassure her, his own conflicting emotions kept him from doing so. Giving her the wrong impression of what he was capable of would hurt her even more. So his bad mood had begun.

And it permeated the entire weekend.

While he was at Nicole's, he helped with the heavy lifting and tried to be his cheerful self, but she had erected her own walls of protection and had a round robin of people helping her around the house. After a while, he wondered if she'd even notice if he hadn't come by at all. He'd have realized it, though, and missed her.

On his last trip, he ran into his sister on Nicole's driveway.

"Hey!" Erin gave him a kiss on the cheek. "Where are you off to?" she asked.

"Interview at the station," he said.

"How's it going in there?" Erin tipped her head toward the house.

Sam shrugged. "Looks like Nicole is settling in and everything's getting unpacked. She sure has enough help to make sure it'll all get done quickly."

"Well, that's good. Moves can be tough. Especially when you do it twice in a short time."

"I guess. See you tomorrow night at Mom's." Sunday night dinner at the Marsden house was a mandatory affair. He turned to go.

"Whoa. Get back here," his sister said.

He tapped on his wristwatch. "Gotta be somewhere."

"It'll wait five minutes. It's not like they can start without you."

"Oh, but they can."

"Sam, stop being obstinate. What's going on? What's wrong with you? You're a grumpy, miserable human, which is more like Mike when he couldn't make decisions

175

about Cara, than you. So what gives?"

He shook his head. "There are things a guy doesn't discuss with his sister."

"You're kidding. You screwed things up with Nicole already?"

Unable to meet her gaze, he shrugged. "I didn't *do* anything." He was just conflicted because he knew Nicole wasn't completely satisfied with things between them, and he wasn't sure how much he was willing to give in order to change things.

"Maybe you *should* discuss these things with your sister. Then you wouldn't make colossal mistakes."

He rolled his eyes. "Because you and Cole did so well in the beginning? Besides, I told you, I didn't do anything wrong. It's just complicated."

A wide smile took hold. "If ending up like me and Cole is your final destination, then you go ahead and screw up now as much as you want."

He growled at her in a way he hadn't since they were kids. When she was little, she'd run screaming.

Now? She merely laughed.

"What was that for?" she asked.

"You nailed the issue on the head. I don't want to end up in a serious relationship."

"And she does?" Erin studied him with

her perceptive hazel eyes, so like his own.

"I didn't think so when we started. Now I'm not so sure."

"Huh." Erin sighed. "Well, then, here's what you should do."

He leaned in, grateful for any advice that could help him keep Nicole in his life and not be tied in knots.

"It's simple," his sister said. "Just say uncle now and give her up to Tyler. Save everyone the time and the aggravation." She shrugged as if the suggestion made perfect sense.

The growl that escaped him this time made his sister's eyes open wide. "Ah, so it's like that. Fighting yourself, are you?"

Sam clenched his hands, wanting to throttle her as he had so often when they were kids. "Did anyone ever tell you that you're a pain in the ass?"

"You. All the time." She rocked forward and treated him to another peck on the cheek. "Go get to your meeting. Continue in denial. It suits you."

Before he could reply, she waved and strode down the driveway and through the open garage.

If Sam's mood was bad before, it was positively brutal now.

EIGHT

Nicole approached the Marsden home uncertain what she was doing here. Erin had invited her for dinner at her parents' house, insisting she come because family dinners were weekly events and guests kept them from killing each other. Somehow, Nicole didn't buy it. In the short time she'd been in Serendipity, she'd heard nothing but glowing praise for each of the Marsdens, from Ella and Simon, whose longtime marriage had withstood crises and even his cancer diagnoses and treatment last year, to the siblings.

The invitation meant a lot to her, and since Erin promised Sam was working a case and wouldn't be there, she was more comfortable attending. She was still trying to convince herself she could abide by the rules they'd set and keep things casual, continue to have sex with no strings, nothing serious.

What had she been thinking? She'd had sex with one person when she lost her virginity to her college boyfriend, and they'd broken up soon after. She'd come home for a school break and reconnected with Tyler, and though it had taken them years to get serious, he was her one long-term relationship and she'd almost married him. What made her think she could do casual, she asked herself for the millionth time.

No matter how potent Sam's touch, no matter how much she enjoyed his company, no matter how explosive the attraction, Nicole had spent too much of her life accepting less than she deserved from her family. She'd broken up with a good man because she didn't want him to settle for less, any more than she was willing to. So she admitted to herself now that she needed Sam to step up, at least in little ways — small, basic ways — if she was going to continue to sleep with him.

They needed to agree they would be exclusive.

He needed to be affectionate in public, acknowledge her as his girlfriend. She wasn't asking him to marry her, for God's sake, but she couldn't just be a fuck buddy. If that was all he wanted from her, even after their last time together, then she'd have to walk away before she became invested even more. The thought caused a sharp pain in the region of her heart, but she was prepared to stand up for what she needed.

First, though, dinner with his family. She rang the doorbell and was greeted by a barking ball of white fluff and an older, attractive woman. From the similar auburn hair coloring, despite the obvious highlights in Ella Marsden's hair, to the eyes, to the warm smile, she was obviously Erin and Sam's mother.

"You must be Nicole," she said, opening the door. "Welcome."

"Thank you for having me over, Mrs. Marsden." Nicole handed her a bouquet of wildflowers she'd bought in town.

"I appreciate these. I love flowers, but next time, just bring yourself. And call me Ella."

Her smile was so sweet and genuine, she couldn't help but respond in kind.

"Who's this?" she asked of the dog.

"Meet Kojak."

Smiling, Nicole bent to pet the dog, who was bouncing up and down in excitement. With Kojak at her heels, she followed Ella into the house.

A few minutes later, Nicole had met Simon, the onetime police chief, and settled in with the family to talk and share a drink before dinner. Cole was in the family room and, to Nicole's surprise, he greeted her with genuine kindness for the first time. Obviously his wife had spoken to him, or he was coming to see that she truly was nothing like her sister. Mike Marsden was here without his wife, who was working with Sam, and even he seemed determined to get to know Nicole for herself.

It saddened her to think that many people, Cole and Mike included, probably wouldn't give Victoria a second chance, despite how far she'd come. But those thoughts drifted away as she was included in the family conversation and joking.

She turned to Erin. "Can I hold that adorable baby of yours?"

Erin handed over the little girl dressed in a pink onesie and swaddled in a white blanket with pink satin trim. The pink brought out the coloring in her skin, making the baby seem even more girly. She smelled like the most delicious baby shampoo and quietly lay in Nicole's arms, making smacking noises with her little lips.

Nicole hadn't thought about having kids, but as she held Angel in her arms, a strange feeling of intense longing welled up inside her, catching her off-guard. "She's so sweet."

"You should hear her when she's hungry at night. Or wet. Or cranky after six P.M. — but of course only in our house; in her grandparents' house she's the Angel we call her," Erin said, laughing. The love in her voice and her expression were obvious.

Cole slid closer on the couch, wrapping an arm around his wife's shoulder. "Says the woman who sleeps while I get up and take care of her midnight feedings?" His deep chuckle also belied his words.

These two were clearly in love, and another, distinctly different wave of need swept through Nicole. She swallowed hard and refocused on the less painful feelings.

"Hey, little girl," Nicole said softly, stroking a hand down the baby's chubby cheek.

Without warning, the front door opened. "We made it," Sam said, stepping into the house, Cara behind him.

Nicole's stomach tightened at the sight of the man she couldn't get out of her head, looking handsome in a sport jacket — obviously he'd been at work — and his gaze took in the room, settling on her, his surprise evident.

She swallowed hard.

"Sam! I didn't expect you tonight," Erin said.

He shot her a strange look. "I told you I'd get things wrapped up early today."

Mike rose to greet his wife.

Ella clapped her hands, obviously thrilled to have her whole family together.

"Come pour yourself a drink," Simon said to his son.

And Erin busied herself with a nonexistent thread on her shirt, refusing to meet Nicole's gaze. She'd obviously lied to get Nicole to come, knowing her brother would show up.

Though she wanted to be mad at Erin, she couldn't be. Erin obviously had her brother's best interest at heart.

Sam said hello to his parents and siblings, kissed his mom and sister, and slapped Mike and Cole on the back, and she couldn't help comparing her own family's stilted dinner parties with this one. No jokes or kidding with the others, no hugs or kisses, no genuine concern over how each person's day had gone.

Lost in thought, she didn't hear Sam approach, but she smelled his cologne and her skin tingled as he kissed her cheek, his lips lingering a hint longer than they had with his relatives.

She trembled at the light touch, acknowledging her body's immediate recognition and desire for a more thorough, more tactile hello.

"This is a surprise," he said to her.

"Same for me." She didn't want him thinking she'd come here expecting to see him. "Erin said you'd be working."

"Now that she's happily married, my sister's a busy little matchmaker," Sam muttered. But he couldn't deny he was pleased to see Nicole here; at the same time, her presence at a family gathering was a little too close for comfort. Sam didn't bring women home to the family, and he definitely didn't invite them to Sunday night dinners. "But I'm glad you're here."

She tipped her head to one side. "Are you? I don't want to invade your home territory. I know we agreed —"

He reached for her hand. "I said I'm glad, and I meant it. As for the rest . . ." He trailed off, unsure of what to say.

"I want to talk about it. Maybe not here and now, but later. I need to clarify a few things between us." She raised her chin in what he took to be a gesture of defiance.

She wanted to change the rules. He felt it in every pulse of tension vibrating off her body.

"Dinner," his mother said, before they could get into details of what Nicole meant.

Leave it to his mother to have impeccable timing, Sam thought.

"Ready?" he asked Nicole, knowing he wouldn't taste a bite of his mother's delicious cooking. Not while he wondered just what Nicole wanted to discuss. Or why he felt like he was at war with himself and the things he always knew to be true about who he was and what he wanted.

Nicole discovered Ella Marsden was a fantastic cook. Her daughter, she learned, could barely crack an egg. Cole did most of the cooking in their house, a fact Nicole could barely reconcile, but she found it endearing that the gruff man clearly doted on his wife and child. Sam too knew how to fend for himself in the kitchen, and so could Mike. Since Nicole had a slew of recipes of her own, she and Ella hit it off well and discussed everything from basic cooking to Nicole's favorite subject, desserts.

"Tell Mom about your shop," Erin said. "She already knows you bake, but fill her in on the details."

Nicole patted her mouth, and placed her napkin in her lap. "Well, Lulu Donovan and I have an appointment at the bank this week

185

to discuss our business loan request," Nicole said, excited at how quickly things were moving along. "Nick Mancini offered us a very fair rental for the old bakery next to Consign and Design. Other than aesthetics, the infrastructure is already there. And Faith Barron is going to help decorate. My head is spinning," Nicole said, laughing.

"When did you make all these decisions?" Sam asked.

"All weekend, while moving in, discussions came up, and Aunt Lulu is so prepared, she's hard to say no to — she makes so much business sense, I don't want to."

Erin went on to fill everyone in on her new job as an attorney at Nash Barron's firm. He had flexible work-from-home hours, and she was happier than she'd ever been.

"What about you?" Simon asked his younger son. "Case almost finished?"

"Wrapped it up today, right?" he asked Cara, who Nicole thought seemed quiet and out of sorts.

She nodded. Her face was paler than before. "Umm . . . excuse me," she said, and darted out of the room.

Mike took off after her.

Eyes narrowed, Sam followed their quick departure. "Is she okay?"

A semi-smile lit Ella's gaze, surprising Nicole. "Something tells me everything's all right."

Nicole met Sam's gaze. They shrugged at each other, and soon Cara returned but Mike insisted they head out so she could get some rest, and nobody argued.

The rest of the meal passed pleasantly enough and the subject turned to an upcoming art festival, for which Nicole had seen flyers posted around town.

"I love seeing new artists," Nicole said.

"Me too. And Tess Barron has a showing there," Erin said. "She's only sixteen and she's an amazing artist."

"That girl has been through so much. I'm happy for her," Ella murmured.

Nicole knew there was a story there and figured she'd ask Sam another time. "I'd love to go. There's a place in my new bedroom that needs a picture."

"Oh, let's go together, then," Erin said. "Cole hates those things, so he can watch Angel." The baby was sleeping in a crib Ella and Simon had set up in a spare room. "Sam, you can keep Cole company. Maybe change a diaper or two."

"Or three," Cole said, offering up the opportunity like it was the chance to win a gold medal.

"I think I'll leave that to you," Sam said to his brother-in-law.

"Chicken," Cole muttered.

Ella laughed and rose to her feet. "On that note, I'll clean up. Dessert in a few."

Nicole pushed her chair back, prepared to help.

"No, no, you're our guest. Sam, take her out back. The patio furniture's all cleaned and we have citronella candles burning so the mosquitoes won't eat you alive."

Nicole heard the definitive tone and knew better than to argue. Apparently Sam felt the same way, because he rose and held out a hand.

Suddenly nervous, she slipped her palm into his big, warm one and followed him outside. The bluestone patio reminded her of the glimpse she'd gotten of Sam's backyard. Four lounge chairs, an outdoor bar with three stools, a rectangular table and chairs with an umbrella in the center, and a fire pit. The surrounding lawn was green and lush, the plantings and flowers perfectly placed.

Everything about the small Marsden house called to something deep inside Nicole, the empty space never filled by her cold parents or their large house full of expensive things but lacking in warmth and love. In the short time here, she'd felt more welcomed and cared for than she ever had by her own family.

Her chest filled with a heaviness she fought against.

"What's on your mind?" Sam asked perceptively, as he settled into a recliner and pulled her down with him.

She settled in beside him, resisting his attempt to pull her back against him so they could cuddle, her back to his front. She wanted to see his face when they talked, needed him to see hers. To understand.

"You're lucky." She wondered if he knew just how much more he had in life.

"How so?"

"Love. You were surrounded by it. Your parents are present in your lives. Not just physically but emotionally."

Sam heard the catch in her voice and knew tonight's conversation was important because she was going deep into herself, giving him insight into who she was and why.

"I'm not sure I ever thought about it that way," he admitted. "Mike did because Simon adopted him."

"Really?" She leaned in closer.

"Yeah. We've always been thought of as the perfect family, but we have our own secrets too. Not so secret, actually. Mom got pregnant by Mike's father and when he bailed, Simon stepped up. Turns out he'd been in love with her all along."

Nicole's eyes grew wide on hearing the story. "That's beautiful. They seem so in love now."

"They've been that way for as long as I can remember."

She made a murmur of acknowledgment. "They're lucky too, then."

"What about your parents? I know you said they don't care much about what you do unless it's to benefit them, but how do they feel about each other?" Having divulged his parents' past, he felt comfortable asking about hers.

She swallowed hard. "Let's put it this way. When I told my mother I couldn't marry Tyler because I wasn't in love with him, she asked me what love had to do with anything, and when that didn't sway me, she followed up with, just when did she tell me that fairy tales ever came true."

Even Sam, who'd stopped believing in that result, at least for himself, winced. What kind of parent disillusioned her daughter? He thought of the way his parents had boosted Erin's confidence and spirits, and convinced her she should at least try to go after what she wanted in life. Even after she'd gotten pregnant by a man determined to leave her and Serendipity behind.

The summer breeze blew around them and lifted Nicole's hair from her shoulders. He met her gaze and wished he could put the stars back in her eyes and convince her that anything was possible. Maybe it was. Just not with him.

"So about us," she said, as if reading his mind.

"I take it you don't want to just pick up where we left off last night?" His chest hurt at the thought she might actually walk away.

"Actually I do — with some modifications or qualifications." She looked down at the slats on the chair, not meeting his gaze. "It turns out I'm not so good at this sex-without-emotion thing after all."

His breath caught in his throat, but he was determined to hear her out. One night with her hadn't been nearly enough, but what happened next? It all depended on what she asked for.

"I need us to be exclusive while we're together."

He let out the breath he'd been holding. "I can do that."

She lifted her gaze to his. The vulnerability in her expression sucker-punched him but good. Everything about her hit him in new ways.

Scary ways.

"What else?" he asked.

She bit down on her full lower lip. "I need to know where you stand. Is this thing between us just sex? Like, when we're out in public are you going to pretend we're just friends? Because I couldn't handle that." Her huge blue eyes bore into his.

"Hell no! Just because I'm not looking to settle down and get married doesn't mean I don't understand what it means to be with someone. I want to *be* with you, to acknowledge it in public, to let everyone know we're together. And I sure as hell don't want anyone else with you either."

Her lips parted in a soft O, and he was unable to resist leaning forward and kissing her face with its surprised expression.

The thing he was drawn to most about Nicole — looks and attractiveness were a given — was her innate honesty. Her vulnerability tugged at his heart, making him want to protect her. Be her white knight, as ridiculous as he knew that was.

He couldn't help but respond to her and licked her parted lips. She sighed into his mouth, and he slipped his tongue inside. She'd had a glass of wine with dinner and

192

he tasted the fruity flavor, but most of all he tasted her and he didn't want the moment to end.

Unfortunately, his brother had other ideas, as he called out from the door off the kitchen. "Coffee and dessert! Unless you're already getting some of your own."

Nicole pulled back and ducked her head, an embarrassed smile on her face. "Geez."

"That's what brothers are for," Sam muttered.

She laughed. "Sisters aren't much better."

"True." He glanced at her flushed cheeks. "Everything okay now?" he asked.

She didn't pretend to misunderstand him. "Will you come home with me?" she asked. "Christen my new bed?"

Yeah, he thought, everything was just fine.

Tyler stepped out of the shower and wrapped a towel around his waist. As he pulled out clothes for his dinner with Macy, he ignored yet another call from his father. He couldn't bring himself to disappoint the man by telling him he hadn't made any inroads in getting Nicole back and bringing her home.

The Nicole to whom he'd been engaged had been quiet and easy to persuade to do whatever he needed in pursuit of career or family bidding. She wore designer dresses and suits, not tight jeans or cropped shorts and shirts. The woman he'd found in Serendipity was not someone he'd have become engaged to, and he had the definite sense she was finding herself now and liking the woman she was becoming. He admired her attempt to break free.

He glanced at the new blue jeans on the bed and the casual T-shirt and frowned. What the hell was he doing, changing who he was in order to fit into a place where he had no intention of remaining? The minute he figured out how to fix the mess in his family business, he was heading back to Manhattan. Except this small town was growing on him. And so was one woman in particular.

He grinned as he thought about where he and Macy were going tonight. Miniature golf. He shuddered at the thought. Yet he'd agreed because doing anything with Macy was something he knew he'd enjoy.

No sooner had he dressed than he heard a knock on his door. He opened it to find the woman who'd been on his mind. Macy stood before him, petite compared to his six-foot frame, wearing patterned shorts, a denim blouse tied over a white tank, and a pair of white Toms on her feet.

"Hey, all set to go?" she asked. Her gaze slid over him. "What are you wearing?" she asked, her smile turning downward.

He swallowed a laugh at her look of dismay. "My clothes."

She scowled at him. "But you're not going to be comfortable outside in those pants and that shirt."

"You mean I'm overdressed for miniature golf?" he asked, unable to suppress a grin at how cute he found her.

"That too. I can wait downstairs while you change."

He shook his head. "Not happening."

Lines formed between her brows. "Why? We went shopping for all those clothes. Just throw on a pair of cargo shorts and we'll be good to go."

He braced one hand on the door frame and stared down at her, doing his best to ignore the swell of her breasts above the tank top. "Macy Donovan, are you embarrassed to be seen with a well-dressed man?"

"No!" She sputtered at him. "If you want to be hot and sweaty all night, be my guest. I was just trying to look out for you."

"And I decided I'd rather be myself."

"Fine." She raised her hands in defeat. "Are you ready to go?"

He nodded and slipped his hand through

hers. "Come on, hot stuff."

He pulled her into the hall, shutting his door behind them, and started for the stairs.

Macy stopped, planting her heels and refusing to walk farther. "What's going on? Why are you flirting with me?" she asked.

He met her gaze and shrugged. "I'm just acting naturally around you."

She raised an eyebrow. "Are you saying I bring out the flirt in you?"

He couldn't contain yet another grin. He'd smiled more in the last five minutes than in the last six months. "Could be."

"Well, rein it in. You're trying to win your ex back and tonight we're just killing time while she's at Sam's parents' house for dinner," she reminded him, turning away so he couldn't see what he felt sure would be the hurt look on her face.

Even though they both knew what their time together was all about, and he appreciated her willingness to hang out with him, there was something between them.

Or could be if not for Tyler's complicated life. At least she was smart enough to remember that.

Macy was the one who'd told him why he couldn't go out looking to run into Nicole tonight in the first place. She'd also tried to encourage him to go back to New York and not set himself up for further hurt. Or embarrassment, she'd gently added. The last thing he wanted was this woman's pity, but he couldn't tell her the truth: that he'd already accepted that things were over between him and Nicole before he'd been coerced into coming up here to *win* her back.

If he hadn't been, seeing the new Nicole would have convinced him. What he didn't understand was why *this* woman, who was even more outspoken than his ex-fiancée, who dressed more provocatively, and who was even more comfortable being contrary than the *new* Nicole, revved him up so damned much.

His mother would take one look at Macy and have Tyler committed, all the while reminding him that his feelings for this woman were inappropriate because she wouldn't fit into his world any more than he, in his khakis and polo shirt with long rolled-up sleeves, fit into hers.

"You're right," he told her. "But I just want us to relax and have a good time. Isn't that what you told me to do while I'm here?"

"Yes. Just don't do it by flirting."

"Fine. I'll try to behave." But it wouldn't be easy, because she was adorable and so easy to be around, even when she was giving him a hard time — something people in his real life rarely did. It was refreshing. *She* was refreshing. He was actually looking forward to miniature golf, of all things.

His cell phone buzzed in his pocket. Setting his jaw, he ignored it, and promised himself he'd focus on this woman who made him feel good and try to ignore his problems, if just for this one night.

At his parents' dining room table, Sam hid a raging erection beneath his napkin and under the tablecloth, suffered through a dessert he didn't taste, and barely paid attention to the conversation surrounding them. Finally, finally he and Nicole were the first to say their good-byes.

He sped home, daring one of his own to pull him over, and parked in Nicole's driveway. Once they reached her house, the polite dance they'd been doing around each other ended. She closed the door and was in his arms in an instant.

This wasn't the smooth seduction of the first time. He sealed his lips against hers and backed her to the nearest wall, dying to be inside her again. She threaded her hands through his hair and held on as he devoured her mouth. He needed her more than he needed air to breathe, and as he wasn't used to the feeling, he ignored it in favor of the hot sensations that were much more pleasurable.

She hooked one foot around his leg and pressed her lower body against his. Knowing exactly what she needed, he ground his hips into hers, nestling his cock into the warm vee of her legs.

A low moan escaped her throat and he trailed a wet kiss down her cheek and sucked on the flesh of her neck, so when she let out another sexy sound, he felt the vibrations against his mouth.

She slid her hands beneath his shirt, and the feel of her soft fingers trailing over his abdomen made him shudder and grow harder. He let out a curse, lifted her into his arms, and headed for the bedroom upstairs.

"You like this caveman thing." Nicole laughed, obviously feeling playful.

"If I were a caveman, you'd be over my shoulder."

"The carrying thing, then."

"I like carrying *you.*" This routine wasn't something he'd done before, but she was right. With Nicole, he always seemed to be impatient, wanting to be naked and inside her.

She grinned, settling her face into the

199

crook of his neck, first kissing him, then nuzzling with her nose and mouth, and finally taking a nip with her teeth.

He felt the kick of that bite in his groin.

He tossed her onto the bed and her eyes opened wide, then glazed over with aching desire. He pulled off his shirt. She took the hint and worked at her own clothes until she lay spread out before him. Instead of rushing to claim her, he decided there were other things he wanted to do first.

He braced his hands on her thighs and lowered his head, breathing in her musky scent before sliding his tongue over her sex. Her hips arched upward in a silent plea for more. Yeah, that he could do, he thought, and began to earnestly work at giving her pleasure. It didn't take long for him to learn her body, what she liked: long, leisurely laps of his tongue around her damp folds, and what really sent her over the edge — a nip directly on her clit.

He'd never tasted anything sweeter, never wanted to give someone pleasure more. He was solely focused on Nicole, her short pants of breath, the soft cries when she edged closer to coming. He slid one finger deep inside her and she came apart beneath his hand and mouth, and a deep sense of satisfaction filled him.

He prolonged the sensations until her muscles relaxed and then he kissed his way up her lithe body, ending with her lips, letting her taste herself on his mouth.

His erection was rock hard against her thigh, and he braced his arms and lifted himself over her. "I need to be inside you."

Her eyes dilated even more. "So what are you waiting for?"

"Not a damned thing." He kissed her deeply as he raised his hips and thrust deep. She clenched him tight in her hot body, skin to skin, and realization dawned.

Shit. "Condom." He started to pull out quickly but her fingernails dug into his shoulders, stopping him.

"I'm on the pill and we — I always used protection." Nicole stared up at Sam, unwilling to use Tyler's name while she felt Sam's thickness in every part of her body.

He expelled a long breath. "Same. Especially since my sister got pregnant . . ." He hung his head, drawing an obvious breath, and then, without warning, he pressed his hips against her, filling her even more.

Small pulses of desire electrified her, from where their bodies joined so intimately to the farthest reaches of her fingertips and even into her throat. The man was so potent and each time they came together, he breached another protective wall she'd tried to erect against him.

Without a condom, she had an even more difficult time differentiating between sensation and emotion. She'd have to sort her head out later, but right now, looking into his gorgeous hazel eyes so intent on *her,* she didn't want to think at all.

And when he began to move inside her, his thick erection spiking her arousal, her brain shorted out and pure passion took over. His thickness aroused nerve endings she didn't know she had, and her sudden orgasm came quickly and fast, taking her by surprise.

"So responsive," he said as she came back to herself.

"Not usually." The words slipped out and he grinned, obviously pleased.

He pulled out and despite just having come, she felt empty until he flipped her over. "On your knees," he whispered in her ear.

Arousal flooded her anew and she complied. He placed his hand on her back and she lowered her head to the pillow as he slid back into her once more.

"Oh God." He was deeper now, and she couldn't hold back a moan.

"You feel amazing."

So did he.

He pulled out and thrust back into her. She closed her eyes and his smooth strokes ignited her nerve endings, stimulating her everywhere. With his body cocooned around hers, taking her, grinding into her over and over, she felt consumed. Owned, even. And as he picked up a faster rhythm, she began the steady climb from being sated once more.

"I'm close, Nic," he said, his rich voice stroking her body and her heart. His fingers bit into her sides. "Come with me," he said, his hips slamming hard against hers.

His rough groan of completion set her aflame and she shattered, her body splintering into tiny shards around his. And as she came back together, she was afraid she'd lost a piece of herself to this very contained man.

He collapsed on top of her, eventually rolling off but never breaking contact as he wrapped himself around her. His rapid heartbeat thrummed hard against her back and they lay in silence as she caught her own breath.

"How come?" he asked, breaking the quiet around them.

"How come what?"

"If you're on the pill, how come you used

protection with your ex?" Sam asked.

A valid question, but not an easy one. Not now, although it had seemed so simple at the time she'd made the decision.

"Even though it's never been said, I don't think my parents are faithful to one another." She'd barely admitted this truth to herself over the years. Even when her mother asked her what love had to do with anything, Nicole hadn't wanted to face what had always been on the edges of her mind.

She swallowed hard. "I was on the pill before Tyler and I started sleeping together, and once we did, he didn't ask about protection, he just used it, so I didn't offer the information."

Because she hadn't trusted him enough, she realized now. "If my parents weren't faithful to each other, I didn't think I should risk it for myself."

Yet she'd taken that risk with Sam. Nicole was afraid to question what that leap of faith could mean. And from his silence, she took it to mean he had no interest in finding out either.

NINE

Nicole soaked in a hot bath in her new claw-footed tub. After her night with Sam, her body ached in the best possible way. She leaned her head back and let her mind drift to the many aspects of the man she was coming to know. He could be tender and sweet one minute, hard and demanding the next. She hoped he'd stick with her long enough for her to learn more.

Her eyes drifted shut and she thanked her lucky stars she'd met him before her wedding and was grateful she'd found the strength to end her engagement. If not, she wouldn't have spent last night in her bed. With Sam. She smiled and sank deeper into the bubbled water.

She trailed the loofah over her calves and her knees and up her thighs before picking up the handheld shower massager to clear the soap. The sweet scent of strawberry soap prickled her senses. And as the water teased her clit, arousal swept through her. With thoughts of Sam on her mind, she settled the light spray between her thighs, placing just the right amount of pressure on her sex, creating a delicious friction, before easing one of her fingers between her slick folds.

She moaned at the same time her phone rang, jarring her into awareness. She glanced down and caught sight of Sam's name, and her stomach flipped in awareness and embarrassment. She dried her hand on a towel and slid the bar across the screen to answer.

"Hey," she said, hoping her tone didn't give her away.

"Hi."

His voice oozed sex and sin, and the heaviness between her thighs increased tenfold. She drew her knees up and squeezed tight.

"What are you up to?" he asked.

She looked down at the shower massager, a reminder of how close she'd been to bringing herself pleasure she'd rather he give her. "Umm . . . I'm in the tub."

He expelled a harsh breath. "You shouldn't have told me that."

She grinned, glad she wasn't the only one affected. "Then you shouldn't have slipped out before I woke up." But he'd been a gentleman and left a note, which enabled

206

her to fall back to sleep without believing he'd done a one-eighty in his thinking or pulled a guy stunt and carelessly skipped the morning after.

It almost made her trust that he was capable of more than he thought when it came to relationships, but he'd been up front with her. So she knew better.

"I promised my father I'd help him around the house. You were out cold and I didn't want to wake you."

"So what can I do for you now?" she asked.

He laughed, low and deep. "That's a loaded question while you're naked in the bathtub, sweetheart."

Her breath caught at the easily used endearment.

"Actually you can join me for dinner later."

A flush of happiness rushed through her. "I'd love to."

"See? I can take you out like a gentleman," he said, causing her heart to tighten in her chest. "Dress up."

"Okay."

"And be good in that bath."

Her face flushed and she wondered if he knew just how bad she planned to be.

The rest of the day passed quickly, with a

trip to the grocery store, and then she spent the better part of the afternoon doing her favorite thing: baking. Nothing made a house feel more like a home than the fresh smell of homemade *anything,* and now that she had her own equipment, this small house was beginning to feel like a real home to her.

She settled on macarons, the currently in-vogue French cookie. The recipe for these cookies was deceptively simple, but in reality, it was intense and time consuming and took lots of patience, of which she had plenty.

For hours, she lost herself in a process she found soothing. She knew just how soft to make the peaks of the egg whites before adding another ingredient, then whisking once more. Then came the pastry bag and the painstaking creation of rounds without peaks by bringing the pastry tip to the side.

She made chocolate ganache and Swiss buttercream filling, so Sam would have a choice, keeping an eye on the oven as she worked. Another part of the process involved a careful watching of time, lowering then raising the temperature for the next batch. A bomb could have gone off in the next room and she wouldn't have noticed, and when she finally lifted her head to glance at the clock, she realized she didn't have much time to shower before Sam arrived to pick her up.

Dress up, he'd said.

She chose a soft pale blue skirt and flowing tank top loosely belted, and a pair of metallic sandals. She blow-dried her hair, but parts were still damp and she decided it could air-dry. A hint of blush and lip gloss, bangle bracelets, a long necklace, and dangling earrings, and she was ready with minutes to spare.

Then her cell phone rang. A glance told her it was her sister, which was unusual and off the set schedule.

"Hello?" Nicole asked, aware she was holding her breath.

"Hi! I have the best news!" Vicky said, sounding more excited than Nicole could remember.

Very *up,* and a prickle of nerves assaulted Nicole.

"What's up?" she asked as she settled onto her bed.

Vicky squealed in excitement. "My doctor said if I keep progressing like this, I can take a day trip out of here. You know, like a test run to see how I handle being back out in the world."

Nicole swallowed hard. It was one thing

to think about her sister getting better, another to contemplate her being out. "Are you sure you're ready?"

"I am. I just need someone to agree to be my guardian for the day."

Another nervous flutter took up residence in Nicole's stomach, and she shivered.

". . . But I'm sure Mom or Dad will agree," Vicky continued, obviously rambling with excitement.

"I just don't want you to set yourself up for disappointment," Nicole warned her.

"It's one day. Twelve hours. Less even."

Nicole shook her head at how Vicky tended to hang on to her optimism when it came to their parents, mostly because her mind ran toward the delusional. "We'll see, I guess."

"Oops! Gotta go. My time's up. Bye!" her sister said, and disconnected the call.

Nicole prayed their parents would step up, but she had her doubts. Which meant Vicky would ask to visit Nicole for the day instead, and nobody in Serendipity would want to deal with that. Especially not the Marsdens.

She closed her eyes, thinking of Sam's family. They'd been kind to her about her sister, but that was easy when Vicky was out of sight. Faced with her return? Nicole shuddered at the definite conflict inherent in that situation.

The ringing of her doorbell interrupted her thoughts. She glanced out the window by the door and smiled when she saw Sam in khaki pants and a collared shirt. He oozed male confidence and sex appeal, his scruffy hair untamed despite obvious efforts.

She let him in and he greeted her with a warm kiss on the mouth. His lips lingered and she sighed into him.

"Mmm, that's nice," she said, running her tongue over her lips.

She could be so happy here and she didn't want her sister to ruin what she was building in Screndipity, she thought, then immediately felt guilty and selfish.

"Just nice?" Sam asked, his brows wrinkled.

"Very nice," she amended, chiding herself to push thoughts of her sister and her problems out of her mind.

She had a hot man waiting for her and she wasn't about to waste time thinking about things that might not happen. There was always the chance that her sister's doctor wouldn't allow her to come to Serendipity at all.

And if he did?

Nicole would stand by her twin. They

were blood. She had no choice.

Sam narrowed his gaze. Nicole's preoccupied tone set off warning signals that something was up. Especially since he didn't think his kissing skills had gone south since he saw her last. She was barely paying attention when usually she couldn't keep her hands to herself when they were alone.

"What's wrong?" Although she'd definitely dressed for their date, looking hot and sexy, her mind was somewhere else.

And when she glanced at her phone before answering him, she confirmed his suspicions.

"I just spoke to my sister."

He preferred not to think about her mentally ill twin, but as he'd told his brother, they were two different people. "Is everything okay?"

She rolled her shoulders and sighed. "Her doctor says she's ready for a day visit, and she's hoping my parents will let her come home."

His gut cramped at the thought of her twin out and about in the world. "Why wouldn't they?"

Nicole pinched the bridge of her nose. "You know what? Let's not discuss my dysfunctional family."

He placed his hands on her shoulders,

massaging her tense muscles in the hopes of getting her to relax. "You can talk to me," he said, meaning it.

She shook her head. "Nobody should have to handle my load but me. I appreciate it, though." She shifted her gaze. "So where are we going for dinner?"

He ought to not just respect her need for privacy, but be happy with her unwillingness to share. The more distance they kept between them, the better. She was too easy to fall for. But it bothered him that she wouldn't confide in him about her problems and feelings. Shit. No feelings. He shook his head and forced himself to take her cue and move on to the rest of the evening.

He'd made a reservation at a steak house about twenty-five minutes outside Serendipity. Once there, he'd requested a quiet table in the back, where he held her hand and plied her with good wine, and visibly she relaxed. The tightness in her expression eased and her eyes, which had seemed so troubled earlier, were clearer and focused on him.

Their secluded table consisted of a booth in the back corner and let him sit beside her, not across the table. He could lean in and inhale her floral scent, watch her enjoy her meal, and shift positions so their thighs aligned and touched throughout the various courses.

They talked about nothing and everything and Sam learned how much they had in common, from enjoying all the new police procedural shows on television to the occasional raunchy comedy — which surprised him — to classic rock tunes. They differed on sports. She hated football, which only made him determined to teach her the workings of the game and change her mind this upcoming season.

Finally she placed her fork and knife down on her plate and let out a pleased sigh that went right to his groin. "The best steak ever," she said.

"Worth the trip," he agreed, for more reasons than the food. He'd do just about anything to keep the satisfied smile on her face, not to mention the way she looked at him, unable to take her eyes off him for a second. The feeling was more than mutual.

She finished her second glass of red wine and the waiter immediately came around asking if she'd like a refill. "No, thank you." She covered the top of the glass with her hand.

"Tipsy?" he asked.

She smiled. "Pleasantly buzzed."

He, on the other hand, was perfectly sober

and driving them home, but he could freely admit to being high on her alone. There'd never been a lull in the conversation. Everything she talked about, from her plans for the bakery, which she hoped to have the keys to next week, to stories of how she'd managed to raise big money for Tyler's mother's campaign for borough president, both charmed and interested him.

"Enough about me. What makes Sam Marsden tick?" she asked.

"Right now, *you're* making me tick," he said, leaning in close and nuzzling his nose into the crook of her neck. He wanted to get inside her skin.

"Flatterer."

IIis hand slid to her thigh and a blush rose to her cheeks as she squirmed beside him. "We're in public."

He glanced around the darkened corner of the restaurant. "Umm, no we aren't. And nobody can see." Inch by inch, he slid the material of her long skirt up her legs, until his palm touched the bare skin of her thigh.

Leaning in, he whispered, "Relax." Then he licked at the small patch of skin behind her ear.

She rewarded him with a full body shudder and her nipples tightened into buds visible beneath her top.

"You're a bad boy, Sam," she said, her voice husky and raw.

"It's only bad if we get caught. If we don't, it's all good."

She looked up at him through eyes half open. "Why?"

"Because you were stressed and need some relief." And because he desired her and he couldn't wait until they got home.

She studied his face, making him wonder not only what she was looking for, but if she'd find it. Then to his surprise, she relaxed, the muscles in her legs gave way, and she opened for him. The trust inherent in that one move humbled him — and truly frightened the young man inside him who'd had his heart and his own trust ripped to shreds one October morning.

The only way he could ignore his rapidly beating heart was to focus on Nicole's pleasure. Around them, he heard the sounds of a busy night at a restaurant. Busboys loading trays, waiters checking in at tables, conversations between patrons.

He'd paid and tipped for privacy, and until he asked for a check, they'd be alone. He kept asking himself why he was putting in the extra effort to wine, dine, and seduce her, and all he could come up with was Nicole. She'd been afraid he was in it for sex only, and he wanted to take her out in public and reassure her. Treat her like the lady she was.

He told himself it didn't have anything to do with her fancy ex-fiancé, but he wasn't so sure. A part of him figured this was his way of competing. Not that she'd made him feel like Tyler was in the running, but she deserved to be wined and dined.

Pleasured.

Beneath the tablecloth, he drew her skirt up over her thighs and cupped her completely, her damp heat pulsating against his palm. Her breath caught and her eyes opened wide, but she didn't stop him as he pushed aside her flimsy underwear and slid his finger along her slick folds.

Her lips parted and she sighed.

"Shh," he said, brushing her hair off her cheek. With his hidden hand, he shifted positions until his fingertip touched her clit. Her hips jerked in response and he turned her head toward him, sealing his lips over hers.

He kissed her while he stroked the tiny bud, all the while aware of her increasing wetness and building desire, the hushed moans he devoured with his mouth, and the way her smaller hands gripped his sides. He kept up the pressure, her feminine juices

217

coating his finger. His dick wanted inside her so badly he could barely breathe, but that meant he had to get her home. So first she had to come.

He stroked her harder, more insistently. Circled his finger over and over her clit until he silenced her cries with his mouth, thrusting his tongue inside her in the same rhythm he used to control her orgasm with his finger.

Soon he gentled the kiss as she came down.

He touched his forehead to hers. "Okay?" he asked her.

"Sublime."

He tilted his head back and met her hazy gaze. "Beautiful."

Her cheeks were pink, her lips swollen. "Mortified."

He brushed his thumb over her mouth. "Don't be. Nobody knows but us. And now that you've had dessert, it's time for the check."

"Maybe I've had dessert, but you haven't." She smiled at him then. "Hurry up so it can be your turn."

In that instant, Sam knew he was falling for this woman and there wasn't a damned thing he could do to stop it.

■ ■ ■ ■

As the art festival and the weekend approached, Serendipity grew more crowded with people Sam didn't know or recognize. Mike put more cops on foot patrol and Sam was grateful he'd made detective or he'd be working even longer hours. He hadn't seen Nicole since spending the night at her house after their date. He did, however, have enough memories to keep him going.

They hadn't slept much and he discovered that despite the occasional shyness, she was a match for him in bed as well as out. She'd made him breakfast, the best egg and cheese omelet he'd ever eaten, and sent him home with cookies she'd obviously baked the day before and had ready for him when it was time for him to head home to shower and go to work.

He'd never slept at a woman's place nor had one stay over at his for obvious reasons, yet doing it with Nicole felt right. Despite the fact that he was feeling uncomfortably domesticated, he couldn't get her out of his head. He called her that day and again during the week, and damned if hearing her voice didn't add something to his long day. Even when working, he found his mind drifting, her blue eyes and the sounds she made when he was deep inside her staying with him wherever he went.

She and Aunt Lulu had taken a booth at the art festival, and Sam headed home to change so he could attend the big event downtown. Normally he wouldn't go near an art festival, but like everything else when it came to Nicole, he was drawn there and he planned to be one of her first customers.

Things moved fast in a small town because people were willing to work on faith and trust. The bakery itself was in pristine condition, the equipment fairly new. Having a partner to share the workload helped. Aunt Lulu had all the information about inspectors and licenses and had agreed to handle the business end of things. Meanwhile, Nicole called Kelly Barron, a paralegal in town, to discuss having partnership papers drawn up, while the bank manager assured them their loan would be approved sometime next week, and the landlord had allowed them into the shop in advance of papers being signed.

With a few phone calls, they had the electricity and water turned on and Nicole spent the day Friday baking for Saturday's art festival. She hoped to give the good people of Serendipity a taste of what was to come when their bakery opened. Aunt Lulu would bring pies and cakes to their booth, and she posted signs around town.

As she readied for what she considered her debut, Nicole was finally starting to feel like she belonged somewhere. Other than Tyler still hanging around, calling and stopping by, all of which she blatantly ignored, praying he'd get the message, life was looking up.

Tyler met Macy at her family's restaurant, and together they planned to go to the art festival. He had to admit she was a good sport about being his sidekick, considering she believed his main goal was to win back Nicole. What Macy didn't know was that Tyler knew a losing battle when he fought one. He understood Nicole was serious about living her own life. He even got that she was involved with another man. Hell, she didn't return his calls and he'd be a fool to think otherwise.

"Earth to Tyler." Macy waved a hand in front of his face. "You alive?"

"Just thinking," he told her.

She hopped onto the stool next to him. "About what?"

He glanced over and met her gaze. Hon-

221

estly interested blue eyes stared back at him. She was so different looking from Nicole, less exotic, her pale face making her large eyes stand out. But it was her genuine concern for him that made him feel something different than ever before.

"Have you ever been torn between doing what's right and family loyalty or expectations?" he asked.

She propped her chin on her hand. "Not the way you probably mean. Family comes first, but we're all so strong-willed, we always clash when it comes to what we want. Like Aunt Lulu got all upset last year and quit here to go work for a supermarket. Then she got hurt and my family circled the wagons and took her back immediately." She shrugged. "But I'm thinking whatever's bothering you is bigger than that."

"What makes you think something's bothering me?"

She raised her eyebrows. "Do you really think I'm buying this whole Nicole-and-I-are-meant-for-each-other thing? One look at you and I get the sense that it's killing you to chase after a woman who isn't interested."

With her insight, the anxiety that had been riding him since he'd arrived in town eased somewhat. "You got that, huh?" He leaned in closer.

She didn't pull away.

"Yeah, I did. So why are you doing it? What kind of family would have you sacrificing yourself and your dignity?"

She was so close, he wanted to lean in and kiss her. More than that, he wanted to explain his motives, but doing so would put her in danger and he already had one woman to look out for. He couldn't drag another into his problems.

"Let's just say that the rich are different, and I don't mean that in any insulting way." With regret, he forced himself to straighten up and pull away.

Disappointment flickered in her eyes. "Sucks for you," she said in her blunt way, looking at him with pity.

And making him feel uncomfortable in his own skin.

She sighed. "I'd rather just make ends meet than suffer with that kind of obligation."

"Me too," he said, surprising himself.

He must have shocked her too, because she smiled at that.

"But I can't," he said.

"Why not?" she asked, still interested, but the light in her eyes had dimmed.

He hated disappointing her, but he knew

that he had. "That obligation runs pretty deep."

So deep that he'd sacrifice himself for his father? He asked himself outright for the first time. Before now, he'd gone about blindly doing as his father asked, but Tyler wanted more for himself than a family business built on corruption and lies. More than a woman who didn't love him — and whom he couldn't love, if he was responding to Macy this way. So no, he thought, he wasn't willing to sacrifice himself for his father.

But before he could extricate himself, he needed a plan. He even wondered if talking to Nicole's cop was an option.

"Ready to go?" Macy asked, when he didn't elaborate on the situation.

"Sure." He pushed the idea of talking to Sam aside, to mull over before doing anything rash.

Macy headed to the back of the restaurant to get her bag. He was coming to know her routine as well as he knew his own, he mused.

As she returned, he couldn't tear his gaze away. Her tanned legs were long beneath the cutoff shorts, and on her feet was electric blue toenail polish. Her white sandals had a heavy fringe. She was dynamite in a petite package, and he enjoyed every minute he spent with her.

They arrived downtown, parking and walking from far away. Obviously the festival was a huge draw. Macy liked art and so did he, which gave him a rush, thinking finally they had something in common. As they passed the various artists set out with their canvases and work, Macy's eyes lit up and she paused at every landscape they saw.

And when she homed in on an artist and piece she wanted, she headed straight past Nicole's food booth, barely waving at her friend.

Although Tyler knew he should stop and talk to Nicole, gauge her mood, and hope maybe she was having trouble with Sam, he focused on Macy. She was talking to the young man who'd painted the beautiful panorama of a small town at the base of a mountain range; he was caught up in Macy's enthusiasm and excitement.

She'd asked about price when he caught sight of two men he recognized. Both blond, dressed casually so they would blend in with the casual tourists, but Tyler knew better. He'd met both men when they came to his Manhattan office to meet with his father. Tyler had sat in on the discussion, as they were new clients and he always tried to be aware of their investors.

On the surface, both men, L.A. art dealers, weren't out of place at an art show, where they routinely discovered new talent. If he were to dig deeper, he knew that there were thousands of similar shows across the country and even in the northeast each weekend, and it was no coincidence they'd chosen the innocuous town of Serendipity at the same time both he and Nicole were here. If Tyler had to guess, his father had gotten tired of waiting and made a preemptive move by alerting them to possible trouble with Nicole.

Tyler tried not to panic, but he knew he had to alert Nicole to potential danger.

"Tyler, what do you think of the price?" Macy asked him. "It's too steep for me, but do you think we can get him down?" she asked in a hushed voice.

Shit. He hadn't been paying attention to the conversation. "How much did he say?"

She frowned at him and pulled him aside. "He started at two hundred. I can splurge at one fifty. I want to hang it in the hall when you walk into my place. What do you think?"

He wasn't focusing, that was for sure. "Not too bad," he said, thinking off the top of his head.

He turned back toward Nicole's booth

only to find she was gone. A look at where the men were standing told him they'd disappeared as well.

With a muttered curse, he grasped Macy's shoulders in both hands. "I have an emergency. Don't do anything until I get back."

Her gaze shot from him to where Nicole had been, and the light in her eyes dimmed. "Sure. Go on."

Heart in his throat, he left Macy and went in search of Nicole.

TEN

Sam scanned the booths at the art fair, looking for Nicole. Of course, this being Serendipity, he didn't get far before someone in his family stopped him.

"I didn't think you liked art!" Erin nudged him with her hip.

He glanced over to find her holding his niece, dressed in a pink frilly tank top dress and a floppy hat to protect her fair skin from the sun.

He smiled and held out his hands. "Come to your uncle, baby girl."

Erin handed him her bundle and Sam settled his niece in his arms. "Did you miss your uncle Sam?" he asked, kissing her soft cheek.

He was rewarded with a baby gurgle and blowing bubbles.

"I'll take that as a yes." He shifted Angel in his arms. "So where's your other half?" he asked his sister.

She frowned. "Cole's away for the week-end. An important job," she said. "He tries to assign the out-of-town security installations, but sometimes they request him."

He caught the hint of wistfulness in her tone. "Can I take you for dinner?" he asked. "Help pass the time?"

She squeezed his arm. "You're a good brother. But Sunday will be here soon enough. I don't want to put a crimp into your social life."

He rolled his eyes. "I always have time for you. And if I didn't, I'd make time."

Erin smiled. "I'm fine. Go find Nicole."

"How do you know that's who I'm here for?"

Erin merely stared at him, holding out her arms. "Who else would bring you to an art show?"

With his cheeks burning at being so obvious, Sam placed his niece back in her mother's arms. "Have you seen her?" he asked.

Erin nodded. "Her booth is at the far end of the street." She pointed farther down than he'd gotten so far.

"Thanks. I'll see you later."

He turned and started to work his way through the crowds once more, when a hand grabbed his shoulder and spun him around.

"Hey!" Instinct had Sam reaching for his holster as he came face-to-face with Tyler Stanton. "Jesus Christ. Didn't anyone ever tell you not to sneak up on a cop?"

"We need to talk," Tyler said.

Sam was not in the mood to deal with the other man. "Not now."

"It's about Nicole."

Sam stiffened. "When is it not, Stanton?" It was time he got rid of this asshole once and for all.

"This time is different." Stanton stood way too close, his posture straight, his attitude determined. "Look, I'm not here to win her back. I know better. She's interested in you, not me. But I need her to come back home for her own good."

Sam shook his head, knowing he'd never understand this guy without a detailed road map. "Explain."

"Nicole's in danger."

With those words, he caught Sam's attention. Sam eyed the other man warily. "Talk to me."

Tyler drew a deep breath. "Before I came here I found out my father has been taking money from the Russian mob and running it through our investment business," he said, his voice low. "He thinks Nicole overheard him talking to his accountant and knows enough to put him in jail and give the feds a good lead on his so-called investors."

Sam closed his eyes and swore. He'd never imagined her secrets were this big.

"And I just saw the owner of the biggest art gallery in L.A. and one of his associates standing near Nicole's booth. He's one of my father's Russian investors, and I can guarantee you he's not here to find the newest artist in your small town."

Sam stared at the man standing in front of him, disbelief and rage filling him as he put together everything Stanton wasn't saying. "Your fucking father sent him after Nicole?"

"I don't know for sure. But by the time I extricated myself from Macy so I could find out, he was gone. And so was Nicole."

Extricated himself. This son of a bitch with his expensive clothes and fancy words was going to be the death of him, Sam thought, shoving Stanton away.

"You'd better hope I find her, and when I do? She'd better be in one piece."

Main Street in town had been shut down to traffic, and along the route, artists had set up stands and easels showcasing their work.

Trisha from Cuppa Café was sharing the long booth at the end of the street with Nicole and Aunt Lulu, where she sold iced coffee, sodas, and bottled water. The day was hot and they almost always had a line for the drinks as well as the pastries by Nicole and mini cakes by Aunt Lulu.

Nicole had made sure to have a wide variety for people to sample in order to entice many palates. And she'd kept her audience in mind, including parents who'd brought their kids for a day outdoors. As a result, some of her more popular items included the fried apple fritters and chocolate caramel doughnut holes. Of course, the churros and cream puffs were big hits too.

The morning passed quickly and Nicole was riding a high from the response to her baked goods. When she added the general welcome she'd received from just about everyone who stopped by her booth, she was feeling not only like she belonged in Serendipity, but optimistic about the success of their soon-to-be-opened bake shop.

The only thing that could make the day better would be seeing Sam. He'd promised to stop by but had texted her to say he'd been delayed by a call from the station and said he'd find her later.

After the long morning on her feet, she

took advantage of a lull in the crowd and turned things over to Aunt Lulu while she treated herself to a much-needed break. It was the first time she'd had a chance to check out the art fair, and she found herself impressed with the talent on display. The general look of the fair was similar to the street fairs in Manhattan, with a warmer feel because the people were so friendly.

She didn't want to leave Aunt Lulu alone for much longer, but before returning to work, she decided to take a quick bathroom trip. Joe's wife, Annie, had stopped by the booth earlier and told her to feel free to come around back and use the bar's office restroom.

Anything to avoid the long lines at the shops, Nicole thought, and she cut down the alley leading to the back of the stores on Main.

She was almost at the back lot when a male voice spoke to her. "Excuse me?"

"Yes?" She turned and looked up at a handsome man with blond hair and a severe expression.

"Didn't I see you at the bakery booth earlier?" he asked.

"Yes. I'm running it with my partner, Lulu Donovan. Did you taste something you liked?" she asked hopefully.

So many people had come back for seconds or to inquire whether she'd be carrying the various items she'd prepared once she opened the store.

But this man didn't answer, merely studied her intently.

In the wake of his long silence, she grew increasingly uncomfortable. She didn't like being alone in the alleyway with a stranger who'd stopped her but was less than chatty.

"I enjoyed the cream puffs," he said at last.

"Well, I'll definitely be making those a staple in our new place. I hope you'll come try them again. If you'll excuse me, I've got to get back to the booth."

She'd stepped around him when he spoke again. "You're Nicole Farnsworth, yes? You used to be engaged to Tyler Stanton." He didn't ask.

He *knew*.

Every warning instinct Nicole had told her to flee, but he held her there with that hard stare.

"You should get back together with your fiancé," he told her. "If you're smart and don't want —"

"Nicole!"

Sam's voice interrupted the man, and she gratefully turned toward the sound.

"I've been looking everywhere for you!"

He came toward her from the direction of the parking lot, reaching her with quick, deliberate strides.

Her heart was racing so fast her chest hurt. She glanced back to see that the stranger had disappeared.

Relieved beyond words, she threw herself into Sam's arms.

As he enfolded her in his strong embrace, she realized she was trembling.

"Who was that guy you were talking to?" Sam asked.

She swallowed hard. "I don't know. He approached me in the alley. At first I thought it was about the bakery, but he knew who I was. He knew about Tyler."

Sam's hold on her tightened. "Call your ex. Tell him to meet us at your place now."

Nicole pushed out of his arms. "No! I can't do that. I have to work the booth. Besides, why —" Her voice trailed off as she looked into the eyes of one very pissed-off man.

"That guy who cornered you? He's a Russian art dealer," Sam informed her.

"Oh my God." Nicole's knees went weak, and Sam bolstered her with an arm around her waist.

"You and Stanton have pussyfooted around each other long enough. And whatever you two are hiding? I want that information too or I can't keep you safe."

Nicole's breath caught in her throat. "You know? Tyler knows?" She couldn't begin to process how or why or even when either man had found out.

"I don't know nearly enough," Sam muttered. "But I'm going to find out. Now grab your phone and call him."

Normally Nicole would balk at taking orders, but her old life was closing in on her and at that moment, she accepted that she didn't have a choice.

As per Sam's instructions, Nicole called Aunt Lulu and explained she had a family emergency and wouldn't be able to make it back to the booth. She was riddled with guilt over not being able to help for the rest of the afternoon or with the cleanup, but Aunt Lulu claimed that was what family was for and she'd have plenty of hands to pitch in. She wished Nicole well, and Nicole promised to keep in touch.

Sam stewed the entire ride back to Nicole's, and she didn't offer anything in the way of conversation. Until she knew how this whole situation happened — how Sam came to be involved, and what exactly Tyler knew about . . . everything, Nicole wasn't talking. She still had her own family's knowledge or lack thereof to worry about too. Not to mention what she'd do now that the Russians were definitely involved. She grew dizzy just trying to figure out all the angles and implications.

They finally arrived at her house, and Tyler pulled up in his Porsche a short time later.

Sam's scowl deepened. "Could he be any more conspicuous?" he muttered.

Nicole knew better than to answer.

They settled in separate corners of the living room, Nicole on the charming floral sofa the Browns had left behind, Tyler on a solid cream club chair, while Sam leaned against the wall, arms folded across his chest.

"I don't understand what's going on today." Nicole spoke first.

Tyler met Sam's gaze.

"Tell her," Sam said, issuing a direct order in a tone she'd never heard from him until this afternoon.

Her ex-fiancé rose to his feet. "I'm not here to win you back. Well, I was, but not because that's what I wanted."

Nicole narrowed her gaze. "It never did make sense to me that you'd chase after me after I ended things. And once you saw there was someone else . . ." She shook her head. "It made no sense," she repeated.

He shoved his hands into his pants pockets. "When you broke up with me, I was floored. I admit I didn't see it coming, but I accepted it."

Sam took in Tyler's words, and Nicole knew he was putting himself in Tyler's position because he had been there when his fiancee ended things the morning they were to get married. She hated that either man had to go through this awkward reliving of events.

"Then why come to town?" Nicole asked.

"The same afternoon you ended things, my father called me to his office. He was in a panic. Afraid you'd overheard certain information about his business dealings and could destroy him if you went to the police." Tyler's gaze shifted from Sam — the cop now in the equation — to Nicole. "Did you overhear them?"

Her breath coming in stuttered spurts, she managed a nod.

To Sam, it was obvious Nicole was thrown. Not to mention in over her head. Sam wanted to walk across the room and pull her into his arms, but he needed a clear head to untangle this mess and find a way out for them both. He couldn't do that if he let his feelings for Nicole get in the way of thinking like a cop.

Sam stared at the other man. "Let me guess. Daddy sent you after Nicole to win her back? Why? Because he didn't think she'd turn him in if you two were still engaged?" Sam looked at Tyler with disgust, wondering what kind of man ceded to his father's bidding. Especially once he realized he was into something illegal.

Tyler ran a hand over his perfectly cut hair. "Because he thought he'd have more control over her if she was still my mother's campaign manager and my future wife, and if she was more invested in the family dynamic again."

Nicole sucked in a startled breath. "Why didn't you just come to me? You could have asked me what I did — or didn't — know."

"You could have done the same thing," Tyler shot back.

Sam held up one hand. "You first." He turned to Tyler. "Why not talk to her?"

"I'd think that would be obvious. Because if she didn't know, I'd be putting her in danger by telling her."

"But I did know. And I've been torn up with guilt, wondering if you knew, how you could let it go on. And if you didn't, same answer you just gave. Your mother's campaign is partially funded by the firm. That's illegal money and would taint her so badly

239

she'd have to step down and not run again. Then there's my father. I had to decide what I thought he knew — if I could destroy his firm, his livelihood, and everything that's important to my parents. I might not like them much, but they're my family. And speaking of family, what about Victoria?" she asked, her voice rising along with her obvious distress. "Who would take responsibility for her once she gets out if my father ends up in jail?" She turned to Sam. "Don't you see? There's more at stake than just my morality."

Tears shimmered in her eyes, and the sight hit Sam in the gut.

Sympathy flashed in Tyler's expression. "Well, I just found out too. And I have many of the same questions you do."

"Nice mess," Sam muttered. "Do you think your father sent those men to hurt Nicole?"

Tyler shook his head, then stopped himself and shrugged. "I hope not. I want to believe he intended to make a statement to me, to get me to step things up. I have to believe that hurting Nicole is a line my father wouldn't cross. Threaten to, maybe, but not cross."

"What if *they* don't have any such boundaries?" Sam asked, meaning the Russians.

"I'm hoping they don't know everything, that they're just doing my father a favor," Tyler muttered.

Nicole wrapped her arms around her waist, and Tyler swore. "I have to go home and find out what my father told them," he said.

"What about *my* father?" Nicole asked.

"I'll see what I can uncover."

Sam nodded. "That's the right place to start."

Tyler inclined his head. "But I have to talk to Macy before I go. I can't just disappear without an explanation," he said, not meeting Nicole's gaze.

Sam wasn't surprised that Tyler had feelings of some kind for Macy Donovan. He'd seen Macy's interest and Tyler had quickly fallen in line, from changing his style of dress to following her around town.

But he'd been sent here to corral Nicole into going home with him, and he stood to watch his father go to prison while the family business he was due to take over was destroyed by greed. Sam didn't envy Tyler. But his only concern was Nicole.

"Tyler, don't you dare hurt Macy," Nicole said. "You have commitments in New York, and she's not a city girl who can slip into the role of society wife."

"Like you did?" Tyler asked, unable to hide his obvious hurt.

Sam swallowed a groan, knowing exactly how Stanton felt being dumped by the woman he thought he'd spend the rest of his life with.

Nicole's eyes softened in sympathy. "I'm sorry. But I ended things as soon as I realized I wouldn't be happy. I didn't lead you on. And I just don't want you to set Macy up for a fall by making her believe she has a chance with you when all you want or can give her is a fling."

Tyler straightened his shoulders. "Don't take this the wrong way, but my love life is none of your business. Not anymore."

Sam had to admit, he liked these two at odds much more than Tyler chasing after her.

"Before you go, leave me names," Sam instructed Tyler. "I want to have Mike run a check on these Russian guys. Meanwhile, head home and try to get a handle on things there. I'm taking Nicole out of town for the rest of the weekend. I want the Russians gone and Serendipity back to people I know and recognize before we return." He pinned Nicole with his gaze, daring her to argue with him.

To his amazement, she didn't.

Apparently, having the mob show up in town had scared her into easy cooperation. That would help for now. Sam didn't have any delusions that she'd keep following his directions, especially when he informed her that their next step had to involve the authorities. His brother, Mike, or Cole and his contacts, Sam wasn't sure which yet. First step was keeping Nicole out of sight until the festival ended and strangers left town. After that? All bets were off because he'd do anything to keep her safe.

Sam waited until Tyler left and he had Nicole alone before changing the focus of the conversation to them. She sat in the club chair her ex had vacated, her entire body stiff. He wasn't sure if she was upset about the Russians being in town today or the fact that he was still vibrating with anger. If she were smart, she'd go with the latter.

Although they'd agreed on casual, he was still hurt over the fact that she'd kept all this inside her from the minute they'd hooked up. He was a cop. Didn't she think he could help her? Protect her?

"How —"

"I wanted to tell you," she said, cutting off his question.

He flexed his fingers, his tension still high.

"Then why didn't you?"

She rose from the chair and walked over. He couldn't tear his gaze from the long legs protruding from her white lace skirt. "You're a cop."

He raised his eyebrows. "My point exactly. Who better to look out for you? To help you figure out what to do?"

She braced her hands on his waist, and his frustration began to recede at her soft touch. He didn't understand his reaction, but he focused on her face and her sincere expression.

"Because you're a cop, I assumed you'd have to report whatever I told you about illegal activity. I didn't want to put you in a compromising position. Now you're there anyway." She shook her head and looked away. "How did you find out?"

"You were looking out for me?" he asked, addressing the most important part of what was racing through his mind, first.

"Don't sound so shocked."

She pulled away and walked back toward the fireplace, staring at the photos on the mantel. Sam looked over her shoulder. Pictures of Nicole and her twin through the years. None of her parents. No friends. Obviously she didn't extend herself to others easily. Yet she'd done so with him.

And she'd taken him off guard with her admission. He was so used to looking out for others — by profession and by family code — he wasn't used to being on the receiving end of someone putting him first. And it humbled him that she'd think of him when her entire life was imploding.

But that didn't change the facts. "Look, you weren't far off," he started to explain to her. "I do have to act on the information but not without a plan. Not without coordinating with you. We can spend the next few days implementing a strategy, but to do that, I need to pull in some people."

"But —"

He held up one hand. "People I trust. Like my brother, who has contacts in Manhattan, and my brother-in-law Cole."

"He hates me," she blurted out.

Sam shook his head. "No, he's just a tough nut to crack. Once you get to know him better, you'll see what I mean."

"Maybe *hate* is the wrong word. But he equates me with Victoria. I'm not so sure he'll want to go out on a limb to help me."

Sam crossed the space dividing them and pulled her back into his arms. "When it came down to it, you helped Erin. You can be damned sure I'll remind Cole of that fact. Not that I think he's forgotten. He's

245

just wary."

"Well, I can understand that." She let out a sigh. "You really trust them not to automatically turn my father or Tyler's over to the police?"

He tilted her chin up and brushed his thumb over her cheek. "Those two? I'd trust with my life. And yours." Leaning down, he did what he'd been dying to do since she flung herself away from danger and into his arms.

He pressed his lips over hers. He meant the gesture to comfort both her and himself, but the fire between them sparked immediately. She licked her tongue over his lips, and his cock jerked in response. He gripped her waist, digging his fingers into the soft indentation, and held on, kissing her like he'd been starving for days.

And he had. He'd had no time to get together, no nights burying himself deep. Just the memory of sliding into her without a condom and losing every bit of sanity he had left.

Then today, Tyler telling him she was in danger and the sight of the menacing Russian looming close to her in the dark alley. His fingertips bit harder into her waist at the thought, and she moaned, shaking his composure.

He wanted nothing more than to sink into her body, but his sense of responsibility made his bigger, more level head prevail and he forced himself to push her away.

"What?" She looked up at him with desire-filled eyes.

"There'll be plenty of time for that once I get you out of town," he said gruffly. Because it was his turn to look after her.

ELEVEN

Sam waited until it was late at night before they headed out. He wanted anonymity and darkness. The timing gave Nicole the chance to organize herself, as well as talk to Aunt Lulu, whom she still felt like she was abandoning for the weekend. Aunt Lulu had no problem with Nicole's sudden trip, understanding family emergencies better than most, she'd said.

While Nicole packed, Sam headed home to his place to do the same. He also took on the job of arranging for a place for them to stay. The goal, he'd explained, was to remain gone until they could return home to a quiet Serendipity on Monday.

To Nicole, it felt like running away, but he insisted on doing things his way. She let him. She'd been carrying the burden of information alone for so long, doing nothing but mull over what to do, so she was grateful to have someone else in charge for a change.

She'd hoped they could talk about what would happen next while in the car. She was afraid that by involving Mike and Cole, she'd lose any chance to get ahead of this mess, but as soon as they hit the highway, the day's events caught up with her. Nicole fell asleep, dozing for almost the entire ride.

When she woke up, it was pitch black outside and the clock on the dashboard told her she'd been asleep for almost two hours.

"Hey, sleepyhead."

She turned her head toward him. "Sorry. I didn't mean to leave you to your own thoughts the whole trip."

He shrugged. "I can handle it. You needed the rest."

She nodded. "Where are we?"

"Saratoga Springs."

"Oh! Home of the horse races."

"And a casino, and shopping, among other things. Unfortunately, I don't want to be out in public. We're better off lying low. Just in case." In case someone followed them, she thought, but didn't say so. She was just glad to be away with Sam.

Once off the highway, he drove back roads, seeming familiar with the route. Eventually he pulled the car into the driveway of a large house set back on a large chunk of property, and parked in one of two extra guest spots.

Surprised, Nicole turned toward him. "This isn't a hotel."

"No. It's not." He shut off the motor and climbed out of the vehicle.

She followed, stepping out into the dense summer humidity, meeting him by the back of his truck. He'd insisted on leaving what he termed her *more conspicuous* car in her driveway so no one, the Russians especially, would jump to the conclusion that she'd left town.

Sam slid his duffel bag over his shoulder, picked up her suitcase too, and started up the walkway to a set of double doors.

"Where are we?" she finally asked.

"At an old friend's house."

"Oh. It was nice of him to let us stay over."

Before Sam could reply, one of the large wooden doors opened and an attractive blond woman answered the door.

"You made it!" She pulled Sam into a long embrace, obviously excited to see him. "I'm so glad you're here."

"It's good to see you, Sara." He returned the hug without reservation before stepping back and studying her.

Nicole took the opportunity to do the same, struggling with the uneasy feelings

she didn't recognize as she took in Sam's . . .
friend. The woman wore a long, emerald silk
robe that covered her appropriately, but it
was obvious she had a long, lithe body in
addition to the pretty face.

Sam finished with his appraisal and
grinned before squeezing her forearm. "You
look great."

With the compliment, Nicole no longer
had any trouble naming the emotion eating
away at her. Jealousy, green and unwelcome,
filled her at the sight of Sam and this
woman.

Unaware of Nicole's thoughts, Sara shifted
her gaze away from Sam. "You must be Nicole," she said warmly. "I've heard a lot
about you."

Nicole's face felt frozen as she replied. "I
wish I could say the same."

Sara shot Sam a chiding look. "When we
were in high school, we used to call him
Silent Sam. I see that much hasn't
changed."

He merely arched an eyebrow her way.
But he didn't meet Nicole's gaze, so he
obviously knew he'd made a mistake in how
he'd handled things.

"You had a long drive, so come on in,"
Sara said, gesturing with her hands.

Nicole stepped into the entryway and Sam

followed. Although the house appeared huge from the outside, and square footage–wise it probably was immense, the interior offered a more intimate and welcoming appearance. Hardwood floors and a country-styled area rug immediately bespoke a cozy home.

"Your home is beautiful." Nicole forced a smile despite being blindsided by this woman and her obviously close relationship with Sam. "I appreciate you letting us stay here. Especially on such short notice."

"Uncle Sam!"

Nicole turned toward the unexpected loud, female shriek that was quickly followed by the sound of feet pounding down the center staircase. A nightgown-clad child, more whirling dervish than little human, flung herself toward Sam.

He caught her easily and swung her around before setting her on her feet. "Hey, short stuff!"

Sara looked down at her daughter in Sam's arms with such love in her eyes, Nicole couldn't help but be affected, softening toward the woman who'd been nothing but pleasant to her. As Nicole had never been on the receiving end of that kind of look from either parent, Sara immediately won points with her.

"How old is she?" Nicole asked.

The child turned to Nicole and held up one full hand and one finger on her other hand. Her long brown curls hung in disarray around her flushed face as she smiled and said, "I six!"

"You're a big girl." Kneeling down to her eye level, Nicole met her brown-eyed gaze. "I'm Nicole. What's your name?"

The child smiled wider, revealing two dimples. "I Sammy."

Startled, Nicole swung her gaze toward Sam.

"I'm her godfather," he quickly explained. But from the glances between Sara and Sam, there was more to the story, and Nicole's stomach cramped uncomfortably as she rose to her feet.

Sara placed a hand on her daughter's back. "Sammy, I let you stay up for your uncle. Now it's back to bed, like we agreed. Say good night to our guests."

"Good night," she chirped cheerfully, practically vibrating with excitement that her uncle was here, making Nicole doubt the child would be falling asleep any time soon.

She was the cutest little girl and those big eyes probably let her get away with a lot more than just staying up late, Nicole thought, amused, despite the questions this visit had caused.

"I'll show you to your rooms," Sara said to Nicole and Sam, and Nicole's stomach pitched in disappointment.

Sam had alluded to picking up where they left off earlier today, but Sara made it clear they wouldn't be sharing one bed in her house. Nicole didn't get the sense that Sara was mean, manipulative, or deliberately keeping Nicole and Sam apart. They were obviously old friends. Good enough friends that Sam was her daughter's godfather. But where was her husband, Nicole wondered, disliking the jealousy pounding away at her.

Once Sammy ran up the stairs, Sara turned back to face them. "You guys can share the guest room downstairs," she said, keeping her voice low. "I just didn't want to mention it in front of Sammy."

Relief swept through Nicole.

Sam nodded. "I know the way, so you can go on upstairs. We'll catch up tomorrow." He leaned over and kissed her on the cheek. "Thanks again for taking us in at the last minute."

She studied Sam intently. "Hey. I owe you and you know it."

He shook his head. "You know it's the other way around."

Her cheeks flushed and she looked away. "Mark should be back from his business trip on Sunday." An obvious subject change. "He'll be glad you're here. You don't visit often enough," she chided, before turning to Nicole. "Make yourself at home. I'm taking Sammy to gymnastics in the morning and we'll be back around eleven."

"Thank you," Nicole murmured.

"My pleasure. Night." With a wave, Sara turned and headed for the stairs.

"Ready?" Sam lifted the bags, and Nicole nodded.

All the tight knots inside her had eased at the mention of one room, combined with her husband's imminent return. But that didn't mean Nicole wouldn't have some choice words for Sam, for bringing her here without explanation or advance warning about this other important female in his life.

Once alone with Sam in the large bedroom, a pretty room set up for guests, Nicole unpacked her suitcase, using the empty dresser drawers for her clothes, and placed her toiletries on the counter in the bathroom. Sam, in typical guy fashion, said he'd deal with his things as he needed them.

She washed up and changed into a pair of boy shorts and tank top for bed, then opened the bathroom door and paused in the doorway. Sam had stripped down to his boxers and stretched out on the queen-sized mattress.

She couldn't help but take in the sight, and her gaze slid over his tanned, muscular legs, up to the bulge in his boxer briefs, and over the flat planes of his stomach. Her nipples tightened and moisture pooled between her thighs, desire for him overwhelming everything else she'd been thinking and feeling.

Yes, she was so weak that despite the unanswered questions, despite her jealousy over Sara and her exhaustion from the day, he could make her forget everything but him. Her only consolation was that he studied her the same way, his hot gaze perusing every inch of her body as he leaned back against the pillows, one muscular arm behind his head.

But she refused to allow attraction to distract her. She wanted to talk, and she hoped he'd explain about Sara without her having to ask like the jealous woman she'd suddenly become.

"There's a big pool out back, so you'll be able to relax tomorrow," he told her.

She blinked in surprise. "Seriously? That's what you have to say to me?" She leaned against the door frame and folded her arms across her chest.

"As opposed to what?" he asked.

Dense man. "Like why aren't we staying in a hotel, for starters."

He raised his shoulders. "It's racing season. I couldn't get a room and then I realized it made more sense to stay with a friend where we're not registered anywhere. No credit card, no trace."

That made sense, she silently acknowledged. "Why didn't you tell me ahead of time? You've never mentioned Sara before, yet she's obviously a *very* good friend."

His eyes narrowed at her tone and emphasis on that one word. "She is. We go way back to high school."

Nicole sighed. Obviously he was going to make her drag it out of him. "So just who is she to you? And what's with the *I owe you, no it's the other way around* stuff?"

His gaze shuttered. "It's ancient history."

Hurt worked its way through her at his refusal to share. "Not so ancient it didn't come up tonight." Her heart squeezed further at his obvious intent to shut her out. "Look, I'm not the type to pry into things you don't want me to know, but we're here with *your* friend who knows about me while I know nothing about her."

Nicole really resented him for putting her

in this position. She really disliked being an outsider, a feeling she suspected would only get worse as the weekend wore on. Unless Sam let her in.

"Come here," he said in a gruff voice.

She pushed herself off the wall and strode over to the bed, sitting down beside him.

He placed his hand over hers, and warmth traveled through her body at his touch.

"Sara and I have a deep history. As *friends.* I made a poor judgment call a long time ago that affected her life and I owe her. That's all."

That wasn't all, Nicole thought, looking into eyes that held hidden stories and secrets. But it was obviously all he'd reveal tonight. They had a long weekend for bigger revelations. She hoped.

"I'm tired," she said on an exhale, wanting nothing more than to crawl into bed and forget everything that had happened today.

He nodded in agreement. "It's been a long day."

"It has. And it's my fault. I've brought a lot of drama into your life," she said, feeling guilty for dragging him into her problems, which had ended up showing her just how it felt to be on the periphery of his life.

He tipped her chin upward until she met

his gaze. "You bring a lot *to* my life. Period." Those sometimes green, sometimes brown eyes held an intensity that affected her straight down to her soul.

She couldn't help but believe him. After all, he'd stood by her through everything. Even when he hadn't known if she was any different from her twin, he'd defended her against Cole's accusations, and Nicole had trusted Sam to have her back. And he had. Their connection had been that solid.

But in the present, he fought any emotional bond with Nicole, and she'd accepted that that was how it had to be. Because being left at the altar had scarred him. Yet tonight she'd seen that he shared that kind of bond with Sara. Their relationship might not be sexual, but there was a trust and a commitment between them, and it hurt Nicole to know he wouldn't open himself up that way to her.

She pushed herself away from him and rose from the bed, pulling down the covers on her side. He stood and did the same. Soon they were under the comforter together, but Nicole wanted the same distance between them physically that he'd put up emotionally.

"Night." She grabbed her pillow and curled into a ball, facing away from him.

She heard the click of the lamp and the bed dipped and moved as he got comfortable, but he didn't bridge the distance between them. A painful lump formed in her throat, but she forced herself to breathe slowly and soon she fell asleep.

Sam woke up with the same heavy feeling in his chest with which he'd fallen asleep. He also knew why. He'd botched last night, mishandling everything with this trip and hurting Nicole in the process. He really thought bringing her here would be good for them both. An under-the-radar place to stay and a chance to see his goddaughter. Why hadn't he realized all the questions that would come up just by being here?

Because, as his sister Erin often said, he was such a guy.

Which meant he'd screwed up and now he owed Nicole an apology as well as an explanation. He could handle the apology better than the other, and that was saying something. He reached out only to find the other side of the bed empty. And cold.

With a groan, he swung his legs over the side. He glanced at the clock on the nightstand. Ten thirty A.M. Sam couldn't remember the last time he'd slept so late. Sara would probably be gone with Sammy to the little girl's gymnastics lesson, so if he wanted time alone with Nicole, he needed to hurry.

He showered quickly and headed to find her. She wasn't in the kitchen, although he did manage to grab a peach on his way out the back door, eating in a few bites. He opened the sliding glass doors and stepped outside, and his breath caught — having nothing to do with the damp humid air.

Nicole lay outside in a bikini, displaying a body that made his mouth water. Just because he'd seen her before didn't mean he couldn't appreciate the view all over again. He started toward her, reacquainting himself with her long legs, curvy hips, breasts that more than filled his hands, and a face that stayed with him from the moment they'd met. Was it any wonder he was struggling with distance?

"You're blocking my sun." She pushed herself up to a sitting position.

He inhaled and caught the scent of coconut sunscreen. It was a scent he'd liked as far back as childhood. He liked it even more now, and his body responded to it in very adult ways.

He sat down on her chaise, taking up not just her sun but her personal space. He finished off the peach he'd been working on and rolled the pit into a napkin on the table before sliding in closer.

"What are you doing?" she asked.

"I need to talk to you before Sara gets back."

At the mention of the other woman's name, Nicole stiffened and pushed her back against the chair, away from him.

He hung his head. "And that's why I'm sorry. If I'd told you about Sara before we came here, if I'd explained, you wouldn't be so defensive now."

"I'm not defensive." She straightened her shoulders and met his gaze. "Fine. I am defensive. But do you blame me?"

"Not in the least. So hear me out?" He reached out and tugged on a lock of her hair. "How else can I apologize?"

Nicole sighed, feeling herself softening toward him.

He was here with the answers she wanted and the apology she hadn't expected. "Okay, fine." She relaxed and hugged her knees to her chest, giving him more room on the chair.

"First things first. Last night, when you said you were sorry you brought so much drama to my life?"

She nodded. "I was serious. We've gone from dealing with my sister stalking yours to money laundering and threats. I'm the reason we're hiding out here for the weekend."

He braced his hand around her ankle. "I don't need an excuse to hang out with you, so no apologies. And as for the drama, do you think I chose my career because I like peace and quiet?" he asked on a laugh.

She smiled. "I didn't know that meant you like it invading your personal life too."

He squeezed her leg tighter. "I like *you* invading my personal life."

"Liar," she said softly.

His lips quirked in a grin. "Okay, you've got me there. But I'll let you in anyway. No matter how uncomfortable it makes me." He drew a deep breath. "Back in high school, there were four of us. Four best friends. Me, Jenna, Brett, and Sara."

She leaned closer so she could absorb not just the story but his emotions about his past as well. "Were Brett and Sara boyfriend and girlfriend too?"

He shook his head. "Just friends. But after — after Jenna left me for Brett and they moved out of town, it was just me and Sara. Not in a romantic way or even a sexual one. We were really good friends."

She nodded.

And he continued. "Long story short, I

went to the academy in Albany and I met this guy, Frank Dalton. He and I became close. He seemed decent. I met his parents. I figured I knew him pretty well. I trusted my instincts and introduced him to Sara." He drew another deep breath, his body trembling.

"It's okay. You don't have to relive it." Nicole saw how difficult it was for him to talk about his past. It was enough that he was willing.

"You need to know," he said, his voice strong.

"Okay." She was grateful. "Okay."

"Frank and Sara hit it off right away. They dated and next thing I knew they got engaged. He wanted to be a city cop and she was ready to leave Serendipity, so they moved to Albany."

Nicole had seen the connection between them. "I bet you missed her."

"A lot. Mostly because we lost touch." His facial features grew taut.

Nicole glanced at his tense expression. "Why? That doesn't seem like the Sara I met. Even two seconds in her presence and I could tell when she loves, she loves big."

"Yeah. And she was there for me after Jenna left, so I couldn't figure out why she would pull back and disappear from my life.

Then one day, she called me. She was hysterical. She said she needed me so I got in the car and drove to Albany."

"What was wrong?"

A muscle ticked in his jaw. "Frank had been in a car accident. Drunk driving and he was in a coma."

"Oh no!" Nicole reached for him, but he shook his head.

"There's more."

She could barely breathe, waiting to hear the end of the story. "When I saw Sara again, everything she didn't want me to know came pouring out. From the day they married, Frank had been a controlling son of a bitch and when he drank, which was often, he was verbally abusive. He didn't like how close we were and he cut her off from me, from anyone who could see what their life together was really like. I never saw that side of him or I wouldn't have introduced them."

"Of course not!"

"But I did. Because my personal judgment sucks, something I've proven twice over. And you know what they say about the third time."

"Third time's a charm?" she asked, trying to lighten the mood.

"More like three strikes and you're out,"

he muttered.

Nicole knew better than to argue with a thinking pattern he'd had too long to believe in and let stick. "Did Sara blame you?" she asked instead.

Sam shook his head. "No. But she should. The night she told him she was pregnant, he was furious. They hadn't planned for a kid. He wasn't ready and — he hit her before taking off in their car. She packed, planning to leave, but she got a call that he'd been in an accident. And you know the rest."

"What happened to her husband?" Nicole asked.

Sam glanced up at the clear blue sky. "He died of his injuries."

"And she was free of him."

He nodded.

"But you weren't. Because you still blame yourself."

He inclined his head.

It wasn't hard to understand his thoughts. A man who was raised in a family of cops, who protected others, had felt like he'd failed himself and his best friend.

She met his gaze. "You have to see that Sara has remarried and clearly has a wonderful life. How can you be so hard on yourself?"

He groaned, running a hand through his hair. "When it comes to making decisions for myself or people I care about, my judgment is suspect."

"Because Jenna betrayed you too? And you didn't see it happening?"

"Both Jenna and Brett. And then Frank." He clenched and unclenched his hands.

She placed her hand over his, stilling his movements. "That's on *them*. The only thing that's on you is being a good, trusting person."

"Yeah, fucking perfect," he muttered.

She blinked in surprise at the vehemence in his tone. She wanted to crawl into his lap and tell him that to her, he was perfect. He was everything good and decent, especially compared to her own family, and she felt lucky to have him in her life. But from the tight set of his jaw, she sensed he wouldn't hear her, let alone believe.

But somehow she had to convince him that not only did she trust him, but he could have that same faith in himself. Otherwise this push-pull sexually was all they'd ever have together. And she already knew it wasn't nearly enough.

Macy prided herself on being smart when it came to men. Not so smart that she'd landed herself one for good, but smart enough not to be taken in by the jerks of the world. Until Tyler Stanton. Yes, she knew Tyler had only been spending time with her while pursuing his agenda with Nicole, but they'd grown closer. He'd flirted even after he'd promised not to. At the very least they were friends. And friends didn't dump each other at an art fair and run off looking for another woman.

After getting a ride home from another friend and stewing for an hour after that, Macy decided it was time she got some answers from Mr. Tyler Stanton. He didn't answer his phone, so she headed over to the Serendipity Inn. She pulled her little Mustang up to the house and parked on the street.

As she walked up the driveway and path to the front door, she waved to Joanne Rhodes, the owner, who was on her knees, weeding in her flower beds.

"Hi, Macy. How are you this fine day?"

"I'm fine, thanks. Did you get over to the art festival?" Macy asked her.

Joanne nodded. "This morning. I wanted to spend time with my flowers this afternoon. Here to see Tyler?" she asked.

"Yes. Is he in?" A stupid question because his car was parked in the extra spots in the back of the driveway, but she forced herself to make polite conversation before she could head in.

"Upstairs. I have to admit, he's such a nice, polite man. I'm sad to see him go."

Macy stiffened but forced herself not to ask her for details. Those she wanted from Tyler. She didn't want to think he'd leave without saying good-bye, but after the way he'd dumped her at the fair, maybe she shouldn't give him that much credit.

She managed a smile. "I'll go talk to him."

Gathering her anger as well as her courage, she headed inside and upstairs to his room. She knocked once and the door swung open.

The Tyler who answered the door didn't look anything like the composed, put-together man she was used to seeing. Instead, his normally neat hair was messed, having apparently been attacked by his fingers, and his eyes were a bit wild, his focus clearly scattered.

"Macy." To his credit, he sounded happy to see her.

"We need to talk," she said, pushing her way into his room, only to see his suitcase open on the end of the bed. Her stomach plummeted at the sight.

She turned to him, folding her arms across

her chest, pinning him with her most determined glare. "Tell me you'd planned on saying good-bye."

Tyler stared at her, wishing he could give her the answer she wanted. But the truth was, he'd heard what Nicole had to say about not hurting her. He also knew there were people in town watching him. And he hadn't wanted to put her in any danger. So he'd planned to go home, settle things with his father, then come back here and see what could be — with Macy.

"You. Suck." She shoved his shoulder, her blue eyes flashing with hurt and anger.

He grabbed her wrist and met her gaze. "Yeah, I do. And you deserve a hell of a lot better than getting involved with me."

She jerked out of his grasp and sat down on the bed. "We're not involved, Tyler. Maybe there's chemistry between us, but I'm not stupid enough to put any stock in you. Not while you're here chasing after another woman. But I at least thought we were friends."

"Oh, we're friends."

Chin high, she glared at him, but Tyler knew her better by now and he saw beyond the bravado and the words. Like it or not, they were both involved, more than either wanted to be. He'd just wanted to come back to explore it, no baggage holding him back from her.

"Friends don't take off on each other without a word. We were together, looking at paintings, no mention of you needing to deal with Nicole. Next thing I know, you're focused on her and leaving me — without a ride home. Not cool."

No, it wasn't. And he'd been so thrown by the Russian art dealers, he hadn't once thought about the fact that he'd abandoned her there. One minute they'd been looking at landscapes, and the next his entire life and Nicole's flashed before him.

"I'm sorry." He drew a deep breath. "Like I said, you deserve better than to have to deal with me."

Silence followed and he knew he'd lost her.

"I didn't peg you for a coward," she said at last.

If she knew what he was dealing with, she might cut him some slack, but he didn't want her pity. "I'm going to ask you for something. Something I have no right to ask of you."

"What?" she asked, sounding wary.

Rightly so.

"Wait for me."

"What?" Her soft lips parted in question.

He took advantage, leaned in, and settled his lips over hers. His intent? To give her something to remember him by. To entice her to hold out for him, despite having given her every reason not to trust him or want him to return.

The result? One taste and she imprinted herself on him for good. She rubbed her tongue against his and with a groan, he pulled her up, wrapped his arm around her waist, and aligned his body with hers. He allowed himself this brief moment, holding her, feeling her, giving himself something to work toward when dealing with the nightmare back home. She softened against him, responding in ways he couldn't have imagined. He wanted nothing more than to bury himself inside her, but not now.

Not until he was completely free.

He braced his hands on her waist and pulled her away from him. "Wait for me," he said once more.

"I don't understand." She looked up at him, eyes glazed, confusion quickly replacing desire.

He touched his forehead to hers. "It's better that you don't know. Not until I've put it all behind me."

Her gaze narrowed. "You'd better not be playing me," she warned him.

Which was exactly what he liked about her. He grinned and slid a finger down her cheek. "When I'm playing you, you'll know it."

Now, he thought, looking at Macy, he had even more incentive to head home and fix the mess that was his life.

TWELVE

Nicole kept Sara company in the pool while she watched her daughter play in the shallow end. Today was the first day of a heat wave — the temperature was due to hit over one hundred degrees by this afternoon — and the water felt good against her heated skin. Sara was warm and friendly, and now that Sam's revelations had taken the sting out of their relationship, Nicole found that she liked his high school friend. More, she respected the other woman for surviving and thriving after all she'd suffered.

She glanced around, taking in the high fence and the heavy shroud of trees behind it, an unnecessary blockade since they obviously owned acres of land. No neighbors in sight. Nicole loved the house and the grounds, the lush greenery making everything out here as warm and welcoming as the interior décor and the owner herself. She couldn't imagine not liking Sara's husband either.

The sound of Sam's phone ringing cut into the silence. He grabbed his cell, talking from where he lay on a lounge chair, eyes closed, as he relaxed. His chest was broad, his abs well defined, his golden skin spattered with just the right amount of hair, which tapered into the swim trunks he wore. The muscles in his arms and the obvious strength in his legs made her mouth water. He looked delectable, but the truth was, the outside was just packaging for the equally spectacular man within.

Every day that passed, she learned more about him. Not just a good cop, he was also a decent man, and he'd dedicated himself to her protection. For the first time since the eavesdropping incident outside her father's office, she felt safe and protected. Because she trusted Sam.

"You've got it bad," Sara mused.

Nicole cut her gaze away from Sam, her cheeks heating up at being caught staring. "It's not like that between us."

Sara's eyes twinkled, her expression indicating she knew better. "It's *something* because he told me ahead of time you'd be sharing a room. And I've known Sam for many years and he's never brought a woman here. Never even mentioned one in passing.

Not even when I've pushed and prodded for answers."

Nicole studied the pretty blonde, surprised she didn't resent her for being so blunt or intrusive. However, she knew now how much Sara cared about Sam.

"Yes, it's *something,*" Nicole admitted, knowing it would be foolish to deny the obvious. "But he's not into relationships. And coming off a broken engagement, neither am I."

Without warning, a huge spray of water hit them both, and Sara turned toward her daughter. "Sammy, watch where you splash!" she called out.

"Sorry!" The little girl bounced up and down in the water. "Mommy, when can I go to Rebecca's?"

Sara smiled at her daughter. "We'll go after lunch."

Satisfied with the answer, Sammy retreated back into her own world to play.

"Sorry about that," Sara said, turning back to Nicole.

"Don't worry about it." Nicole liked observing the mother-daughter bond between these two.

The whole concept was such an anomaly in her life that watching them caused an ache near her heart, making her acutely aware of everything she'd lacked growing up. She wondered if she'd get the chance to be a mother, and if so, she was determined to do a better job than her own had done.

Sara pushed herself up onto the edge of the pool and Nicole joined her, their legs dangling into the water.

"Now where were we?" Sara asked. "Oh yes. You said Sam's not into relationships. And I beg to differ. He only thinks he doesn't want to get emotionally involved."

Nicole glanced at the handsome, self-contained man on the lounge chair and sighed. "You have to admit he's got good reasons to avoid one," Nicole said, knowing Sam was afraid of being hurt again.

Sara raised her eyebrows. "So did I." She swept her hand around, gesturing to the beautiful home and the little girl babbling to herself a few feet away, as if to say, *But look what I have now.*

"You're miraculous," Nicole said, meaning it in every way.

The other woman flushed. "No, I'm just a survivor. So I take it Sam told you about my first husband?"

Nicole nodded. "I hope that's okay." She'd hate to get him in trouble for betraying a confidence.

Sara met her gaze. "It's fine. Sam knows I

volunteer at the hospital, talking to domestic abuse groups, so sharing is what I do."

Nicole stuck by her view of Sara being an incredible woman, but she wouldn't embarrass her by saying it again. "I'm glad you and Sam are still close," she said instead. Because Sara seemed like that rare person — trustworthy and loyal — and Sam deserved a friend like her.

She smiled. "The feeling's mutual and I just want him to be happy. He's refused to open himself up to the idea of love. It's like he shut down, and to be honest, I was beginning to think he'd always be alone. But just the fact that he brought you here tells me he's changing."

Nicole shook her head, not wanting Sara to formulate the wrong idea about her and Sam. "I'm only here because I'm in trouble and we needed to get out of town for a few days." Sam had mentioned that he'd been vague but honest with Sara about Nicole's situation when he asked her if they could come stay.

"Well, he could have brought you to a hotel."

"He tried. It's racing season."

"So why didn't he choose another location?" Sara smirked, sure of her conclusions. "Instead he brought you here, to an old friend who knows him better than anyone. That tells me he's more invested than even he knows."

Nicole's heart squeezed tight, longing and hope threatening to rise, and she ruthlessly quashed the emotions. Sam had made himself clear. No matter how attached she might be getting, and she'd be a fool to deny it to herself, she couldn't set herself up for pain and heartache. They were neighbors. And when things between them ended, she'd have to live in his small town and make their friendship work.

"Sara —" Nicole wanted to stop the speculation and conversation, but the other woman was on a roll.

"Now, maybe you're not ready for a relationship, as you said," Sara went on. "Or maybe that's an excuse because Sam told you up front that he isn't interested in one. I don't know. But I like you. And I like you with Sam."

"Thank you," Nicole said, not knowing what else to say.

Sara tipped her head up toward the sun. "I'm just calling it like I see it. Sam's relaxed around you. He watches you and smiles when he thinks you're not looking."

"He does?"

It took every ounce of Nicole's self-control

for her not to turn around and sneak a peek at the man and see for herself.

Sara merely grinned.

Which led her to wonder what she'd do if Sam Marsden suddenly decided he was all in and wanted more. The answer, which she'd never admit to out loud, had her wanting to dive in and submerge herself in the pool.

Sam glanced over to where Nicole lounged at the edge of the pool, talking to Sara. Water droplets glistened on her sun-drenched skin, her dark hair a contrast to her paler flesh. She simply took his breath away, bringing up emotions he knew he'd have to deal with at some point, but not until the threat against her was gone.

As the women spoke, their conversation broken only by Sara's reprimand at her daughter's splashing, he caught discreet glances coming his way. He didn't know what, specifically, they were discussing, but he could take an educated guess that he was the general subject.

"Women," he muttered, amused despite himself, as he lay down and shut his eyes against the glare of the sun.

His mind kept replaying last night's talk with Nicole, the revelation and discussion of things he'd avoided discussing or thinking about for years. Yet revealing himself to her felt right. And he was forced to admit that talking about his biggest failures in life helped ease the burden he'd been carrying for years.

He might not trust his personal judgment, but Sara had no such problem, even after Frank, and the result was a great marriage to a decent guy. Mark Stein owned a couple of luxury-car dealerships, hence this beautiful house and pool, and Sara's ability to be a stay-at-home mom to her daughter. Sam couldn't be happier for her, knowing what she'd gone through to get to this point.

His cell phone rang. At a glance, he saw it was his brother and he answered on the second ring. "Hey, bro. What do you have for me?" He'd given his brother the names of the Russian art dealers Tyler had passed on to him.

"I took the names you gave me to Cole, who went to his contact with the feds. They ran them through their database, and this is big for them. They want to set up a sting. Have Nicole wear a wire while talking to Robert Stanton. Once he confesses to money laundering on tape, they can leverage that information and get him to testify against the Romanovs. They want the big fish, which will take care of Nicole's problem."

Sam swore and glanced out at the pool. Nicole's laughter rang out as she splashed with Sammy in the water. He couldn't help but grin at the sight even as his stomach churned at the thought of asking her to do as Mike asked.

"I don't like it."

"And I don't blame you, but you've got no choice."

He knew that. "I'm not telling her until it's time. She doesn't need to worry or panic."

Mike paused before answering. "That's your call. But aren't you worrying a hell of a lot about this woman? I know you look out for those who can't do it for themselves. And you're seeing her, that I know. But how involved are you?"

"It's none of your business, Mike."

"That's enough of an answer. And *I* don't like it. Look, she's a nice woman and all, but given who her sister is, don't you think that's going to make Thanksgiving dinners awkward?"

Sam nearly choked on his own saliva. "Dammit, Mike. I'm sleeping with her, not getting married."

"It always starts in bed," Mike muttered.

"Trust me. I know."

"It's not like you and Cara."

Mike burst out laughing.

"What's so funny?"

"That's what I said when I was fighting myself."

Sam rolled his eyes. "You don't know what you're talking about."

"So I can tell Cole you'll handle persuading Nicole to wear a wire with Tyler's old man?" Mike asked, changing the subject.

"Yeah. But not until we're back in town," Sam said. "How's Cara feeling?"

"Not good. Can you talk to her when you get back? I get the feeling she's shutting me out. I don't understand, but maybe you can get through to her?"

Sam knew what it took for his brother to ask. "Sure thing. Once I'm home, I'll make it a priority."

"Thanks. I'll be in touch."

Sam disconnected the call and joined the women in the pool, where he spent the next half hour having water fights with a six-year-old and carrying her around on his shoulders around the pool. More than once, he caught Nicole watching him, with an expression he'd never seen before on her beautiful face. He didn't know what to make of it, but damned if he didn't like it.

A little while later, Sara announced it was time for Sammy to take a bath, and then she could go to her friend's house for the rest of the afternoon and for dinner.

The little girl squealed in excitement, dumped her uncle Sam, and ran for the house.

"Wait for a towel! You'll drip water everywhere!" Sara took off after her, towel in her hand.

Nicole laughed, leaning her head back against the chair in which she sat. "Oh my God, she's so cute."

"A firecracker," Sam said.

They lay in companionable silence, enjoying the afternoon, and he was glad Nicole was able to put her problems aside. And if she wasn't, at least she was making an effort to enjoy as much as possible. He dreaded the time when they'd have to head back to reality, but that was a while off.

Sara stepped outside to tell them she was leaving, and she pointedly mentioned she wouldn't be back until Sammy's bedtime at eight.

Good friend, he thought wryly, letting him know he had the all clear. Which was perfect, because he couldn't keep his hands off Nicole for much longer.

■ ■ ■ ■

The sun beat down overhead and beads of perspiration pooled on Nicole's chest. She groaned, knowing that the weatherman's prediction of one-hundred-degree temperatures had to have come true.

"I'm roasting out here," she murmured.

A few seconds later, she squealed at the unexpected cold shot of an ice cube trailing over her stomach. She bolted upright, but Sam's firm hands pushed her shoulders back down.

"Shh. Let me cool you off."

His husky voice aroused her in an instant and she did as he asked, relaxing back into the chair.

He outlined her bikini top with an ice cube, first tracing the band around her chest, then moving over the swells of her breasts, taking his time, leisurely caressing her skin.

The ice, a stark contrast to her heated flesh, melted on contact, leaving droplets of water in its wake, and she arched into the cooling sensations. Sam added texture to his ministrations, brushing his thumbs over her already distended nipples, awakening her nerve endings that begged for a harder touch, but he didn't linger in any one spot.

Instead he retrieved another cube from the Lucite bucket and worked his way down her stomach, her muscles rippling and clenching at the icy trail he created. He outlined the top of her bikini bottom, sliding the ice along her lower abdomen, keeping his fingers in the mix, stroking her aroused flesh everywhere — except where she needed it most. Every touch, every brush of his callused fingertips might as well have been directly on her sex, because the tiny bud throbbed and ached as if he were physically touching her, and she arched her hips, seeking deeper contact.

Sam pressed his lips to her stomach, lapping at the droplets of water and kissing her skin. She moaned at the intimate touch, unable to hold back the sounds of pleasure.

Forcing her heavy eyelids open, she caught sight of his golden-brown hair, his face lost to her, buried against her.

"Sam," she said, his name escaping, the word more a plea.

"Right here." Which sounded like a promise, and moisture dampened her bottoms even more.

He hooked his fingers into the sides of her bikini and slowly slid the bathing suit down and off her legs.

Bared in broad daylight beneath the afternoon sun, she ought to be embarrassed, but she knew they were alone. And with his green-gold gaze darkened with desire, she didn't care about anything except the pulsing needs of her body and his.

"So damn sexy," he said, lowering his head to her body once more.

Only this time he slid his tongue directly over her damp sex and began to work her in earnest. No more teasing, his tongue slid over her outer folds, giving each one thorough, loving treatment, before sliding his tongue briefly over her clit.

Her hips jerked and she gripped his head, centering herself, unable to hold still as the beautiful sensations built inside her. "Sam, God. Don't stop."

One long swipe of his tongue was her answer.

Then he grasped her thighs and slid his tongue inside her. She pulled at his hair, thrusting her hips against his eager mouth. He gripped her legs tighter, playing her body faster, flicking his tongue back and forth over her clit, then easing off long enough for her to catch her breath, only to start up again.

He brought her close and pulled back, close and pulled back, until she writhed beneath him, a frantic mess of need, every nerve ending in her body screaming for the release he deliberately denied her.

Then suddenly, he nipped at her clit and then pressed his tongue down hard and flat against her and she shattered, her body imploding in the most mind-blowing orgasm that seemed to go on and on, until she could swear she saw bright, colorful stars behind her eyes.

She'd barely come back to herself when a shadow loomed over her. Sam stood before her. He'd shed his swim trunks and his big, beautiful body stood poised at her entrance.

He glanced down at her and groaned. "The damned lounge chair is too low. I need to fuck you and I can't do it on that flimsy thing." Before she could blink, he lifted her up and into his arms.

"Then get us inside," she said in a husky voice she didn't recognize.

He nodded and headed into the house, her still-throbbing heat rubbing almost painfully against his hard erection as he carried her to their guest bedroom.

She pressed her lips against his and wrapped her legs around his waist. "I could get used to being carried around naked by you," she said, nuzzling her face into the sweat-slickened skin of his neck, reveling in his masculine scent and heat.

He stiffened at her words, but before she could react, he had her flat on her back, pulled her to the edge of the bed, and thrust home. He was big, thick, and she needed him inside her more than she'd realized. Her body tightened around him, pulling him in deeper.

She opened her eyes just as he slid out and thrust back inside. She felt him everywhere, and she moaned her approval. "More," she said, arching her hips.

"You sure?"

She nodded.

He closed his eyes and took her harder, pounding into her with renewed determination. The muscles corded in his neck, his jaw set tight, and she marveled that she made him lose control this way. The very thought had her body reacting, and she welcomed the insistent pleasure that began building all over again.

As he took her hard, she was lost, and knew the last of her walls had crumbled. She'd always known she could fall hard for him even as she'd agreed to nothing serious between them. And as he played her body so well, bringing her over the edge once more, she took that final tumble into love.

Sam opened his eyes and watched Nicole's face, taking in the soft expression as she came hard, again, for him.

"God, Sam, I'm still coming." Awe and passion etched her words, his willing partner in every way.

He held on by a thread but wanted her to finish, to milk every last bit of her pleasure around his cock before he let go.

She arched, her body clamping around him, her inner walls rippling. With her gorgeous face open and honest as pleasure consumed her, his body tightened and her final cry triggered his release and he poured himself into her, pounding over and over until he was done, spent, gone.

He collapsed on top of her, breathing heavily, until he felt her fingers sift through his hair. His heart beat hard in his chest and he knew it wasn't just a physical response to phenomenal sex. Although it had been that.

The usual fear of commitment and ultimate rejection threatened to set in, and he fought it back. For right now, what they shared was solid. Not to mention how much she needed him to stand by her throughout this mess with Tyler's father and his business.

He couldn't predict the future but if nothing else, he could damn well enjoy the present.

A while later, they'd shared a shower, which had been a repeat of their earlier coupling, this time standing up in the small stall. Afterward, Nicole said she had a phone call to make, and he'd left her alone, giving her privacy, promising to find them something to eat.

Sam shook his head, unable to remember the last time he'd been with a woman, stayed to shower, planned to eat with her, then headed back to bed. If he wasn't careful, he was afraid he'd be calling what he and Nicole shared a relationship.

Shit.

He turned his focus to the fridge in the kitchen. Sara loved to cook and she always had extra meals in the fridge. Sure enough, he found lasagna with a note to him to heat up whatever they wanted. It was easy enough to preheat the oven before heading back to let Nicole know they'd be eating in about forty minutes.

He walked down the hallway, pausing outside the bedroom door at the sound of Nicole's voice.

"Yes, it's Nicole Farnsworth. I've been on hold to talk to my sister, Victoria?" A pause, then, "No, it's not our regularly scheduled time, but it's our birthday — I mean, we're twins. So I wanted to call and —"

Silence followed, while Nicole listened to the other person on the phone. "Yes, I'll hold for her doctor," Nicole said.

Sam leaned against the wall, surprised by what he'd heard. The whole day had passed and he hadn't known it was her birthday. Her phone hadn't rung. Nobody had called to wish her well. He ran his hand through his hair, remembering what she'd told him about her parents. How they rarely remembered she was around unless they needed something from her.

A painful knot formed in his chest as he thought of his parents and siblings, and the birthdays he'd had, both growing up and as an adult. Nicole's utter isolation gave him a completely new appreciation of family. Of the love and caring he'd always taken for granted. He'd had no way of knowing, understood she wouldn't be upset with him, but he doubted a belated *Happy birthday* would take the sting out of the day and wondered what he could do to make it up to her.

"Hi, Dr. Templeton. What's going on?" Nicole asked.

More silence, during which Sam wondered what was happening with her sister.

"I thought . . . I mean, last time we spoke Victoria said she was getting better. That you were talking about giving her a day pass, to see —" Nicole's voice brought Sam out of his introspection, followed by that damning quiet as she listened again, Sam thought.

"I see." Voice lowered, Nicole's pain and disappointment filtered through to Sam. "Sure. Okay, yes. Thank you for explaining everything to me yourself. Good-bye."

A loud sob followed, and Sam pushed open the door without knocking.

Nicole spun around at the sound of his entrance and immediately wiped her eyes with her hands.

"Don't pretend nothing's wrong."

She visibly stilled. "I'm fine."

He shook his head and stepped closer. "No, you're not. I heard your end of the call. Whatever's wrong with your sister, you don't have to hide it from me."

"But —"

"But I'm here for you. End of discussion." He slid his arm around her waist and pulled her against him. Ignoring how his body lit up at contact wasn't easy, but she needed more than sex to make her feel better now. "Talk to me."

Nicole pushed out of his embrace. "My

sister isn't getting better. She's fighting the meds, and when she told me she would have permission to come out on leave? That was her being delusional."

"I'm sorry."

"Don't be." She let out a harsh laugh. "It protects your family from having to deal with her any time in the near future."

She spun away but he caught her arm, halting her emotional retreat. "Hey! Don't run away from me."

She turned, her glassy red eyes kicking him in the gut.

"I've always dealt with Victoria's issues and problems myself."

He nodded. After she'd broken her engagement, she'd been alone. She'd chosen to move to Serendipity. Alone. And now she'd taken this hit from her twin, expecting to be — alone.

His heart broke a little more as he realized how solitary her life had been. He didn't want her to be alone right now. Not when she had him.

"Come back here." He extended his arms.

She hesitated a brief second, then launched herself into his embrace. He brought her to the bed and let her cuddle into him, stroking her hair as she cried.

"She's in a good place," Sam said of her

twin. "You know she's getting help, not out on her own, where she could possibly hurt herself."

Nicole hiccupped in an attempt to catch her breath, and she managed a small laugh. "I know that. I do. I guess —" She trailed off, obviously not wanting to explain.

"Come on. Let it out." His hand cupped the back of her head, urging her to talk to him.

She sighed. "I let myself start to think about the possibility that she'd come out whole and healthy, ready to live her life. And maybe then I'd have someone there for me always. Like sisters are supposed to be. Like family is supposed to be."

He heard the hurt and disappointment in her voice and ached for her. "I get it. But you're making solid friends in Serendipity, right?"

She pushed back, turning to face him, propping herself up with one hand. "I am. It's still new, but I feel comfortable and welcomed."

"What about your friends at home?" he asked, curious about her past life.

"They're all caught up in the social scene I grew up in. I kept up appearances when I was working for Tyler's mother's campaign because I needed their support, but after I broke off the engagement and moved away . . ." She shrugged. "I didn't keep in touch with them and vice versa."

He reached out and rolled her on top of him. She was wearing an oversized T-shirt that hiked up on her thighs. And though he had on a pair of cargo shorts and a soft T-shirt, he was suddenly hot and felt overly constricted in his clothes.

"You're brave, do you know that?" he asked, focusing on what was important and what she needed from him now, not his body's aggressive demands.

"If you consider running away brave."

He brushed her hair off her face. "I consider walking away from a life that didn't suit you brave. Same with picking up and starting over in a new place."

Her eyes warmed at his compliments.

"And holding all your problems inside? That's pretty —"

"Stupid. Do not say *brave.*" She grinned, and he knew he'd broken through her sadness.

"Since you had your reasons, I suggest we let that one go."

"Thank you," she murmured.

"For what?"

"For not letting me get so deep into my own head that I forget all the good things in my life. And Sam?"

"Hmm?" With her body bracketing his, her scent teasing him, her feminine warmth arousing him, he was finding it harder and harder to concentrate.

"You're one of those good things." She tugged at his T-shirt and he shifted, helping her yank it over his head.

He tossed the garment onto the floor. She pulled at his shorts next, and those followed the same path. He removed her shirt too and discovered that she was nude beneath it.

"Oh, man," he muttered, taking her in. Pale breasts stood in contrast to the rest of her now-tanned body, and he groaned at the sight.

He reached out and tweaked one nipple, and she responded with a soft moan. His cock twitched at the sexy sound. He maneuvered himself into a sitting position, intending to suck that tempting peak into his mouth, but she scooted down on him instead.

"My turn," she murmured, and leaned close, swiping the head of his cock with a lick of her tongue.

He swore. Her pleasuring him was not what he'd had in mind when he set out to make her forget her troubles, but from the hazy look in her eyes, she was wholly focused on him and nothing else. So mission accomplished, he thought, falling back against the pillows at the same time she enclosed her mouth over his aching shaft and sucked him deep.

Buried in the moist recesses of her mouth, he felt the suction all the way into his balls before she released him, licked her way back to the tip and started all over again. He just might die if she kept up the rhythm. He'd never gone from zero to sixty so damned fast.

His orgasm threatened and everything inside him knew it would be the most explosive one he'd ever had. Maybe it was the way she focused on her task, licking and eating at him like he was the tastiest treat. Or maybe it was the way she gave of herself in the process. He'd placed a hand on her back and her entire body shook, letting him know she was enjoying this as much as he was. But he had the scary feeling that the only thing that mattered was the fact that it was *Nicole* selflessly giving him all those things, at a time when he should have remained focused on her.

Somehow he managed to pull himself out of her mouth, flip her over, and pin her on her back before he came.

"What's wrong?" She lay beneath him, large eyes opened wide, mouth swollen and wet.

"Not a damned thing except I'm not inside you," he said at the same time he rectified the situation, notching himself at her entrance and thrusting inside.

"Oh, Sam." His name sounded like the deepest groan in the back of her throat, taking him impossibly higher.

"Look at me," he said, managing to listen to the voice in his head directing something other than his cock.

She forced her heavy eyelids open.

He eased out of her, deliberately slow, wanting her to feel every last inch of him.

"Nic?"

He watched as she forced herself to focus. "Hmm?"

"Happy birthday, sweetheart," he said, before thrusting back inside.

Sam didn't remember much of their joint frenzy to completion, but long after he collapsed on top of her, after they'd showered again and eaten dinner, and after she'd fallen asleep, he lay awake. And remembered the tears that moistened her face as he made love to her for the first time.

THIRTEEN

Sam walked into the kitchen the next morning, shocked by the explosion of baking stuff all over the usually pristine counters: bowls, a mixer, pans, flour, and God knows what else spread across the granite. Sammy sat on a stool, her little body leaning over, listening intently to Nicole's explanation.

"So now mix the dough until there are no more lumps. Let me get you started because the flour's heavy like paste." Nicole took over the task for a few seconds, until she was satisfied Sammy could handle things. "Okay, here." She handed the little girl the wooden spoon. "Take your time, okay?"

" 'Kay." Sammy began to stir in the contents of the bowl. She bit down on her lip, concentrating on her job, eager to please Nicole. "Is it ready?" she asked after about three or four stirs.

Grinning, Nicole looked down. "Nope. Still lumpy." She dipped her finger into the mix and placed a dot on Sammy's nose. "Keep going."

Sammy giggled and bent back down to work.

Sam watched in silence, his admiration for Nicole growing. Her ability to relate to his goddaughter, her caring nature, her patience with a little girl, all showed him a depth he'd always known was there. How she managed to be this warm, giving woman in the face of all she'd lacked in life astounded him — and his heart opened to her a little more.

Uncomfortable with his thoughts, he cleared his throat. "Morning," he said, making his presence known.

"Uncle Sam! Look at what we're baking!"

Nicole looked up, met his gaze, and blushed. In her face, he saw the replay of last night in her head. He knew exactly what she was feeling. He couldn't look at her and not *want.*

"I see, Pumpkin," he said, using his favorite nickname for his goddaughter.

"We're not bakin' pumpkins, silly! It's gonna be cookies!"

Sam grinned and pulled up a stool, joining the party. "So what's the occasion?"

"Daddy's coming home today. So we're baking." Sammy still mixed the dough, but

Sam noticed her movements slowing, her arm obviously getting tired. And there were still massive lumps in the mixture.

"Hey, I want a turn," he said, nudging Sammy lightly with his arm.

She looked up at him through big brown eyes. "Mommy says we're 'posed to share." She pulled the spoon out of the bowl and handed it to Sam, trailing cookie dough over the counter.

He met Nicole's amused gaze, not missing the warmth there, heat and tenderness, just for him.

He glanced away and took the spoon from Sammy. He began to stir, making the dough smooth and much easier for the little girl to finish the job.

"Look at that," Nicole said, pointing to the cookie dough. "We're almost ready to put them on the pans. My assistants did great jobs."

"Yay!" Sammy clapped her hands together. "Can I have a taste before we turn 'em into cookies? And can I lick the bowl when we're done?"

Nicole smiled at the little girl, so charmed and in love with the child. She was so glad she'd woken up early and found her coloring a card for her dad's return. This had been one of the best baking sessions she'd ever had. Coming on top of the hottest, most special night she'd ever shared with a man.

She shivered at the memory of Sam buried deep inside her. *Happy birthday, sweetheart.* Goose bumps broke out over her skin as she replayed the low timbre of his voice in her head, as she'd been doing over and over again.

She'd awakened early, her body sore, her heart full, and forced herself out of bed, all the while reminding herself that by wishing her a happy birthday that way, he was just trying to make up for her pathetic life. Just because she felt so much more every time they were together, it didn't mean he was becoming more emotionally involved. And, further, just because she didn't want her heart to go getting any stupid ideas, she reminded herself that even if he was falling for her too, he'd made himself perfectly clear. No ties. No relationship. No future.

"Nicole, can I lick the bowl?" Sammy asked again, bringing her back to the present.

She forced herself to focus on the little girl. "Well, I don't know. You might have to fight your partner there for bowl rights." She caught Sam's eye, unnerved by the warmth and approval she saw in his expression.

Sammy's eyes grew wide. "But . . . but . . . it's my cookies!" she said, panicking at the thought of losing her anticipated treat.

"Relax," Sam assured her. "I could give up my rights for . . . how about a kiss?" he asked Sammy, but his gaze drifted to Nicole's.

Before either of them could react, Sammy threw her arms around Sam and planted a big kiss on his cheek. The result of her impulse was to spread the dough that was still on her nose across his cheek.

Sammy jumped back to her seat, a satisfied look on her face. "Uh-oh," she said.

"What's wrong?" Nicole asked.

"I have to pee. Nobody touch my cookies!" Sammy yelled, and ran out of the room.

Laughing, Nicole walked over to Sam and ran a hand down his cheek, scooping up the dough. His eyes darkened at her touch. And when she slid her finger into her mouth, taking a deliberately long time to suck and lick the sweet dough, his big body shuddered.

"Cut it out," he said in a gruff voice.

Feeling playful, she pulled her finger out with a deliberate pop. She listened for Sammy's voice or footsteps before leaning close and licking the rest of the dough off Sam's cheek.

He let out a low growl, one she was coming to recognize as his *I'm close to losing control* sound. She liked that she could do this to such a strong, normally composed man. He turned his head and caught her lips, his minty taste mingling with the dough she'd been sneaking.

"Break it up, you two," Sara said, joining them.

Nicole ducked and Sam swiped at the remaining dough on his cheek. A few seconds later, Sammy came skidding back into the room.

"Didya wait for me to put the cookies on the pan?" she asked.

"I did. Let's get to work."

She busied herself teaching Sammy how much dough to scoop and proper placement of cookies on the sheet, but her tingling body reminded her that Sam wouldn't be easily forgotten.

The rest of the weekend passed quickly, and too soon, Nicole had repacked her things and was back in Serendipity, in her new home. Sam had dropped her off, explaining that he had to meet up with his brother, and she'd promised to remain at home until he knew the status of the Russians.

While she unpacked from the weekend, she reflected on her time away. Considering she'd left to escape trouble, she'd enjoyed herself way more than she should have. Nicole had gotten used to living with Sam — making love at night, sometimes waking up and doing it again in the morning. He'd let down his guard with her, and she saw a different side to the man.

He was a doting godfather, a solid friend to Sara, and a guy's guy with her husband, Mark. With Nicole, he'd been attentive, and she'd enjoyed their time alone together and with Sammy, listening to her chatter. When Mark came home, she was treated to a firsthand look into the married couple's dynamic. They were obviously in love, and their family with Sammy was one Nicole envied and knew she'd want to replicate if she ever had the chance to have a husband and child of her own.

Because her own family didn't exist. Her parents? Hadn't called her on her birthday. Her twin? Was still psychotic and delusional. Any friends she had? Were better off in New York City with their fake lives. Nicole's throat swelled and she pushed back the pain. Pain she ought to be used to. But the more she let down her walls with Sam and his friends, the more she began to feel. She hadn't realized just how much she'd shut off those emotions over the years, but here they were, rearing their ugly, unwanted heads.

Especially the ones involving Sam. And that was something she couldn't allow. So as soon as she wrapped up the mess with Tyler's father, she'd turn her focus to creating her new life in Serendipity. She had a house of her own, a business to start and build, and friends like Macy to cultivate. Sam could be her sex buddy, but she'd be a fool to let down her walls any further, only to end up with her heart sliced out of her chest.

Sam walked into the police station and headed directly to his brother's office. He knocked once and let himself inside, shutting the door behind him. For a man who'd fought the idea of settling down in Serendipity, Mike had done so with seeming ease. The office used to belong to their father, Simon, and all the pictures on the walls were the same, depicting their hometown over the years. But the photographs on the desk belonged to Mike, and those were of himself and Cara. Some were facing inward, but others faced out, and Sam only had to look at the happy couple to know his brother had changed.

Sam, of all people, knew it hadn't been easy for Mike. He also remembered being one of the people to help his brother see what he could have with Cara. Ironic, since Sam didn't believe in the same kind of thing for himself.

But something had shifted inside him after this weekend with Nicole. It felt deep and profound, and yet Sam couldn't put a name on it. He couldn't bring himself to examine it too closely.

"Hey, you called and asked me to stay so we could talk. Are you going to stand there? Or did you have something on your mind?" Mike asked, breaking into Sam's thoughts.

He'd come directly from dropping off Nicole at home. His own suitcases were still in the trunk. He'd needed to talk to his brother.

"All quiet in town after I left?" Sam asked.

Mike nodded. "The festival ended and everyone cleared out. Stanton left town, as you know. The Russians hadn't checked into any nearby motels and were gone by nightfall. I didn't see them around again, and believe me, I had an eye out."

"Has Stanton been in touch?" Sam had

given Tyler Mike's number and told him to fill his brother in on any progress or lack thereof at home.

Mike nodded. "He tried to talk his father into coming clean, but his old man is more afraid of his clients than the cops. He knows the Russians could get to him in jail or out. So he's refusing. Told Tyler if he could get Nicole back home and under his thumb, everything would be fine."

Sam let out a low, threatening sound.

"Yeah. We all know that's not happening," Mike said, chuckling. "His old man's delusional."

Sam nodded.

"I told Stanton the feds want Nicole to wear a wire with his father. He balked. Wants to do it himself."

Sam raised an eyebrow, feeling a surprising swell of admiration for Nicole's ex. Maybe Stanton wasn't such a jerk after all. "I'd rather he take the risk than Nicole. When do the feds want this to go down?"

"They're watching Romanov. He headed back to L.A., so not for a while. You'll be the first to know when I do."

Sam nodded. "Thanks. I'm keeping quiet about all this until Nicole needs to know. No use getting her worked up over something that may not come to pass."

"That's your call." Mike folded his arms across his chest and met Sam's gaze. "Speaking of Nicole, how's your girl?"

"She's not . . ." He caught his brother's raised eyebrows and look of disbelief. "Yeah, umm, she's fine."

Mike laughed. "I never thought I'd see this day."

"You haven't. It's just . . . it's good. For now."

Mike took his suit jacket off the back of his chair and slung it over his shoulder. "Whatever you say, little brother. I'm heading home to Cara."

"I'm meeting up with her for breakfast before work tomorrow."

"Good. Maybe you can figure out what's going on with her. I'm sure there's something she's not telling me, and it makes no sense."

"And it bugs the hell out of you that you need me to dig." Sam understood his brother's way of thinking. He wouldn't like it if he needed to find someone else for Nicole to confide in.

"You can say that again," Mike muttered.

"I'm on it." He slapped his brother on the back. "It can't be anything terrible." Mike and Cara were solid.

Like Sara and Mark. Erin and Cole.

Like Nic . . . Sam shook his head and pushed the thought down deep, far from the light of day.

The following morning, Cara was waiting for Sam in their usual booth at The Family Restaurant.

"Long time no see," he said, settling into the seat across from her.

"I've missed hanging out with you." She smiled, but the emotion didn't reach her eyes.

"Okay, talk to me. What's wrong?" He covered her hand with his.

It wasn't just that she'd lost weight or her skin was pale. Dark circles shadowed beneath her eyes and she lacked the vibrancy he usually associated with Cara. "You still don't feel well?" he asked.

She shook her head. "No." She gestured to the tea in a cup in front of her, a decaffeinated wrapper lying beside it.

Sam gestured to the waitress. "Coffee, please," he said, before refocusing on Cara.

This illness had been going on too long, reminding him of when his sister had had a never-ending stomach bug before discovering she was pregnant. He wondered if the problem was that basic.

He leaned in close. "You know, the last

woman who didn't feel well for so long was Erin, and she turned out to be —"

"Don't say it!" Cara said, cutting him off with a wave of her hand.

Sam narrowed his gaze. "Is that it? Are you pregnant?"

She shrugged. "I'm afraid to find out," she admitted in a half-whisper.

"That's not like you. And it makes no sense. You're married. You're happy. In love, yes?"

She nodded, blue eyes wide . . . but not happy.

Which was crazy. Of all the women he knew, she'd make the best mother. She worked with abused women at a shelter and had a huge heart. Not to mention, Cara faced life and problems head-on.

"What's going on?" he asked.

She opened and closed her mouth, as if building up the courage to explain. "I'm worried about your brother."

"What about him? He *loves* you." Hell, Mike had fallen so hard for Cara, even Sam had been envious of the intensity between them, knowing he'd never have that for himself. "Not to mention he's worried about you. He asked me to pump you for information, and that's wrong. You need to talk to him."

She sighed, her eyes sad. "But he took so long to come around to the idea of settling in Serendipity — with me — and when we talked about kids, it was in the future. A baby now wasn't part of our plan."

Sam shook his head at her attitude. "*Mike* wasn't part of the plan for my mother. Angel wasn't part of Erin and Cole's plan. Life happens. You of all people know that. If you're pregnant and he's going to be a father? He'll be thrilled because it's with you."

"You really think so?" she asked, her hand already cupping her belly in a protective gesture he'd seen with his sister.

"I may not be an expert on love, but I know my brother. It's going to be okay."

She swallowed hard, eyes glistening. "You're right. I don't know why I'm so emotional." She wiped at her damp eyes.

Sam rolled his eyes. "Do you really need me to explain?"

That earned him a smile. "I probably don't need to take that test," she muttered. "But I will. I've been carrying two of them around with me for a week."

He squeezed her hand. "That's more like the Cara I know. Always prepared and ready for anything."

"Well, I'd better be, right?" She glanced

313

down at her stomach, hidden beneath baggy sweats, and her expression softened.

"Better?" he asked, hoping he'd helped her come to terms with things.

"Yeah. I'm glad we didn't lose our friendship when I married your brother."

"No chance of that happening."

She smiled, seeming more at peace. "So I think I'm going to go home and do this before I lose my nerve," she said.

He rose, as she stood. "Good luck." He leaned over and kissed her cheek, watching as she made her way to the front door of the restaurant.

Sam headed out after her, arriving at work in time to discover there had been an assault downtown, and the case took over the rest of his week, including most nights. His hours were erratic, which meant he didn't see Nicole despite living next door. She hadn't called him in the time they'd been back, and he gave her the distance he assumed they both needed.

The natural separation ought to be a relief, given the intensity of the weekend they'd spent together, but damned if he didn't miss her. In a few short days, he'd grown accustomed to another warm body in his bed. He liked waking up to her snaked around him, as if they shared a twin bed instead of a double. He hadn't even been bothered by her female stuff all over the bathroom, and his toothbrush at home looked lonely by itself.

Pathetic.

But true.

With work keeping Sam busy, he was grateful Mike had taken charge of the situation with Tyler. He had a patrol car doing drive-bys of Nicole's house and the bakery, where she was preparing for opening. He didn't mention it to her. She was wary enough. But with the art show over, Serendipity had gone back to normal and anyone new would stand out. Tyler stayed in the city, catching up on work and taking the opportunity to look for evidence that could implicate his father or, even better, the bigger fish the feds were after. So all was quiet for now.

If and when things blew up, Mike would let Sam know to be ready.

Sam finally found time for himself late Saturday. Instead of heading home, he walked from the station to Nicole's bakery.

The door was unlocked and he let himself in. The smell of fresh paint assaulted him first. A cheery yellow replaced the original gray, and a royal blue trim bordered the white ceiling. Both her and Lulu's welcoming personalities were clear everywhere he looked. They'd accomplished a lot in a short time, and a feeling of pride filled him at the sight.

No sooner had the bells rung overhead than Lulu greeted him at the entrance, her long gypsy skirt sweeping the floor as she walked. "Well, hello, handsome."

He grinned at her lack of formality. "Hello to you too. How are things going?" he asked.

She smiled wide. "Amazing, as you can see. We're on track for a grand opening in two weeks!"

"Congratulations."

"Thank you."

"I'm thrilled for you."

She reached out and pinched his cheek. "I bet you are. Your girl is putting down roots here."

His throat constricted as Lulu used the same words his brother had used recently to describe Nicole. "Where is she?" he asked, changing the subject.

"In the back. I was just heading out for the night. I'll lock the door behind me."

"Have a good one," he said.

"You too. Don't do anything I wouldn't do," she said, laughing over her parting words.

Sam rolled his eyes. The Donovan family

bred them bold and outspoken, he thought.

He walked through the back and into a small office and caught sight of Nicole, changing her clothing. He glimpsed her long legs and barely-there top.

"Hey," he said, causing her to shriek and pull her miniskirt over her nearly naked body.

"Relax, it's just me," he reassured her.

"Oh my God! Aunt Lulu said she was leaving and would lock up behind her." Nicole's heart pounded a thousand miles an hour in her chest. "I thought I was alone."

"She sent me back to you," Sam said.

His hot gaze traveled over her and her body reacted, her nipples tightening, her sex contracting.

"Well, I'm changing to go to Joe's." She waved her hand at him in a gesture indicating he should turn around.

"Oh, come on. I've seen you in less." His sexy grin merely complemented his scruffy look. He hadn't shaved in a few days and he only looked hotter.

She rolled her eyes and pulled on her skirt, then added a flowing tank top with ruffles at the bottom.

"You look as good in clothes as out."

"Thank you. So what brings you by?" she asked casually, feeling anything but. Because she'd missed him. Badly.

He raised an eyebrow. "I came to see you," he said, as if it were obvious. But it wasn't. There'd been a sudden distance between them this week, reminding her not to get too attached.

He edged closer and she breathed in. The sheer male scent of him wreaked havoc with her hormones.

"It's been a long week," he said in a husky voice.

Didn't she know it?

She cleared her throat. "It has, and I've been busy." She'd returned to her new home and spent the week alternating her time between getting the bakery in order and decorating her house with her own touches. She didn't have much downtime and fell into bed exhausted every night. Already she knew her life here in Serendipity would be full. But she'd missed him too much.

Considering she didn't know if he felt the same, and feeling like he'd caused the separation, she wanted him to know she didn't need him to be happy.

"Lulu and I ordered all our supplies; they're due in early next week. We're planning a grand opening and I have to tell you, I have a really good feeling about this." Not even her worries about them or even the reality of a daily four A.M. wakeup call brought down her anticipation about success.

"I'm glad." He sounded . . . proud. "Tell me something. While you were busy being an entrepreneur, did you find any time to miss me?" He brushed her hair off her shoulder, and she trembled at his light touch.

For a woman who'd always considered herself independent, it threw her, just how often she'd thought of him. But since he obviously wasn't pining over her, she'd decided to keep her own feelings locked up tight.

"I might have thought of you every so often," she murmured.

"Then let me take you out for a nice dinner so we can catch up."

She wished she could say yes, but she'd already made plans with Macy and she wouldn't blow off a girlfriend for a guy. "I can't. I'm meeting Macy at Joe's. I was changing to head over there when you walked in." She'd thought it would be easier to switch outfits here and walk down the street than to take the time to go home.

"I'm disappointed." He leaned in and kissed her cheek, his lips lingering. "But my case didn't wrap up until a little while ago and I had no idea I'd be free."

Her skin tingled where he touched her, and she curled her hands into fists. If she reached for him now, they'd christen her small desk and she really did have to go.

"Come by when you get home." He curled his hand around the back of her neck, his touch electrifying her all the way to her toes.

"It might be late." Though she doubted it. Macy had to work the next day.

"I'll be awake." He tightened his grip and pulled her in for a real kiss.

His tongue slid into her mouth and tangled with hers. Her legs went weak and she leaned against him for support. Of course that aligned their bodies together and awakened her senses, reminding her of just how much she loved him.

Something she'd been deliberately suppressing all week. Something she wasn't going to let herself revisit now. She curled her fingers into his shoulders and pushed back. "I'm going to be late."

Disappointment flickered in his eyes, and after the week of no communication, no matter how legitimate, she took satisfaction in that. "See you later."

She stashed her work clothes in the bag she'd brought and gathered her purse.

"Ready? I need to lock up after us."

He nodded, eyeing her as if trying to understand what was going on in her mind. *Good luck,* she thought. She was still trying to understand it herself.

FOURTEEN

Somehow Nicole and Macy snagged a private table in a corner of Joe's. Music played on the jukebox, but the murmur of the Saturday night crowd was loud and Nicole found it hard to process the music over the din.

"I should have eaten something more substantial than a couple of French fries for dinner. I'm buzzed from half a beer," Macy said, eyeing the bottle.

"Good thing I'm driving home then." Nicole took a sip of her soda. "I didn't eat much either. I had a leftover sandwich in the fridge, but I didn't take more than a few bites." She'd paused to change clothes and then Sam had interrupted.

"What's with the sour face?" Macy asked her.

Nicole sighed. "Not sour. Just confused."

"Let me guess. It's about a man. Or should I say the man?"

Leave it to Macy to cut right to the point, Nicole thought wryly. "It is." Why bother lying? She needed a friend and she finally had a real one.

Macy shifted in her seat. "No confusion allowed," she said, waving a hand in dismissal. "He's into you. I've never seen Sam so into a woman before."

Sara had said something similar. Nicole warmed at the thought and wished things were that simple. "But that doesn't mean it'll change the outcome."

Macy took a long pull of her beer. "You never know. I've seen harder nuts than Sam crack. Just ask Cara. And Erin." She grinned.

"I can't control it, so I'm trying not to worry about it. It's just not easy."

Macy's expression turned sympathetic. "I understand, which is why I have to talk to you about something." Her gaze darted away . . . an unusual occurrence for a very direct woman.

Nicole leaned in close. "What's up?"

Macy drew a deep breath, then let it out again. "What's the story with you and Tyler? The real story."

Nicole blinked, surprised at the subject. Although she shouldn't have been. Macy's interest in Tyler had been all too obvious.

"That was real subtle of me." Macy let out a shaky laugh. "I know there are things you can't tell me, and that's okay. I just have to know . . . you and Tyler —"

"There is no me and Tyler." Nicole reached out and grasped Macy's hand, wanting to reassure her in every way possible. "Not in the romantic sense. I'm . . ." She looked Macy in the eye and prepared to bare her soul. "I'm totally and completely in love with Sam." She shook her head at herself. "And that wasn't hard to say out loud. The point is, I have no hold on Tyler."

Macy closed her eyes, her obvious embarrassment showing. She sat up suddenly, her gaze focused on Nicole. "So you don't mind if I . . . if we . . ."

Admiring her ability to be direct, Nicole smiled and shook her head. "I'd be thrilled if he found someone to make him happy. It'd be even better for him if it was you."

Macy exhaled hard and laughed. "Well, that was as awkward and as difficult as I thought it would be."

"I can imagine." Nicole leaned back in her seat, suddenly exhausted. "Aren't we a pair?"

Macy nodded and treated herself to another long swallow of beer. "Is he coming back?" she asked.

"Tyler?"

She nodded.

"He'll be back," Nicole assured her.

"How do you know? Have you spoken with him?"

"No." But they needed to have a private talk when all this was over. One that put things between them to rest, once and for all.

Macy propped her chin on her hands. "Then how do you know for sure?"

At that, Nicole couldn't help but grin, thoughts of Tyler's time in Serendipity flashing through her mind. "He went shopping. He wore shorts. And he followed you around town. He'll be back."

Macy grinned. "Here's to getting our men." She raised her glass and Nicole tipped hers, clinking them together, toasting as much to Macy's words as to her new friend and her life here in Serendipity.

They spent another half hour talking, then made their way over to a group of people, some Nicole knew, others Macy introduced her to. As much as she enjoyed herself, she couldn't help thinking that she would rather be with Sam. But she needed to make friends and she was Macy's ride home, so she didn't say anything.

"I'm beat," Macy said at last. "Do you

mind if we head home?"

Nicole shook her head, relieved it wouldn't be a late night. "I'm ready when you are."

They walked back to the bakery, where Nicole had parked her car. Once they were on their way, Macy pulled off her high heels and sighed. "Whoever invented these things should be shot."

Nicole grinned. "I wear them a lot less here than I did back in New York, and trust me, I do not miss them." On her feet now were a pair of bejeweled sandals with less than a quarter-inch heel.

"Stay straight on this road for a while," Macy said, obviously remembering Nicole needed directions.

"Are you working early tomorrow?" Nicole asked her.

"Not until lunchtime, thank goodness."

She glanced up at the rearview mirror to check the car behind her, annoyed by the bright lights reflecting there.

"Something wrong?" Macy asked.

"The car behind us is driving too close," Nicole muttered, squinting and keeping her gaze on the road in front of her.

At a four-way stop sign, she came to a complete halt before continuing on. Out of nowhere, another car approached from the right and sped right through the stop sign, plowing into them before Nicole could blink. Her car spun and took another hit from the vehicle behind her, which had obviously stayed on her tail.

Macy screamed. Nicole gritted her teeth and held on to the wheel as the back of her car skidded into a lamppost with a sickening crunch.

Sam paced through his house, moving idly from one room to the next, unable to sit still or get comfortable. He didn't expect Nicole to be at his beck and call, but he'd sure hoped she'd want to see him after a long week apart. He could have gone to Joe's, but that would have been too obvious. *He* might be desperate to see her, but she didn't need to know that.

Another glance at her dark house told him she hadn't come home, although he'd been keeping watch and already knew as much. He was already mentally lecturing her about not leaving inside lamps and the porch lights on. It was safety 101 for anyone, but Nicole wasn't dealing with a normal situation. Just because they thought they knew where all the players were in her situation didn't mean she should be lax with the basics.

He glanced at his watch and blew out a

long breath. Nine wasn't that late and he needed to chill. He started upstairs when his cell rang.

Pulling it out of his pocket, he glanced down, surprised to see the police station's main number. "Marsden."

"Hey, Sam. It's Burnett."

"What's up?"

"Just doing you a solid. I thought you'd want to know your girlfriend was in a car accident at the stop sign on Maple. No serious injuries, but the car's in pretty bad shape. They're lucky."

Sam narrowed his gaze. "They?"

"She was driving Macy Donovan home. Both women walked away relatively unharmed. A damned miracle if you ask me."

Sam was in his truck by the time he wound up the call. On the short drive over, a myriad of situations ran through his mind. Panic and the need to see her were paramount, but his cop brain also was on alert, thinking about Tyler's old man hiring someone to scare Nicole into heading home.

Sam arrived on the scene to find one side of her car crunched, and his stomach twisted painfully. He parked and climbed out of his vehicle.

Burnett met him as he headed for the ambulance. "That was fast."

Sam nodded. "I appreciate the call. What happened?"

"Looks like Mrs. Adler was driving too fast and ran her stop sign. She was driving without a license and wandered off without her daughter knowing."

Sam winced, knowing that Mrs. Adler was in her mideighties.

Burnett shook his head. "Sad when they get old and lose control like that. Anyway, she slammed into Nicole's passenger-side back door. According to Nicole, the car behind her wasn't giving her much space to begin with and couldn't stop in time, causing a second impact."

Sam's instincts went on alert. Was it that the actual accident was a coincidence, but the second occurred because Nicole was being followed?

"Who was the second driver?" Sam waited for a Russian name.

"Drunk driver."

Sam ground his teeth together. "Local?"

Burnett shook his head, and Sam's instincts went haywire. "You're booking him, right?"

"Yeah, but he refused the Breathalyzer," Burnett said, inclining his head.

"Make sure you hold him. I want the chief to run a full check on the guy." In case he had been sent after Nicole, with his inebriated state an intentional diversion.

"What's going on?" Burnett asked.

"No time to explain now. Where are the women?" Sam asked, wanting to get to Nicole.

Burnett tipped his head toward the ambulance. "Being checked out just to make sure they're fine."

"Thanks again." Sam shook Burnett's hand and headed to see Nicole for himself.

Both Nicole and Macy had been released by the paramedics, and as Sam approached, they were being reminded that should they feel anything unusual, they should head to the hospital immediately.

Nicole signed the form the paramedic held out for her, then turned, and her eyes connected with his. Shaking, he caught her in his arms before she could collapse.

"I'm so glad you're here," she murmured.

His heart squeezed tight at the admission, and he held on tight. Turning to Macy, he extended his other arm for her and helped both women to his truck, grateful tonight hadn't turned out so much worse. And with the way his brain had spun out alternative scenarios, he decided he wasn't letting Nicole out of his sight for a good, long while.

■ ■ ■ ■

An hour later, Nicole had showered and now, wrapped in her favorite robe, she sipped a cup of tea and cuddled next to Sam on the sofa in her family room. After dropping Macy at home, Sam called Mike, at which point Nicole realized he believed the drunk driver behind her might have been sent to intimidate her into running back to Manhattan and Tyler for protection.

She had to admit that as the driver hovered on her tail, she'd thought the same thing. But she didn't like Sam being uptight and stressed out, and he was both.

"How are you feeling?" he asked, obviously worrying about her the same way she was about him.

"Sore," she admitted.

His arm around her tightened and she laid her head against his chest, inhaling his masculine scent that was both comforting and arousing at the same time.

"It'll be worse tomorrow," he said, his voice thick as his thumb rubbed comforting circles on her arm.

"I know. The paramedic warned me. I'll take some ibuprofen and I'll be fine." She wasn't looking forward to it, but she'd survive.

He groaned. "Let's go upstairs. You'll be more comfortable in bed."

She narrowed her gaze and shifted so he could move out from under her. She pressed her hands against the sofa, prepared to stand, when he lifted her into his arms. "Sam, this is becoming a habit." One she already knew she liked and wanted to get used to.

He met her gaze, his eyes as serious as she'd ever seen them. "I need to take care of you tonight."

She leaned her head against his chest and sighed. Earlier, when she'd turned from the paramedic only to catch sight of Sam, her knees almost buckled at the sight of him, strong and solid, there for her in her moment of need.

He was her safe haven.

And so much more.

He took care of her. He looked out for her. He understood her. He made her feel everything.

"You make it too easy to love you," she murmured, deciding it was time to let out what was already in her heart. She'd grown up used to hiding her emotions and feelings, and she hated how she felt when doing it.

He stiffened but continued his climb up the stairs. "I don't —"

"Shh." She looked up and placed her finger over his firm lips, rubbing her fingertip back and forth over his mouth.

His hazel eyes dilated at her touch.

He couldn't say it back, and it hurt. So did the fact that he didn't want to hear it either.

"Sam, just because I needed to say it doesn't mean you need to repeat it. And just because I feel it doesn't mean you have to." Although she sensed he did.

But he was running from his feelings because of his past, his fear of being hurt again. Though she had to accept that he might never let himself get beyond those fears, tonight's accident reminded her that life was short. And so she was willing to fight for both of them and hope she could bring him around.

Sunlight streamed through the window, waking Sam in a painful way. He forced his eyelids open and rolled over to face Nicole, finding her watching him.

"How are you feeling?" he asked.

Her eyes filled with pain. "I can't move."

Her groan went straight to his heart, memories of the mangled car coming back to haunt him.

"My whole body feels like I was slammed by a semi."

"Let me get you something to eat and some Motrin. It should ease the aches and pains."

She closed her eyes. "Thank you. Then I'll try a warm shower and see if I can get moving."

In between sleeping and tossing and turning, he'd been fighting a mixture of emotions. Fear at the thought of what might have happened to her in that accident. Rage at the notion that someone might have been sent after her. And a healthy dose of both of those feelings over her words last night.

You make it too easy to love you.

Damned if she didn't do the same to him.

He wasn't sure what threw him more. That she'd said it or that she hadn't pushed him to say it back. Vulnerable yet strong, loyal and so damned gorgeous she took his breath away; yeah, he was probably in love with her.

But the too-rapid pounding of his heart, the sweats and shakes he'd have if he didn't have to concentrate on keeping her safe, and the fear of being hurt again told him he couldn't handle it.

Thanks to her, he didn't have to. "Be right back." He slid out of bed and went to get the supplies to take care of her. That was something he could handle.

A while later, the Motrin worked and she was able to move around, although he saw the pain in her tight expression. While she went to shower, he called his folks to check in, then headed for the kitchen.

He opened the fridge and studied the contents, trying to decide what more he could put together for lunch.

"The shower helped a lot," Nicole said, walking into the room. He turned to see that she wore a summer dress that was light and obviously easy for her to put on. One that was hell on his libido. The white ribbed tank top showed her breasts, perky and bouncy beneath the flimsy and relatively thin material. The light blue skirt flowed around her hips and ass, coming to rest at her shapely calves. She'd wrung out her hair, leaving it damp as it air-dried around her face. Even makeup free, she affected him on a soul-deep level.

He watched her gingerly move around the kitchen and wanted to help, to take her pain as his own. Shit. He knew he was in trouble, and the best thing to do was not to think.

He pulled out his cell and called his brother, walking out of the room as Mike answered on the first ring. "Hey, bro. Any news on the drunk who rear-ended Nicole?"

He listened to his brother and was relieved by the answer. "Got it. Thanks." Mike asked about Nicole. "Yeah, she's okay. Hurting but okay. How's Cara?"

Mike told him she seemed better and thanked him for talking to her, then said good-bye. Sam noted his brother still hadn't mentioned anything about Cara being pregnant.

He wondered if she'd taken the test. Spilled the news. Maybe they'd decided to wait to tell everyone, Sam thought. But he already knew. Well, he assumed he knew. Not that he'd ask.

He disconnected the call and turned, finding Nicole watching him from the doorway of the family room.

"Well?" She stepped into the family room. "I didn't mean to eavesdrop, but I heard you ask about the drunk who rear-ended me. Was he connected to the Russians?"

"No. It was just an accident." Sam shook his head. "I can't believe I'm calling that wreck *just* anything."

She walked over and wrapped her arms around him. "I'm fine."

Reflexively he squeezed back, wanting to be as close to her as possible.

"What else is wrong?" she asked.

"Why do you ask?"

"Just a feeling." She shrugged and pulled out of the embrace.

Immediately he felt the loss. She read him well. "It's a secret," he said.

She raised her eyebrows. "Well, I'm a good listener and I don't blab. But I understand if you want to keep things to yourself."

Oddly, he didn't. Even more shocking, he trusted her not to spread the news. "Let's sit," he said, wanting her off her feet.

He lowered himself onto her couch, which he found more comfortable than the one in his house. "Cara thinks she's pregnant," he said, when they were settled in. "I spoke to her when we came back from Sara's, and she was going to take the test and talk to Mike. But he hasn't said anything, so I was wondering if she worked up the courage."

Confusion crossed Nicole's face. "Does Mike not want kids?"

Sam shrugged. "I'm pretty sure he wants the whole nine yards with Cara, but apparently any conversation they had about it involved it happening some time in the future. And they had a rough road getting

337

together, so she was worried about how he'd take it."

"Umm, I didn't live here, so I don't know what happened."

"Right." For some reason, he felt so connected to her, it was as if he'd had her in his life much longer. "Mike's father isn't Simon." He'd already told her the bare-bones story but wanted to tell her more now. "Ultimately he left town. It was more complicated than that, but I'll save those details for another day. Suffice it to say, Simon had always been in love with Mom and offered to marry her. We always knew Mike was Simon's adopted son, but he never treated him any differently. Still, Mike had . . . I guess a shrink would call it abandonment issues, always felt different from us, like he didn't live up. Until Dad got cancer last year, Mike was rarely home. Even when he came back as temporary chief, he didn't plan to stay."

A soft smile played around Nicole's lips. "Until Cara."

Sam inclined his head. "Until Serendipity got a hold of him, and Cara too. But he fought it the whole way. So she's worried the baby will scare him off. Which will not happen."

Nicole leaned against the sofa cushion and

pulled her knees to her chest, her gaze never leaving Sam's. "For two men raised in a loving home, you two sure go out of your way not to believe in the notion."

Well, that was a fast turnaround, Sam thought, and squirmed being under the spotlight. But she had a fair point. "I guess it's your own personal experience that defines a person more."

"And what about your mom? She married Simon for security. Did she fight the whole love thing because she'd been hurt and abandoned by Mike's real father?"

Sam's head began to pound. "Not according to the legend of Ella and Simon," he muttered, trying like hell to find a way out of this conversation.

"Interesting." Nicole eyed him with curiosity but didn't utter another word.

He decided conversation was preferable to this silent scrutiny. "Are you hungry?"

She laughed and rose to her feet. "Might as well eat. I told Aunt Lulu I'd be in this afternoon if I was up to it. But we aren't getting deliveries until Monday, so I should be okay to rest up today."

Subject dropped, just like that. Damn woman confused and confounded him. She told him, in so many words, she was in love with him; she asked pointed questions about his family and how he ended up not trusting in the notion, and then she left him alone with his thoughts.

"Crafty," he muttered.

"What?"

"Nothing." He followed her to the kitchen, but the doorbell rang, interrupting her chance to eat. Again.

"Expecting anyone?" he asked.

She shook her head.

He made it to the door first and looked out. "Stanton," he muttered, letting him in.

"Tyler! What are you doing here?" Nicole asked, coming up behind Sam.

Tyler pushed past Sam and headed straight for Nicole. "His brother called asking questions," he said, glancing at Sam. "Mike told me you were in a car accident and they needed to rule out foul play."

Nicole took a step back. "I'm okay. You didn't need to drive all the way here to ask me that!"

"I also needed to come here and tell you that I'm going to wear the wire with my old man. Not you."

"What wire?" Nicole asked, still in the dark because Sam hadn't thought it was the right time to tell her yet.

Sam pinched the bridge of his nose and wondered if he'd go to jail if he decked Nicole's ex. It might just be worth it.

Sam cleared his throat and both Tyler and Nicole turned to face him. "We hadn't had a chance to discuss that yet," he said pointedly.

"Shit," Tyler said, realizing he'd spilled those beans.

"Yeah." *Thanks a lot, asshole,* Sam thought. Though it was his fault Nicole didn't know yet.

He'd wanted to spare her the worrying until there was a reason, but from the furious look on her face, she didn't appreciate being left in the dark.

"What's going on? What do you two know that I don't?"

"The feds —" Tyler began, but Sam held a hand up, interrupting his explanation.

"I've got this," Sam said.

"Now. You've got this now," Nicole muttered. "But you've had plenty of time to tell me . . . what?" She perched her hands on her hips and glared at him.

"When Mike and Cole spoke to the feds, they said they wanted you to wear a wire to get information from his father so they could implicate Romanov. He's a major drug dealer and money launderer," Sam explained, as Tyler remained silent.

"And you didn't think I needed to know

about this?" she asked, her voice rising.

Sam set his jaw. "I didn't think you needed added stress right now, no."

"Tell me you didn't make that decision for me." Her eyes grew dark and stormy, along with his mood, and a beat of silence followed.

They both already knew the answer.

Tyler swore out loud. "I didn't mean to cause trouble."

Sam ignored him, drawing a calming breath. "Can we discuss this later? In private?"

Nicole nodded, but her pain-filled expression told him she wasn't up to the news. And he'd known that.

The doorbell rang again and Nicole threw up her arms, wincing in agony. "What now?" she asked, her voice rising. She glanced through the door before swinging it open wide. "Am I glad to see you," Nicole said.

Macy walked in with a cake box in hand. "I was coming to bring you a get-well present from my family. Then I saw the car in the driveway." Her voice darkened as she narrowed her gaze on Tyler, who'd clearly been caught back in town visiting his ex — before he'd told his current . . . whatever Macy was to him that he'd returned.

Now it was Tyler's turn to be in the doghouse, Sam thought, taking no pleasure in anyone sharing his predicament. Having Nicole mad at him ruined his damned day.

"Might as well come in and join the fun," Sam said to Macy.

She rolled her eyes. Handed Nicole the cake. Folded her arms across her chest and glared at Tyler, hurt and fury warring for dominance.

Even Sam winced at what poor Stanton was in for.

Macy had taken one look at Tyler's Porsche parked in Nicole's driveway and wanted to vomit. Of course he'd come *here* before letting her know he was back in town. If he was back. For all Macy knew, he'd planned on leaving again before she even realized he'd returned. But she refused to let him stop her from checking on Nicole and delivering her gift.

Once inside, it took all her willpower to keep her focus on her friend and not the man who'd asked her to wait but couldn't be bothered to keep in touch.

"Anyway, Aunt Lulu said she can take the deliveries if you aren't up to working," Macy said, ignoring Tyler's heated gaze.

"I'm not missing any more work because

of this mess." Nicole sliced a hand through the air for emphasis. "And what about you? What are you doing out and about? You were in that car with me," Nicole said.

"What!?" Tyler stepped forward. "Are you okay?" He reached for her, but she backed away.

"I'm fine," she said through clenched teeth. "Nice of you to ask."

Tyler ran a hand through his hair. "I didn't know. Mike only told me about Nicole. He didn't know you and I . . ." He trailed off, obviously unsure of how to characterize their relationship.

Hurt rocked through Macy, but she didn't want to deal with him now. "What mess are you talking about?" she asked, referring to what Nicole had said earlier. "What don't you want to keep you from work?"

"Umm —" Nicole glanced from Sam to Tyler.

"Macy, I've been trying to keep you in the dark for your own protection," Tyler said, stepping closer to her again.

She turned to face him, lost and confused. "My protection? What are you involved in?"

Sam shook his head and groaned. "Macy Donovan, if you breathe a word of this around town, and I mean one word —"

"Hey! Just because I'm outspoken doesn't

mean I'm a gossip or I can't be trusted," she said, annoyed by the implication. "I can keep a secret. Ask Erin," she said pointedly. She'd kept his sister's pregnancy a secret last year.

"I know. I'm just trying to tell you how important this is. How dangerous," Sam said to emphasize the point.

A chill rushed over her skin and she shivered. "Tell me."

Tyler reached out and took her hand. He then began to explain how his father was involved with Russian money launderers and that he'd come after Nicole to protect her. He'd left Serendipity last week to try to talk sense into his father. That or find evidence of guilt so the feds wouldn't want Nicole to wear a wire to get information.

Macy listened in disbelief.

"Then I heard about Nicole's car accident and I thought maybe they'd sent someone after her. To scare her into coming back to Manhattan. So I came here to see for myself that she was okay. And to tell her if anyone was going to be wearing a wire, it would be me. Not her," Tyler summed up at last.

Macy bit down on the inside of her cheek. So he wanted to put himself on the line. For Nicole. She swallowed hard. Before she could speak, Nicole chimed in.

"And that was the first time I learned about me wearing a wire because Sam thought it was in my best interest to keep me in the dark," Nicole said, her voice low, angry.

"Just like Tyler thought it was in mine?" Macy asked in a sugary-sweet tone she didn't mean.

The two women locked gazes, and Nicole stepped up alongside Macy. "You two. Go away. We need to talk."

"Give me a break," Sam muttered. "You can't be angry because I was looking out for you."

She raised an eyebrow. "Yeah. I can."

"Macy, I just told you everything about me. We need to talk," Tyler said.

"Later," Macy muttered. "If you're lucky."

Nicole met her gaze. "We're taking the kitchen. You two stay here." She grabbed Macy's hand and pulled her into the other room, leaving the two know-it-all men alone.

Macy wanted to laugh, but her heart was heavy because she couldn't separate what she'd learned about Tyler's past from his feelings for Nicole. And unless *he* convinced Macy he didn't have any feelings beyond friendship, she was getting out of this non-relationship before it ever got started.

FIFTEEN

Nicole and Macy retreated to the kitchen; Nicole wanted to make her point to Sam that she was not happy with him making decisions about what she should know and when.

They sat at the kitchen table, staring at each other.

Nicole broke the silence first. "The last thing I want to do is fight with Sam, but I can't believe he kept me in the dark." They'd spent an entire weekend getting closer and all along he knew what her future held.

"Umm, same?" Macy sighed, propping her head in her hands. "Was he even going to tell me he was back in town?"

Nicole looked at her friend. "Honestly? He was probably going to wait until this nightmare was over. I mean, why get you involved in something potentially danger-ous? If he cares about you, then he wouldn't want you hurt."

Macy grinned, and Nicole narrowed her gaze. "What's that smile for?"

"Oh, I'm just finding it amusing that you can justify Tyler's reasons for not telling me things, but you're furious at Sam for doing the same to you. For the same reasons."

Nicole shot her a dirty look. "Fine. Be like that." She glanced down at her hands, knowing Macy was right. "I'm not apologizing for being angry, though. Sam has to know he can't do that stuff to me no matter how good his reasons." Her parents thought they could control her life and decisions. She didn't want anyone trying to pull that on her again.

"So tell him. Talk. Then at least you two can have good makeup sex. I don't know what Tyler wants from me."

Nicole rose from her seat. "Then I suggest you find out."

"Good idea." Macy stood too, her expression lighter than before. "But not until whatever this situation is, is resolved. I want him free. From the past and from you. No offense intended."

"None taken." Nicole understood how her friend felt. She headed back into the other room to find Sam and Tyler sitting in uncomfortable silence. "We're back."

Tyler jumped up first. "Macy, can we please go somewhere and talk?"

She shook her head. "Not now," she said sadly, and Nicole's heart hurt for her. "Come to me when you're free — of everything. Then we can talk." Macy turned and walked away.

"But —"

"Let her go," Nicole said quietly, placing her hand on his arm. She waited until Macy had disappeared out the door before meeting Tyler's gaze. "She has her pride, and this situation is screwed up. She doesn't deserve it. When you're free of your family mess and yeah, of me, then you go to her. And see if you two can start from scratch. Get to know each other and see what happens."

He groaned and nodded. "You're right. Which means this fucking mess has to end."

She blinked, surprised at his choice of words. Tyler Stanton never cursed. "I agree. Sam?"

"On it. I'll go talk to Mike. See if he can make some calls and find out why the feds are stalling on making a move on your old man."

Tyler paled but nodded.

Sam grasped her hand and pulled her through the house and into her bedroom.

"I'm not leaving with you angry."

She sighed. "I don't want to fight with you either."

"Is that what this is? Our first fight?" he asked with an endearing grin.

"Yeah. Because you decided what I should know and when."

He shook his head. "It won't happen again."

"Promise?"

"I'll do the best I can."

She rolled her eyes. "That's such a male answer."

"Hey, I'm a man and a cop. I just want you safe. What do you expect?" he asked in a gruff voice.

Having already decided she'd made her point, she leaned in close and kissed his cheek. "Great makeup sex?" she asked, deliberately light, letting him know it was, in fact, finished.

Unless he pulled crap like that again.

His eyes darkened at the suggestion. "As soon as I get home."

This time it was she who reacted, her nipples pulling into tight points. "Hurry back."

He pulled her against him for a hard kiss. He didn't keep it short, slipping his tongue between her parted lips and giving her a preview of what he intended later on.

A little while later, Sam had left, leaving Nicole alone with Tyler. They stared at one another, the silence stretching between them, merely waiting to be broken.

Tyler walked to the bay window, staring outside onto the street. Nicole used the time to study the man she'd almost married. No doubt he was good looking . . . in a more refined way than Sam's gruff, sexy appearance. And no question he was a good guy. She should never have doubted him. But he wasn't the man for her.

Still, they had history and now they shared something more — the pain of discovering that their fathers weren't the people they thought they were. For Nicole, she'd always known her father wasn't a man she looked up to. He'd never been there for her, not as a little girl, and not as an adult. But did his behavior cross from uninterested, uncaring parent to criminal behavior?

If forced to choose, she didn't think so. At least, she didn't believe he'd let anything terrible happen to her.

Tyler, on the other hand, was first coming to the realization about his parent now. And the knowledge that his father was involved in illegal activity and was willing to go to desperate lengths to keep it secret? That had to be a huge blow.

"Ty?" she said, using her old nickname for him as she walked over and placed her hand on his arm. "I'm sorry about everything."

He turned to face her. "I don't blame you for ending things between us. It hurt, but I realize now that you were right. There was no . . . spark. We were comfortable. Good friends. But we wouldn't have been happy."

She was glad he finally understood. "I don't suppose Macy has anything to do with that realization?"

He smiled, but it was grim. "She has everything to do with it, and you know it."

"I do. And I'm glad. You deserve someone to make you happy."

He cleared his throat. "So do you. It's tough to say, but Marsden's a good guy."

Nicole laughed at his reluctance to admit it. "He's the best." The words slipped out before she could think them through. "I mean —"

"I know what you mean. If I said Macy was the best, would you take offense?"

She laughed again. "No. I guess, it's just, this is awkward."

"But we're going to have to get used to it. Get used to each other being with other people."

"Because you're sticking around?" she asked, curious how he planned to have a relationship with Macy while she was here in Serendipity.

He shoved his hands into the pockets of his slacks. "I'll figure that out when I see what's left of the investment firm in Manhattan when all this is over."

"It'll get easier. But I'm not just sorry about us. I'm sorry about your father. I know it has to be a huge blow and I want you to know, if you need to talk about it to someone who understands, I'm here."

"Thanks." He reached out and squeezed her hand. "I appreciate the offer, but I think you and I have other people to confide in these days."

"Yeah. If I can convince Sam that love exists and *relationship* isn't a bad word."

Tyler raised an eyebrow in surprise. "You deserve someone who is certain and sure. Someone who will stick."

Nicole raised her chin. "Yeah, I do. And I plan on doing everything I can to make sure I get it."

Tyler shook his head and laughed. "The guy won't know what hit him."

She grinned. "That's what I'm hoping for. But if not? I'm doing everything I can to have the best life possible. With or without

Sam Marsden in it." She just did her best not to contemplate the *without* alternative.

Sam strode into the station and found his brother by the coffee machine in the small break room. Mike poured a cup of coffee, the bright orange top of the carafe capturing Sam's attention.

"What's up with the decaf?" Sam asked. Mike was a hard-core coffee drinker.

"What are you doing here on your day off?" Mike asked, ignoring the question.

Sam waited until Mike had added some milk to his coffee before following his brother back into his office.

Mike slammed the door behind him. "Cara said if she has to give up caffeine, so do I," he muttered, and Sam burst out laughing.

"So it's definite?" Sam asked, bringing the question dogging him out into the open. "Cara's pregnant?"

Mike placed his coffee on the desk and looked up to meet Sam's gaze, his brother's eyes wide with wonder, the grin on his face huge. "Thanks for persuading her to talk to me."

Sam strode over and pulled his brother into a big hug, slapping him on the back hard. "I am so damned happy for you."

"I'm in shock. I don't know how — okay, obviously I know how. It just wasn't planned."

"Yeah. I got that much from Cara."

"I can't believe she was afraid of my reaction." Mike shook his head and lowered himself into his oversized chair.

Sam blew out a long breath and settled on the corner of the desk. "Okay, well, you gave her a good run for her money before coming around, but that said —" Mike started to speak, but Sam held up a hand. "That said," Sam continued, "her childhood, her mother remaining in an abusive situation, her having to cut off her emotions in order to protect herself, she was just doing that now. Protecting herself."

"From me?" Mike asked in disbelief.

"From her own fears. Anyway, it's over. She came to you, right? It's all good?"

He nodded. "Yeah. It really is."

Sam chuckled at the goofy grin on his brother's face. "Just keep doing what you're doing. She knows you love her. She just needs to be reminded, that's all."

"Yeah." Mike tapped a pen against the desk. "Enough about me. What's going on with you and Nicole?"

"We're having fun together. Well, we would be if everything in her life weren't so screwed up," Sam muttered.

Mike raised an eyebrow. "Fun."

"Yeah. She's fun. We have a good time."

"And that's all."

"Can we not do this?" Sam asked.

"Like I didn't want to do it when you went after me about Cara? What are you doing, man? I've never seen you so protective over a woman. From the first minute you laid eyes on her, you were different."

Sam pushed himself off the desk and paced the floor. "She gets to me."

"So let it happen. What's the worst result?"

"I get my heart ripped to shreds. Again. I'm humiliated. Again. I've already been the laughingstock of this town once. Everyone looked at me with pity for years after Jenna left me at the altar. Do you think I'm looking to revisit those days?"

Shit. He'd never admitted that out loud. He barely admitted it to himself. But the humiliation of that time had stuck with him.

"Ah, so it's not just about you not being able to trust your judgment. It's about time you admitted as much," Mike said, using his *I'm the older brother and I know best* tone.

"I came here to talk about the wire. Nicole wants this thing over with, and I tend to agree. The sooner she's safe, the sooner everyone can move on with their lives."

Mike stared at him for a long moment, letting Sam know he wasn't happy with the subject change. Sam just waited him out. He had nothing more to say.

"Fine. I'll see what I can find out about why they want to wait and try to move up the timetable. Will it be Stanton or Nicole wearing the wire?"

Sam thought back to the scene earlier. "Still up for debate, but I'm thinking — hell, I'm going to insist on Stanton."

"Yeah, I'd do the same — if it were the woman I loved."

"Mike," Sam said on a low, warning rumble.

"Coming to dinner this week?" Mike asked, wisely changing the subject. "Cara and I are going to tell Mom and Dad the big news."

With the conversation back on Mike, Sam relaxed. "Wouldn't miss it."

"Are you bringing Nicole?"

Sam nodded. "Except for work, I'm not letting her out of my sight until those bastards are behind bars."

"I'll keep your schedule light. No reason why we can't cover you."

"Thanks," Sam said, deciding not to argue. The more time he could look after Nicole himself, the better. "Get back to me as soon as you hear from the feds."

"Will do."

Sam turned to leave.

"Hey, Sam."

He paused at the door and turned to look at his brother. "Don't screw up with Nicole. It's harder to get trust back than to win it in the first place," Mike said.

With his brother's words ringing in his ears, Sam strode out of the station.

Nicole stood across the street from the bakery, staring at the sign above her store. *Her store.* At the thought, a delightful shiver of excitement ran through her.

The new awning and sign had been delivered and installed. *Lulu and Nic's.* Plain and simple. In a small town, everyone would know what products they sold, and all of Serendipity already knew Aunt Lulu from The Family Restaurant. Nicole had no problem giving her top billing.

"Looks amazing," Sam said, walking up to her.

"Well, this is a surprise!" she said.

They hadn't seen much of each other during the day this past week, as she and Lulu had decided to try a soft opening before next Monday's big grand opening. They figured they could test out pastries and desserts, see what people preferred, where the glitches were in service and preparation, all before the advertised open date.

She arrived at the bakery by four A.M. to start baking for the day and often didn't come home until late at night. There was much more to do than she'd anticipated, but she was operating on adrenaline and excitement and wasn't the least bit tired. Sam insisted on being with her at night and she wasn't complaining, even if part of his reasoning was that he wanted to make sure she remained safe.

They fell into a routine whereby they alternated whose place they slept at. He drove her to work in the morning and picked her up when she called him at night. They'd grab dinner in town or one of them would make something light, depending on whose house they ended up in, make love, and fall asleep curled in each other's arms. So whether or not he wanted to admit his feelings for her, she was forging a place in his life. If he wanted her out when the situation with Tyler's father and the Russians was resolved, he was going to have to say so.

In the meantime, she enjoyed every day for what it was, hoping she was showing him what could be. "Are you ready to head over to my parents'?" he asked.

She nodded. "But it seems like such an intimate family moment." Not that she'd know of such a thing. "Maybe you should all be alone when Cara and Mike tell your folks she's pregnant."

He immediately shook his head. "Nobody will mind. It's good news. And I want you there."

"Are you sure you don't just want to have an eye on me?" she asked, only half teasing.

He met her gaze. "Don't overthink. Just go with the flow."

Apparently he found the flow a lot easier to handle than she did. "Fine," she said with forced brightness. "Let's go."

Twenty minutes later, she was welcomed with open arms by Ella Marsden and the yipping dog jumping up and down on his hind legs at her feet.

"I'm so glad you could join us! Sunday family dinners are always more fun when we have company." She enveloped Nicole in a warm, Jean Naté–scented hug.

Nicole recognized the perfume because she'd complimented Lulu's fragrance and learned the name. If it were her own mother, she'd be choking on Chanel. This scent warmed her all over.

"I brought you some meringue puffs," Nicole said, handing Sam's mother a white bakery box with their new Lulu and Nic's logo emblazoned in what she hoped would become their royal blue and yellow branding.

"Thank you, that's so sweet. I can't wait to hear all about how everything's going. I already stopped in, as you know." Ella accepted the box.

"I do, and I appreciate your support."

Ella smiled and turned to Sam, hugging him and kissing his cheek before letting him go.

"Hi, Mom. You look beautiful as usual."

She waved off his compliment. "You just want me to send you home with extra meals you can freeze." She laughed. "Come in. Everyone else is in the living room."

Nicole joined Sam's family and accepted their hellos and warm greetings. She was so grateful they welcomed her so easily, even Mike, who she knew had reservations in the beginning, and especially Erin and now Cole. Her heart had led her to this small town and these wonderful people. No matter what happened between her and Sam, she knew she'd made the right decision settling here.

But she couldn't lie to herself. She didn't just envy the tight family unit he had, she longed for the same thing for herself. Craved it, in fact. Being here today was like a big tease. A tiny sip of water in the middle of a parched desert, only to know it could be snatched away at any moment. She'd be devastated if she lost this personal connection to his family. She pulled in a shaky breath, mortified when a small, distressed cry escaped.

"Hey. Are you okay?" Sam walked up and placed an arm around her shoulder, pulling her against his warm, hard body.

"I'm great. Why wouldn't I be?"

Sam eyed her warily. He'd gotten to know Nicole pretty well and although she said the right things, deep inside, something was brewing. He didn't know what was bothering her, but he didn't like that she wasn't perfectly at ease and comfortable here.

"Do you want to leave as soon as Mike makes the announcement?" he asked quietly. "I can make an excuse and we can go."

She shook her head. "No, of course not. I'm really thrilled to be here." She stroked his cheek with her hand and in that instant, he wanted to make an excuse and disappear so they could be alone. "It's just . . ."

"What? Tell me."

"I've never experienced a real family celebration. One where everyone is truly happy for everyone else. No ulterior motives, no faking it for one reason or another. I'm looking forward to seeing everyone's reactions."

She looked up at him with blue eyes, so open and honest that she took his breath away. He didn't know why she affected him so deeply, making him want to give her everything she'd missed out on in her life. "Okay, then. We stay."

"We have an announcement to make," Mike said, his voice a welcome intrusion into Sam's musings.

Without thought, he reached out and clasped Nicole's hand in his. Her warmth and presence grounded him.

"Michael? What's going on?" Simon asked.

"It's good news," Cara jumped in, nudging her husband in the ribs.

"Well, come on, then," Simon said, sounding relieved.

Sam stifled a chuckle. After the year of his father's cancer, news and updates and problems, he understood why Simon reacted the way he had.

"Okay, grandpa times two," Mike said, unable to contain his smile.

A grin split Simon's face. "You're having a baby!"

"I knew it!" Ella said, launching herself at Cara and pulling her into a hug. "Long bouts of nausea, unable to sit at the table and look at food. I was wondering when you would figure it out or at least fill us in."

Cara hugged Ella back. Her relationship with her own mother was difficult because of the woman's unwillingness to leave Cara's abusive father, so Sam knew how much Ella's love and support meant to her.

"I should have known you would figure it out before we did. There's no keeping secrets from you, is there, Mom?" Mike asked, laughing.

Erin and Cole stepped up next for congratulations, then Sam, who, of course, already knew, and Nicole, who pretended it was her first time hearing the news.

Sam watched as she interacted with his brother, who admittedly hadn't been her biggest fan. But Mike had come around, trusting Sam's feelings for her over his history with her mentally ill sister.

"I'm thrilled for you," she said to Cara. "Are you feeling any better?"

"A little. I think telling people helped my mental state, at the very least." She shot a glance at Mike, who pulled her in for a hug and a long kiss that had even Sam wanting to look away.

Nicole, on the other hand, watched them, a look of pure longing on her face. A look so wistful, like she knew she was seeing something she'd never have. Sam's stomach cramped badly and he glanced away.

"Anyone ready for dinner?" he asked, hoping to break the tension building inside him.

Everyone jumped on the idea of his mom's food, and the meal was one of the happiest and most fun Sam could remember in a long while. Considering his family always ribbed each other, joked, and had a good time, that was saying something. Erin wanted to know if Mike and Cara planned on finding out the sex of the baby. Either way, she was mentally planning baby play dates. By the time they'd finished coffee and dessert — his mom being smart enough to serve only Nicole's meringue puffs and not anything she'd made or bought too — Sam was ready for grown-up time.

Beneath the table, he reached out and placed his hand on Nicole's thigh. Through her long skirt, he felt the heat of her skin against his palm, or at least he imagined he could feel it. His body thought so too, igniting at the thought of getting her home and into bed.

He leaned over and whispered in her ear. "Ready to get going?" he asked, his hand trailing higher.

"Behave," she whispered back. "I want to help your mom clean up."

"Nonsense," Ella said, having heard *that*. "Guests don't clean up."

"But . . ."

"Go," Ella insisted.

Sam rose from his seat. "You heard the lady," he said, pulling out Nicole's chair.

"Thank you for a delicious meal and a wonderful evening," Nicole said.

"Our pleasure," Simon said.

Ella actually snorted in reply. "As if he cooked?" She laughed. "But it is our pleasure. See you soon." She blew a kiss in their general direction.

"Congratulations again," Nicole said to Cara and Mike.

"I'll walk you two out," Mike said, taking Sam by surprise.

He followed them to the front door, where Sam paused, turning to face his brother, Nicole by his side. "What's going on?"

"Change of plans. It turns out the DEA was already watching the Romanovs. They have a guy deep undercover and a sting in place. They want us to stand down and stay the hell out of their way."

Sam glanced at Nicole. Her eyes opened wide. "But . . . what about the money laundering and my father's firm? Tyler? And me? They're after me!" she said, her voice rising.

Sam pulled her tight against him. "You're going to be fine," he said, glancing at his brother for reassurance.

"Mike?" Nicole asked.

He exhaled a harsh breath. "From what I understand, and it's sketchy at best, they hope to have the Russians behind bars by tonight. According to Cole's sources, there's a huge shipment coming in and if they can catch them in the act . . ." He trailed off.

"Okay, and the bit players? Like Tyler's father?" Sam asked.

"The New York City cops will talk to Tyler about giving grand jury testimony and indicting his old man and anyone else involved in laundering money."

Nicole sucked in a breath. "I need to go home and talk to my father."

Sam exchanged glances with Mike. "I'm not sure that's a good idea. The less you're involved, the better."

"But I am involved. I'm the one who overheard the conversation."

"Which probably can't be used as evidence anyway," Mike reminded her.

She sighed. "I still want to talk to him. He deserves a heads-up. He may not have been a doting parent, but I can't imagine he'd let anything happen to me. I couldn't live with myself if I didn't warn him before his world comes crashing down."

Sam admired her loyalty to a man who didn't deserve it, but given what he'd learned of her so far, she was loving and caring and put others before herself. "I'll go with you."

She swung toward him. "You don't need to do that."

"Maybe not, but I want to." He squeezed her shoulder and she laid her head against his arm.

Mike shot Sam a knowing look. "I'll leave you two to figure out your next step. I don't have to remind you to be careful," Mike said before turning and walking away.

Nicole looked up at him with trusting eyes. "Will the Russians leave me alone?"

"Once the DEA arrests them with drugs in hand, you'll be off their radar, believe me. We can go to the city tomorrow and talk to your father."

She studied him, as if gauging his sincerity in wanting to go along. Without warning, she leaned up and kissed his cheek. "Thank you."

"For what?"

She shrugged. "For making me feel better. Now let's go home and I'll make you feel good."

His cock stiffened in response. The things this woman did to him, mentally and physically, defied anything he'd felt before. Grasping her hand, he said, "Lead the way," and tugged her toward the car.

Sixteen

The next morning, Sam found himself driving to New York City. On the ride there, Nicole had been eerily silent, keeping her own counsel, withdrawn into herself. Sam guessed she wasn't comfortable bringing him to meet with her father, but he wasn't letting her go through this alone.

He pulled up to an expensive building on Manhattan's east side. Though out of his element, he refused to be intimidated by her parents' wealth. She was what mattered, not her folks.

"I thought you grew up in a house?" Sam asked, indulging his curiosity as the valet opened her car door.

"I did. On Long Island. My parents still own it, but they also have an apartment in Manhattan, and my father stays here more often than not."

They climbed out of the car and Sam met her by the large revolving door to the building. "Is your mother here too?" He wanted a heads-up on whom he'd be meeting.

Her sigh answered his question.

He didn't expect her to elaborate and was surprised when she did.

"Mom's at the house on Long Island. A testament to *what does love have to do with anything,*" she said without meeting his gaze.

Sam winced, recalling that she'd told him her mother had used that line to try to persuade her to marry Tyler.

"My father is always here on Sunday night, so I figured I'd catch him before he goes into the office this morning," Nicole explained.

"Hence the six A.M. wake-up call," Sam said, covering his yawn with one hand.

She shrugged. "I wanted to get this over with."

Sam grasped Nicole's hand as they walked into the luxury building. Ignoring the mirrors surrounding her, she headed straight for the bank of elevators.

"Still want to do this?" he asked.

She didn't answer right away, waiting until they were in the elevator, the doors closing behind them. "No," she said, as the elevator took them skyward to the penthouse. "But I have to. It's the right thing to do."

"I admire that about you," he said.

She leaned against the wall and treated him to a forced smile. "Thank you."

The doors opened wide and her father, dressed in what had to be a thousand-dollar suit, greeted her in the doorway of the apartment.

"The doorman called up," he said, answering her unasked question. "To what do I owe this early-morning visit?"

No hello. No warm welcome. No hug. For the love of —

"Can we come in?" Nicole asked. "I don't think you want your neighbors overhearing what I have to say," she continued, unperturbed by the greeting or lack of.

Her father stepped aside and Sam followed Nicole past him into the apartment. A glance revealed that the floors were marble, the walls were adorned with thick crown moldings, top and bottom, and the décor oozed wealth. Sam didn't like it here worth a damn.

He noted her father hadn't batted an eyelash at Sam's presence, nor had he introduced himself. Just because they were wealthy self-righteous pricks didn't mean he had to be. His mother had raised him better.

"Sam Marsden," he said, extending his hand toward the other man.

"Sorry." Nicole blushed, embarrassed. "Paul Farnsworth, this is Detective Sam Marsden. Sam, this is my father."

"Nice to meet you, Detective." The older man took his hand in a firm grip. "So to what do I owe this visit?"

Nicole drew a deep breath. "Is everything okay with your business?"

He narrowed his gaze. "Why would you be asking about my business?"

She pressed her lips together, and he was floored by how difficult she obviously found it to shake her father's world in light of how cold the man acted toward her. Didn't every kid deserve love and affection from their parents?

She deserved love and affection, Sam thought, and damned if he didn't want to be the one to give it to her. It was all he could do not to reach out and pull her against him, supporting her completely. The only thing stopping him was the fact that she didn't need the distraction any show of affection would provide. So he kept a respectful distance even though it just about killed him, as he realized his feelings for her were growing exponentially with every minute that passed.

"Would it surprise you to know that your partner is in bed with the Russian mob?"

Nicole asked her father. "And before you ask how I could accuse him of such a thing, you should know I overheard him discussing it with Andre, your accountant." She went on to explain what she'd overheard and when, along with the resulting threats to both Tyler and herself.

Sam kept an eye on her father. His training taught him what to look for, and the older man's expression never registered shock, surprise, anger, or anything else he knew she'd expected over her accusations.

"You already know!" Nicole exclaimed, proving what Sam already knew.

She was smart. Savvy. And one hell of a strong woman to have been raised by this cold, unfeeling man and still come out the warm, sweet woman he loved.

Loved?

Shit. This was not the time for revelations, he thought, breaking into a cold sweat.

"I didn't know specifics, but I suspected something was wrong when I noticed the books were off. That and Robert's been acting strangely, clearly nervous and hiding things. I hired a forensic accountant to look into things." He straightened his tie. "You said Tyler knows too?"

Nicole nodded. "I suggest you talk to him. The police are aware as well, and that's why

I'm here. I wanted to give you a heads-up before they pay you a visit."

He sent her an appreciative look, which was as much emotion as Sam suspected the man was capable of, Sam thought in disgust.

He'd never treat his child like a business associate or inconvenience, which was exactly what this man was doing to his daughter. And she accepted it, clearly used to the dynamic. Sam wasn't, and his stomach churned. He wasn't sure if it was because he'd just thought about the idea of how he'd handle a kid of his own, something he'd never contemplated even in passing before, or because the notion settled in his heart. And stayed there.

"Well, I'm certainly not going to jail because Robert's gotten reckless and greedy." He straightened his tie. "However, I did not know anything about what you heard or that he'd let those animals loose on you."

Sam stiffened at the reminder of the Russians and any danger. He hoped like hell the DEA bust and round of arrests had gone down as planned.

"I know that, Dad."

"No, I don't think you did, or you would have come to me long before now."

Guilt flashed across Nicole's face, which

infuriated Sam on her behalf. "Maybe if she thought you gave a shit about her, she'd have brought her problems to you instead of thinking she had to handle them herself," he said, unable to rein in his anger any longer.

"Sam —" Nicole placed a warning hand on his arm, but he was finished letting anyone treat her with cold dismissiveness.

"Excuse me, but I'd say this is between myself and my daughter," her father said with an air of authority and entitlement.

Oh hell no, Sam thought. "Considering I'm the one keeping her safe, I'd say you'd better include me in the conversation. You're lucky she cares enough to warn you. I wouldn't have been so generous. Now tell me what you plan to do to make sure your partner can't use his connections to hurt Nicole."

Paul Farnsworth stepped back and studied Sam, suddenly seeing him as someone worth assessing. "What are your intentions toward my daughter?" he asked, surprising Sam by turning the conversation to the personal.

"That's between me and Nicole." Sam couldn't help but play this man's game. He didn't like him or his smug arrogance, but mostly he didn't like how he treated Sam's woman.

He reached out and snagged Nicole's hand. Let the man take *that* as an answer. As of this moment, Sam was claiming her, at least in his mind. He'd take the time to sort through what that meant to him later.

For now, he'd deal with the situation at hand. "I believe I asked you a question."

Nicole couldn't believe Sam was engaging her father. For her. She found the whole situation humiliating and embarrassing.

"I'll call the police myself and cooperate," her father said, taking Nicole by surprise. "If they have the evidence from Tyler and me to arrest him, that should protect Nicole." He spoke to Sam as if she weren't in the room, his tone bland, as if he were discussing a business deal, which was the way he always acted toward her.

Her father was the iceman. That had been Vicky's name for him growing up, and she wasn't wrong. To have Sam, who came from a perfect family — loving, caring, kind — see her treated like that . . . She shuddered and wrapped her arms around herself, unwilling and really unable to face him.

"And I'll talk to Tyler and see what we can salvage businesswise when this is all over," Paul continued.

Because after all, that was what mattered most to her father, Nicole thought.

Her father turned his gaze on her. "Now I suggest you and your friend head back to Serenity —"

"Serendipity," Sam muttered, obviously disgusted that the man didn't even know the name of the town where his daughter now lived.

Whatever, she thought. She just wanted to get out of here. "Good luck," she said to her father.

He inclined his head. "Thank you for the heads-up. And thank you, Detective, for your help."

The men shook hands, and none too soon Sam and Nicole were back in the car and speeding home to Serendipity. She didn't have anything to say and kept quiet.

"That went well," Sam said.

She leaned her head back against the seat. "About as I expected."

Keeping his gaze on the road, he placed his hand on hers. Although his touch usually warmed her, today she was ice cold, inside and out, her father's behavior having reminded her of her place, not just in his life, but in Sam's.

Passing through.

"It's almost over," Sam said, and she

didn't know if he referred to her father's business mess or to them. After all, considering what he'd just witnessed, she wouldn't blame him.

"Yeah," she said, keeping her gaze on the passing scenery outside the car window. "It is." She wanted nothing more than to get back to Serendipity and throw herself into her work.

At this moment she was glad he wasn't a man looking for a serious relationship, because after viewing what she knew of love and affection, if he had been looking, he'd run far and fast from her now.

Sam couldn't remember the last time he hit up Joe's on a Wednesday night without looking to see if Nicole was there or knowing he'd be meeting up with her later on. But something between them had changed. He would have thought it had to do with their visit to her father, but after the trip, she'd been distant, not gone.

It was Mike's news the following morning — that the DEA bust had been successful, with the Russians picked up en masse while taking possession of a huge drug shipment — that had caused the shift. Now that Nicole was safe from their wrath, she no longer needed Sam's protection, and she'd pulled away. As if their relationship had been one of convenience, based solely on his need to protect her, and with that need gone, so was she.

Which made no sense to Sam. One day she'd been warm and loving; the next she'd pulled away. He didn't know what to do, so he'd given her the space she seemed to need. He'd backed off, letting her leave for work at the crack of dawn and drive herself home after dark, with no help from him.

And unlike before, she wasn't making time for him afterward. She'd pushed him away. He missed her like crazy and he didn't know what to do about it. With her grand opening coming up on Monday, he gave her the space she seemed to need, figuring he'd regroup and come at her from a different angle.

Since it was still early, Joe's wasn't crowded, the mood mellow. Slow music played on the jukebox and Sam nursed a beer, waiting for his brother to show.

"Problems with Nicole?" Mike asked, joining him at the bar.

Sam shrugged. "You could say that. She wants nothing to do with me."

Mike hauled himself onto the neighboring stool and gestured to Joe. "I'll have what Sam's drinking. And get him another one."

Turning to Sam, he said, "You do something stupid?"

Joe slid two bottles their way.

"Thanks," Mike said to the bartender.

Joe nodded and made his way to another customer at the other end of the room.

Sam glanced at his brother. "It's a sad day when you've become the expert on women," he muttered.

Mike raised an eyebrow. "I've always been the expert on women. It's just that now I'm also the expert on keeping one."

"Good one." Sam let out a laugh before sobering. "Something changed. I don't know if it had to do with me meeting her SOB father or her finding out she didn't need protection anymore, but she froze me out." He took a long pull of his beer, seeking solace in something, even alcohol.

Mike leaned against the old, scarred wooden counter. "When I showed up at a 911 call from a neighbor after Cara's father abused her mother, she was mortified." Mike's scowl reflected just how he felt about the situation.

Sam understood. Cara's entire life had been shaped by the fact that her mother hadn't left her husband.

"Cara didn't want me to know how bad things were, and if it were up to her, it would have been worse between us once I found out."

"How'd you get through to her?" Sam asked.

"That time? I made her sit down with me and talk."

Sam shook his head and laughed. "That doesn't sound like you. At that point, you were running away from commitment."

"You see how well that worked for me. Seems like you're going through the same thing. You didn't want to trust any woman ever again, but as soon as Nicole moved here, you jumped in with both feet."

If his older brother hadn't gone through a similar experience, Sam would be embarrassed to admit his feelings. "She's it for me."

He shook his head, amazed he was so willing to say it out loud.

And even more amazed that he trusted her in a way he never thought he'd let himself trust again.

Sam groaned, deciding to confide in his brother. "Man, you have no idea how bad Nicole had it growing up. Her father barely acknowledges she exists. I always knew we were lucky, but seeing that?" He shuddered at the memory. "I don't know how she ended up as warm and caring as she is."

"Maybe that helps explain her twin?" Mike asked.

"Well, she truly has a mental illness, but having parents who don't give a shit couldn't possibly help her coping abilities. I said as much to her father," Sam said.

Mike's eyes opened wide. "How did that go over with Nicole?"

Sam shrugged. "Not a clue. She was already withdrawing into herself." He vividly recalled Nicole's arms wrapped around her body, staring out the truck window, lost to him on the ride home.

"Do you remember what you told me when you showed up at my apartment after I'd left Cara and Serendipity?" Mike asked.

Sam thought back to that day. "Go big or go home?"

Mike nodded.

"Not that simple. I think Nicole needs me to build the foundation first. I haven't given her that," he said, feeling ashamed.

Mike's eyes narrowed in understanding. "Only you know what your girl needs."

Sam squared his shoulders. "Me. She needs me," he decided, one hundred percent certain. "She has no family that truly cares about her well-being. From what I can see, she's making real friends here for the first time. If either of us has reason not to trust in people, it's her. And I've given her no reason to believe in me. In fact, I told her not to from day one." His gut churned with the knowledge that he'd done nothing but push her away.

Mike leaned back, his gaze fully on Sam. "As someone who's known you your whole life, I can say that *I* trust you. Just throw that Marsden focus her way and you'll be fine."

"That means a lot coming from you. Thanks." Sam tipped his bottle against Mike's.

"Good luck."

"Thanks." Something told Sam he'd be needing it.

Nicole was tired, bone-deep tired, and she knew it wasn't just from preparing for her grand opening tomorrow. But she and Aunt Lulu had done it. They were ready with exactly the right menu for the morning, they'd hired one part-time and one full-time worker, and everything was a GO.

She pulled her rental car into her driveway and dragged herself out of the vehicle, wanting nothing more than a hot shower and hours of sleep. No sooner had she walked to her front door than she heard her name.

"Nicole."

She turned to find Sam striding across the lawn, looking relaxed and tanned, a bouquet of daisies in his hand. "I wanted to wish you good luck tomorrow." He held out the flowers, an endearing grin on his face.

The walls she'd built up since he'd witnessed her humiliating interaction with her father melted easily. "Thanks," she said, accepting the gift.

"Just getting home?" he asked.

She nodded.

"Long day."

"Longer week," she said, surprising herself by laughing easily with him. She'd missed him more than she thought possible. "Would you like to come inside?"

He stepped closer and she inhaled his musky cologne, a warm familiar scent that mocked her attempts at keeping a distance. "I would, but I know you have a big day tomorrow and have to be up early."

She nodded, disappointment filling her.

He stepped closer, tilted her chin up with one hand. "I missed you this week."

His minty breath tested her resolve. "I missed you too."

He slid his lips over hers, once, twice, a third time before settling his mouth over hers. Her eyelids fluttered closed and she sighed into the kiss, knowing she was defeating the need to keep him at a distance before he pushed her away first.

His tongue swirled inside her mouth, finding an answering tug lower in her belly, a pulsing need between her thighs. She raised her hands to his hair, holding on as he seduced her with his talented mouth and tongue.

She was about to insist he needed to come inside when the loud honk of a car horn startled her and she jumped back. She jerked toward the offending sound in time to see a large white BMW pull into her driveway.

"Oh my God."

Sam glanced at the car. "Who is that?"

She swallowed hard, nausea filling her. "My mother."

He swore beneath his breath. She knew the feeling.

Nicole watched in disbelief as her mother's driver stepped out of the vehicle, strode around the back of the car, and opened the door for Marian Farnsworth to climb out. That she'd made the drive to Serendipity at this hour didn't bode well for Nicole, and she straightened her shoulders in preparation for confrontation.

"What's she doing here?" Sam asked.

Nicole didn't answer, already rebuilding

the walls and distance she'd maintained all week. If Sam thought her father was cold, wait until he witnessed her mother in action.

Marian Farnsworth walked up the driveway, her heels clicking as she approached Nicole and Sam.

"Mother, what are you doing here?" Nicole thought it best to get down to business.

Her mother tilted her head, her perfectly blow-dried hair sweeping her shoulder. "I came to ask you the same question. To see what's so attractive about this small town." She glanced at Sam, assessing him and finding him lacking, all with a single dismissive glance.

Nicole did her best not to react.

"Your father told me you paid him a visit. He appreciated the heads-up you gave him about his partner's . . . activities. Personally, I think you should have kept quiet. Discretion being the better part of valor, after all."

Nicole raised her eyebrow. "Too late."

"Ah. You think this changes things? That we no longer need you to come home and fulfill your role?"

"I can't imagine what good you think forcing me to marry Tyler will do."

"Your father and Tyler will rebuild the

firm and our standing in the community with a united front. You, darling, are the glue that will hold the families together."

Nicole felt the weight of Sam's disbelieving stare on both her and her mother. To his credit, he remained silent, at least so far. But shock tended to render a person mute, Nicole thought.

"Nothing has changed," she informed her mother. "Tyler and I are finished. And my life is here now."

Marian rolled her eyes. "Give me a break. Give your father one. It's time to stop playing games and come home. I'm finished humoring your little crisis."

"Be blunt, why don't you," Nicole muttered.

"Well, humoring you hasn't helped."

Nicole stiffened. "Humoring me."

"Yes. Letting you come here to this small town, play house, sow your . . . oats —" Marian flung a careless hand toward Sam, who watched her with an impassive expression. "You've had your fun. It's time to come home and live up to your responsibilities." Her tone lacked any lightness or warmth.

Nicole dug her nails into her hand and latched onto the only important part of her mother's statement. "*Letting me?* You think you let me come here? I'm an adult. You don't own me, control me, pay for anything in my life, or tell me what to do," Nicole said, her voice rising. "And contrary to what you might think, you haven't since I turned twenty-one and my trust fund kicked in."

At which point she'd finished paying for her own college education, so she could have her independence.

"Can we have this discussion in private?" Her mother looked dismissively at Sam.

Nicole would rather not have this discussion at all, but Marian had driven this far, and when she intended to have her say, nothing short of being physically restrained would stop her. Normally, she wouldn't give her mother the satisfaction of doing anything she asked, but the thought of Sam witnessing any more of her family dysfunction turned Nicole's already upset stomach.

"Let's go inside my house."

Her mother turned her nose up, no doubt at the thought of entering Nicole's modest, older home. "Fine," she said, obviously knowing she had no choice.

"Not fine," Sam said, speaking for the first time.

Nicole turned a pleading gaze his way. *Please, please, don't do this again,* she silently begged him. Her mother was just getting warmed up. Whatever she said to Nicole would be painfully humiliating if she was alone, but she'd survive. If Sam witnessed it, she might not ever be able to face him again.

The whole time she'd been speaking with her mother, she'd deliberately shut off the mortification of Sam witnessing her being belittled and talked down to, the weight of her unreasonable family expectations, and the fact that she was a constant disappointment. Nicole's parents stood out in stark contrast to Sam's family's warmth and caring, and she wanted to curl up and die, knowing worse was to come. The longer he stood by her, the harder the fall would be when he was ready for this affair between them to end.

And he'd made it clear that it would.

"Please?" she asked softly.

He shook his head, not speaking but letting her know that no way would he allow her to go through this alone.

Well, that was nice of him, but while dealing with her domineering parents, she'd always been alone. She was the child who'd never lived up to their hopes and dreams and never would. And if this shame was how it felt for someone to be by her side, maybe she was better off by herself after all.

"Sam, just go." Hoping he would comply, she turned, gesturing for her mother to follow, which she did, judging by the clicking sound of her heels against the walkway.

Nicole was disappointed but not at all surprised when Sam stepped into the house behind her mother, closing the door behind him.

"I believe she asked you to leave," her mother said to Sam.

He merely stared at her mother for a heartbeat before extending his hand. "I'm Sam Marsden. One of the things Nicole finds so attractive about this small town."

Oh, he did not just say that.

Nicole closed her eyes, knowing that if she'd introduced them earlier, she could have avoided this, but unlike with her father, when she'd just blanked, this time she'd hoped to spare Sam her mother's direct snub.

When her mother merely eyed him warily, Sam, with his hand still out, explained, "Someone has to be civil."

With a put-out sigh, her mother shook his hand. "Marian Farnsworth. Now may I speak to my daughter in private?"

He glanced between the two women. "I'll wait in the den just in case you need me," he said pointedly to Nicole. He headed to the next room, where Nicole knew he'd be able to hear every word exchanged.

"What does he think I'm going to do to you?" her mother asked. "He's a rude man."

"No, that's you, showing up here uninvited, ordering my . . . friend around and making demands. I told you when I was packing to leave I was serious. It's my life."

Her mother sighed, shifting the chain on her purse to the other shoulder. "You're part of a prominent family, Nicole. Your father's partner was arrested this morning. Tyler and Paul are trying to hold things together and keep their important clients. You have an obligation to help us."

"Why? Because you gave birth to me?"

"Exactly." Her mother's lips thinned. "Bloodlines are important." Marian eyed her, a determined expression on her face. "And this little rebellion won't do anything for you in the long run. Neither will that small-town cop."

"Just stop!" Nicole's voice rose, and she realized she was a heartbeat away from stamping her feet like a child. She drew a deep breath and pulled herself together. "This isn't a rebellion. This is my life. You're standing in my home, insulting me. You're belittling a place with good people, a place you know nothing about. And that small-town cop you're so disdainful of? I love him."

"Oh, Nicole." Her mother's voice filled with pity and dismay. "I told you that you can't build a life that's meaningful or important on love. Love won't support you in the lifestyle you're accustomed to. And this kind of living? It'll grow old. Come home and do what's expected of you now."

Her head began to pound. "Mother, I'm going to say something and for once in my life, I want you to listen. To *hear* me. I'm building a good life here. One I'm proud of. I have friends who like me for me, not the family name or money. And tomorrow I'm opening a bakery in town with a woman I admire. I'll be up at four A.M. preparing the pastries and the baked goods for my customers. If our blood ties mean anything, if my being your daughter is important to you, I hope you'll come and see what I've accomplished."

A myriad set of expressions crossed her mother's face, none of which Nicole could interpret. It would take too much time and effort for her to try. She could only hope she'd made some kind of impression on her mother's implacable will to put her status above all else.

Marian placed a hand on Nicole's shoulder, surprising her and making her wonder if she'd made some sort of dent after all.

"Your sister's ill. She will never be able to step up and be the daughter we need her to be. But you still can. Think about it," Marian said.

Nicole jerked away. "I don't need to think. I know who I am. You're looking at her, Mom. So look. Understand. Come tomorrow and see for yourself." Was she really begging? Nicole bit the inside of her cheek hard.

"You're a disappointment to me," her mother said. "And clearly I came all this way for nothing."

Nicole shook her head and closed her eyes. Her mother hadn't heard one word Nicole said. In one ear and out the other. Her mother had ignored everything that was important to Nicole, words that came from her heart and soul in a last-ditch attempt to reach the woman who was supposed to be her mother. But a mother's job was to love and nurture, and Marian Farnsworth had done none of those things.

When she opened her eyes, she wasn't surprised to find that her mother had gone, cementing the fact that they clearly had very different views on what it meant to share blood.

Nicole swiped at her damp eyes, fully aware that Sam was in the other room. He hadn't rushed in to save the day. No doubt he was still reeling, processing the difference between their families, reassessing what the hell he was doing with a woman who'd grown up with vultures, not parents.

Or maybe he was wondering how to extricate himself sooner rather than later. She wouldn't blame him.

One thing she knew for sure: After that little display, *she* wanted nothing more than to be alone.

SEVENTEEN

And Sam had thought her father was a coldhearted bastard. Sam sat frozen to his seat, shocked that anyone could treat their own child like a pawn in a game. With those two as parents, Nicole was a fucking miracle.

His miracle.

She'd stood up for him to her mother, declaring her love, proving herself much braver than he'd been with her. He was the big bad cop and she put him to shame.

He rose from his seat, sorry that he'd left her alone with her bitch of a mother. Then again, maybe it was better that Nicole think he hadn't heard anything. Less embarrassing for her that way, and he'd do anything to protect her from being hurt any more.

He paused in the entryway, the distraught look on Nicole's face gutting him. Unable to remain silent, he stepped forward. "Nicole?"

She brushed at her cheeks, and he realized she'd been crying. And now she wanted to hide it from him.

"Hey." He strode up to her and grasped her hands. "Are you okay?"

"I'm fine."

He held on to her wrists and stared into her damp blue eyes. "No, you're not. Don't pretend with me."

To his surprise, she jerked out of his grasp. "Don't."

He narrowed his gaze. "Don't what? Help you? Be there for you?"

Her face morphed into a cool mask. "Don't make me think I can depend on you."

"Whoa." He dropped her wrist and raised both hands in a gesture of confusion. "I am here for you. I want to be here."

"Why?"

It was his turn to step up. "You want to know why I want to be there for you when you need me?" He drew on all the courage she'd shown so far, using her bravery to bolster his own. "Because I love you."

Her eyes opened wide, a flash of hope in their depths, before they went . . . blank.

She deliberately shut down her feelings. "No, you don't. You feel sorry for me." She wrapped her arms around her shoulders, her fingertips digging into her skin.

"I don't —"

"Yes, you do. You heard everything my mother said and you pity me. Why else would the man who didn't want anything to do with relationships and who doesn't believe in love choose this moment for a declaration?"

Her voice cracked and his heart squeezed painfully as she deliberately misinterpreted his words.

He'd told Mike he'd prove to her she could count on him. No matter how hard she made it, whether or not she shut him out, he wouldn't bail.

"I'll tell you why. Because I'm an idiot who couldn't get beyond my past to see the amazing woman in front of me. But I see you, Nicole. And I've heard everything you've ever said about what you want and need in life —"

"Oh my God, don't!" Her eyes opened wide, the blue depths filled with disappointment. "Don't use my own words against me."

"I'm using them *for* you. For us." But as he spoke, he recognized the irony. Now that he wanted everything from her, she didn't trust him or his words.

She couldn't because her mother had

shown up and demoralized and destroyed her in an attempt to get what she wanted. And Sam hadn't come to his senses in time.

She turned away. "I have to get up early and I have a long day tomorrow."

"I'll get my things and be right back. We can stay here."

She didn't face him. "That's okay. I . . . I need to be alone tonight."

Sam shook his head and swallowed a groan. "Nicole —"

"Sam, please. I can't do this now. I just had it out with my mother. I can't argue with you too. I'm exhausted," she said, her voice catching.

"Okay." He didn't like it, but he'd respect it. "But set the alarm when I leave."

"I will."

"I'll pick you up and take you to work tomorrow."

She shook her head, still not turning around. "There's no reason for you to be up before dawn just because I have to be."

He rolled his eyes. If she thought she could get rid of him that easily, she didn't know him well at all. "I'll be in the driveway at four. With coffee. See you then."

Because he loved her. He knew for sure. And in his mind, that changed everything.

■ ■ ■ ■

Operating on autopilot, Nicole woke up, showered, and dressed for her grand opening. Her head hurt from lack of sleep, and she wasn't feeling the excitement she'd anticipated for today. She blamed her mother as well as Sam. He was a good guy, trying to make her feel better in the only way he knew how. But she didn't believe he suddenly realized he was in love with her at the very moment he was exposed to yet another ugly side of her family and her life.

He came to her door to pick her up, not looking much better than she felt. He hadn't shaved, his eyes were bloodshot, and he seemed to be moving as slowly as she was. But he still looked delectable to her, and keeping her distance was hard. But she'd gone into self-protection mode. No longer was she willing to expose her heart for people to slice and dice. Even well-meaning people who told her the way things were going to be up front. Like Sam.

They drove to town in silence, punctuated by occasional questions on his end.

"How did you sleep?" he asked.

"Fine." She lied. She'd tossed and turned in her big empty bed all alone.

"Really? Because I didn't sleep at all. I haven't been sleeping all week. I'd gotten used to having you in my bed, and I miss you."

She'd stared straight ahead, not wanting to get into any kind of deep discussion, and he took the hint and was silent for the rest of the way.

He pulled up in front of the store. The lights weren't on yet, which meant she'd beat Lulu here and she could get started on cleaning and sanitizing before prep and baking began.

Sam turned, slinging one arm across the passenger seat. "I'm working today, but I'll come by to check out the line coming out your door," he said, his grin cute and sweet.

"You don't have to do that." She managed a forced smile. "I'll be too busy to be able to talk."

He studied her, his hazel eyes assessing her in a way he'd never done before. Like he was looking beneath her skin and trying to figure out a way to understand this new version of her. Well, she understood herself, and she'd tried to explain it to him last night: She didn't want his pity and she certainly didn't want him saying things he didn't mean because of it.

"Like I said, I'll be by later to check things

out," he said, ignoring her.

She clutched her bag. "Suit yourself. Thanks for the ride." She opened the door and hopped out of the car.

She let herself into the shop, with the car engine humming behind her, as Sam waited until she was safely inside before taking off.

She brought her hands to her face and groaned. What was she going to do with him? The good news was, she had no time to worry about it.

She had a business to open.

Nicole didn't know what to expect from the day, but based on last week's slow build of sales, she had high hopes. Those hopes were exceeded. As Sam predicted, they had long lines during the prework hours, when people would pick up coffee from Cuppa Café and come by for food.

Her cranberry and hazelnut scones were a hit with the moms, and the kids loved the chocolate chip ones. The cinnamon and cream cheese muffins were treats everyone seemed to enjoy. And people ordered Lulu's pies for their weekend barbecues. By the time the day ended, Nicole's legs ached from being on her feet all day, but her emotions were running high with their success.

Then there was Sam. True to his word, he stopped by during the day. Not once or twice but three times, offering moral support and buying food. He didn't stay to talk or hog her attention, but she felt his warm gaze on hers for the duration of his visit. His proud gaze.

And his words from last night came back to her. *You want to know why I want to be there for you when you need me? Because I love you.*

Could he mean it, she wondered? And more importantly, could she trust him, especially after his insistence on not wanting or believing in relationships and love for himself?

Come to me when you're free — of everything. Then we can talk. Tyler never thought the day would come. In fact, up through last night, his father had been refusing to co-operate with the police, proclaiming his innocence and thrusting all the blame on his accountant. Only when Paul Farnsworth had refused to stand by him did Robert Stanton break down and confess. He'd truly believed that his partner, Nicole's father, would understand the need to bolster the firm during tough economic times, no matter the means.

Tyler was still coming to terms with his father's betrayal of everything moral and right. His mother? He didn't think she'd ever forgive her husband, and at this moment she was meeting with her attorneys. Not to delve into the legal status of her campaign funding, but to file for divorce. That was his mother. No second chances.

Before he could go talk to Macy, he had to do some legwork on something he hoped would prove to her that from this moment on, she came first. Whatever happened between them in the long run, Tyler knew it wouldn't be for lack of trying.

Daisies. Sam sent daisies to the store every morning for a week straight. Each day, they brightened up the area by the cash register, and when Nicole ran out of the room, they lined the windowsill overlooking the street.

"Someone's in love," Aunt Lulu said, turning the lock on the door and hanging the *CLOSED* sign from the doorknob.

"Are you talking about me? Or Sam?" Nicole asked her partner.

Aunt Lulu waggled her eyebrows. "Oh, a little bit of both of you."

Nicole bit down on the inside of her cheek. "Is love enough?" She asked the question that had been nagging at her day and night.

"Oh, honey. Of course it is." Aunt Lulu

placed an arm around her shoulders and led her to a small table in front. "Sit."

Not one to argue with this woman, Nicole did as instructed. Aunt Lulu pulled up a seat beside her. "I lost my first love to cancer before we ever got married. If I could have him back, just to experience that love again, I truly believe all would be right in my world." The woman who always seemed so together and strong looked suddenly frail and sad.

Nicole reached for her hand. "I'm sorry. I had no idea."

Aunt Lulu shrugged. "It's in the past. I can't change it, so I just push forward. But I can advise you not to waste one single day." She rose to her feet, obviously finished with sadness and reminiscing. "So aren't you glad we hired people to help with the cleanup?"

"More than anything. I don't know if I could handle it," Nicole admitted, stretching her legs and wiggling her aching feet.

A knock sounded at the door. "Who could that be?" Nicole asked.

Aunt Lulu stepped closer and glanced outside. "A very distinguished-looking gentleman I've never seen before."

Wary, Nicole stood and checked the visitor for herself. "Dad!"

"That's your father?" Aunt Lulu asked. "Nice-looking man."

"Yes." But Nicole wondered what was inside him. "I guess I should find out what he wants." She unlocked the door and let him inside. "You're returning my unexpected visit," she said. "What's the occasion?"

"I have news," he said.

"I see. Well, first meet my business partner, Lulu Donovan. Lulu, this is my father, Paul Farnsworth."

They shook hands, Aunt Lulu lingering too long — more for effect — as Nicole had come to learn about her. She liked being noticed.

But she was also observant and realized that Nicole's father had come for an important reason. "I'll go see to the cleanup," she said, excusing herself.

Nicole waited until Aunt Lulu was in the back room before turning to her father, only to find him wandering around, taking in her bakery with his discerning eye.

"Very nice," he said, surprising her.

She blinked. "Thank you. I take it Mom told you where to find me?"

"Your mother told me she paid you a visit. She was . . . upset about the business and Robert's arrest, and you know how your

406

mother gets when things don't go her way."

"Yes. She tries to manipulate them back the way she wants them."

"She does," he agreed.

"You've done it a time or two yourself," Nicole pointed out.

His mouth twisted in a wry grin.

"It won't work with me. Not anymore. I'm not leaving my life here —"

"I'm not here to ask you to."

Nicole stepped back, taken off guard. "Then why make the trip here?" she asked, her heart suddenly racing, and she couldn't figure out why.

He studied her, as if seeing her for the first time. "Something your boyfriend said."

"Sam's not my —"

Her father burst out laughing, the action and the sound so at odds with the man Nicole knew, she was even more off balance. "What's so funny?" she finally asked.

Her father shrugged out of his suit jacket and placed it over the back of a chair. "Whatever you label the man, he cares about you. Enough to call me out on 'not giving a shit about you.' "

Nicole's mouth went dry and she lowered herself into the nearest chair. "He shouldn't have said that."

Her father took up the chair Aunt Lulu

407

had been in minutes earlier, his big frame awkward in the smaller seat. "Someone needed to point out what should have been obvious."

Nicole glanced down at her hands. "I don't know what to say." And she was rarely at a complete loss for words.

He paused, clearly as uncomfortable as she was. "Your mother and I aren't affectionate with each other," he finally said, surprising Nicole yet again. "It shouldn't be a surprise to me that I didn't know what to do with children. Two girls, no less, and one with a mental disorder. And your mother is not exactly the maternal type."

"You can say that again." If he could state the truth, Nicole wasn't about to hide her feelings. "She told me I was a disappointment." She choked on the word and averted her gaze, embarrassed to show emotion in front of him.

"I'm sorry. From both of us. I realize that doesn't change anything, but at least you know I'm aware now. And that's why when Robert asked me to back him up and help him out of this mess, I refused."

"He betrayed your trust and was using the business to launder money. Of course you wouldn't help him."

"No. I can't say I'm that honorable. If

he'd managed to pull us out of the recession mess we were in without getting caught, I might have turned a blind eye." Her father's cheeks flushed a ruddy color. "But to threaten you because of it? Robert crossed a line that's unacceptable. I don't care if I have to start over from scratch. I want him to pay."

Her father had defended her? Gone to bat for her? Nicole blinked back tears. "I matter to you?" she asked, hating that she sounded like a pathetic little girl seeking her daddy's approval, even if that was exactly what she was.

The child who'd never gotten what she needed. Not when she made honor roll every semester. Not when she'd graduated cum laude from college. Not ever.

Until now.

Her father reached out and — awkwardly — placed his hand over hers. "You matter, Nicole. You and Victoria both do."

She didn't know how badly she'd needed to hear those words until her father said them. She wiped at the tears with the back of her hand.

"Now I want you to do something for me," he said, ignoring her show of emotion.

"What's that?"

"Find a man who deserves you. Someone

warm and caring. Someone *not* like me." His lips turned up again in a self-deprecating way.

She managed a laugh.

"Someone like that detective of yours."

She blushed, unable to answer.

Her father wasn't expecting a reply. He rose from his chair, pulling his jacket back onto his shoulders, and started for the door.

He grasped the doorknob and paused. "Nicole?"

"Yes?"

He cleared his throat. "You've done a wonderful job with this place."

She blinked hard. So many surprises from him, she couldn't take them all in. "I . . . Thank you," she said, to his retreating back as he shut the door behind him.

Macy lived in a garden apartment, a low-rise set of buildings near The Family Restaurant. She loved the location, so close to work, and she also liked being surrounded by people. Her neighbors were composed of a mix of people her own age, married couples, and older folks who'd chosen to downsize from their homes. Macy, being Macy, was friendly with them all, and today was the day she normally checked on her next-door neighbor, Monique Tamm, a recent widow.

Yesterday Macy had picked up sticky buns, Monique's favorite, so she could drop by for a cup of tea and a chat. She didn't know why, but she found it easy to talk to people of all ages and always had, which was why her family had designated her hostess, not waitress, from early on.

She and Monique lived on the ground floor, the last two units near the end of the hall, which had the same apartment layout. Their kitchen windows overlooked the parking lot, which, despite its nature, was surrounded by beautiful flowers and trees. The backyard gave them each a view of a man-made lake.

She brought her bakery box with the brightly colored Lulu and Nic's insignia and knocked. Monique opened the door. Her dark hair with no gray was pulled back in a sleek bun; she had a warm smile on her face and Macy was happy to see her looking relaxed and more at peace than she'd been in a while.

A few minutes later, they settled around the kitchen table, and Macy was drinking the most delicious chamomile tea. As usual, conversation drifted from town gossip to Monique's past. Today she focused on her early dating days with her husband.

Macy couldn't imagine losing someone you loved so much, but at least Monique had had over forty-five years. She wasn't ready to see anyone else, but she was open to the idea of companionship of a sort. Other people, like Macy's aunt, never got over a loss and compensated in other ways, but Macy suspected her aunt was still lonely and often wished Lulu would find herself a nice man. But she preferred to be alone.

Macy didn't feel the same way. She was getting tired of her own company. Her friends were slowly but surely marrying and moving on with their lives. And though she'd fallen for Tyler, she knew her feelings had to be superficial at best. After all, she hadn't spent all that much time with him, so how well could she really know him?

The problem was, what she did know, she liked a lot. Putting his distinguished good looks aside, he was loyal to people he cared about, a good quality even if she was admittedly jealous of the way he looked out for Nicole. He was funny even when he didn't realize it or mean to be, and she appreciated a man with a sense of humor. He clearly had a strong sense of right and wrong, if his current situation was anything to go by. And when he focused on her, he looked at her as if there weren't anyplace else in the world he'd rather be.

The problem was, moments like that were few and far between. She didn't want to hold his problems against him, or the fact that his ex-fiancée was entangled in them too. She just wanted to come first with a man, and until that time, she felt she'd had no choice but to send him away.

"My goodness, you're a million miles away this morning," Monique said, snapping her fingers in front of Macy's face at the same time.

She blinked, startled and flushed. "I'm sorry. My mind was elsewhere, and that was rude of me."

"Nonsense. You're probably bored by the stories I tell you about Charles and our courtship."

Macy smiled. "No way. I love to hear you reminisce. Honestly."

"Well, I appreciate the time you give me. Is there anything I can do for you?" Monique asked.

Macy shook her head. She wrapped her hand around the delicate teacup, absorbing its warmth. "No. Maybe." She laughed. "It's just that I met a guy and I thought we could have something special, but . . . a lot of time has passed and I think maybe he's not really interested."

413

She remembered seeing him at Nicole's, the embarrassment she'd felt at his being in town and not coming to see her. Her face flushed at the memory.

"Well, his loss." Monique patted her hand. "Oh! Are you expecting a delivery?" she asked, her gaze focused out the window over the parking lot.

"No. Why?"

"There's a gentleman walking up the path toward our units with a large wrapped package. It looks like a painting."

Macy rose and walked to the window over the sink. She looked out and gasped.

"What's wrong?" Monique asked, coming up behind her.

"Not wrong, very very right," Macy said, her stomach suddenly in nervous knots. "That's *him,*" she whispered.

"Ah," Monique said, her voice lifting in understanding. "You should go, then."

Macy turned to her and pulled her into a warm embrace. "Thanks for understanding."

She ran for the door, making it to the outside walkway just as Tyler reached up and rang her doorbell. "Looking for me?" she asked, breathless and not from the short sprint into the hall.

He turned, leveling those green eyes her

way. "Hi," he said.

"Hi yourself. What are you doing here?" She rocked on her feet, nervous and happy at the same time.

He rested the package wrapped in brown paper against the wall.

She took a minute to drink him in. His sandy brown hair was combed and lightly gelled; he was clean shaven and wore a pair of tan slacks and a light blue short-sleeved collared shirt. Typical Tyler; he looked every inch the groomed and well-styled man she'd fallen hard for. The only thing different was the nervous glint in his eyes and the uncertain expression on his handsome face.

"You said not to come back until I was free of everything."

Clasping her hands behind her back, she merely nodded, waiting.

She wouldn't have thought she'd want a man to beg for her, but after the way he'd taken off after Nicole, leaving her alone at the art show, she realized she needed him to wonder where she stood. To work to prove himself to her. For her.

What she wouldn't tell him was that he'd won her over by showing up with whatever was beneath the wrapping. She had a hunch she already knew — which meant despite running after Nicole, he'd paid attention to *her.*

"Well, I am. Free of Nicole, my past, the family business and expectations . . . all of it."

As he spoke, her heart lightened . . . a lot. So much that she knew that at this moment, her life just might be doing a one-eighty.

He drew a deep breath. "And so I'm here. Bearing gifts." He grinned. "Or should I say a gift?"

Tyler looked into her bright blue eyes and waited . . . waited . . . and then she gave it to him.

She returned his smile with the first open, honest one he'd seen. "Come on in," she said.

He followed her into her home for the first time. He took in the wild splash of colors, vibrant and alive, and laughed. "This place suits you."

"Yeah? You don't think it's . . . gaudy?"

She folded her arms across her chest, a defensive gesture he couldn't mistake. "Umm, no. If I thought it was gaudy, I wouldn't have said it suits you." He stepped closer and grasped her shoulders. "You, Macy Donovan, are not gaudy. You're outspoken, honest, you don't take crap from anyone, and you're real. Added to that, you're beautiful. You were it for me from the moment I laid eyes on you."

Her eyes opened wide. "But you were still chasing after Nicole then."

He wanted to forget all about Nicole. Hell, he already had. She was his friend, nothing more, but he owed it to Macy to explain.

"I think I told you before . . . Nicole and I were always good friends. When I look back now, I believe we were doing the right thing by getting married. Making everyone happy."

"Were you? Happy?" she asked.

Honest, he reminded himself. "I thought I was."

She tipped her head to one side. "But?"

"She broke up with me and I ran after her, but that wasn't about love. That was about family. Safety. And it's over. From here on out, it's all about you." He ripped the paper off the landscape; he'd gone to great pains to first find the artist, then acquire it.

A soft sigh escaped her lips. "You really were paying attention to me."

"Every minute, even if I did have to run off. Which I handled badly, by the way. I'm sorry."

Her eyes blazed brighter. "I don't want

your apology."

"You don't."

"Nope."

"Then what do you want?"

She walked toward him, placing her arms around his neck. "I want you."

"You have me," he said in a gruff voice he barely recognized. Then he did what he'd wanted to do since the moment they'd met. What he'd only done once, and it wasn't nearly enough.

He kissed her.

EIGHTEEN

When Sam told Mike to go after Cara, he'd been so sure of his advice, *Go big or go home.* Mike had had a point to make: that he wasn't leaving Serendipity or Cara, and most importantly, that he'd changed and wanted to put down roots. So Mike had purchased a house and an engagement ring and gotten his girl. Sam didn't see his situation with Nicole the same way. He was here, he wasn't going anywhere, and she'd shown him what it meant to fall in love. For Sam, it was simple. Except she didn't believe he loved her, and he didn't know what to do in order to convince her he meant what he said.

Frustrated and not in the mood to be alone in his house, wondering what Nicole was doing next door, he drove over to his parents'. He found his mom working outside on her hands and knees in one of the flower beds.

He parked in the driveway and joined her, kneeling down by her side. "Hi, Mom."

"Sam! I'd hug you but my gloves are covered with dirt." Her eyes, so similar to his, lit up as she met his gaze. "What are you doing here?"

"Can't I just come to visit?"

"I suppose you could." She eyed him warily. "If you didn't have that lost-little-boy expression I remember from . . . the time we don't discuss," she said, her voice trailing off.

He shook his head, amazed at how stupidly stubborn he'd been about a woman and a time long past. "You can talk about Jenna," he told his mother.

She stripped her gloves off her hands. "Help me up."

Sam rose to his feet and helped his mother do the same.

"Let's go sit."

He followed her to the front steps and they sat down on the top one. It reminded him of when he and his siblings were in elementary school and they would all wait here for the bus to pick them up. His mother had always been there, day in and day out. He doubted Nicole could say the same.

"What's on your mind?" his mother asked him.

He rested his hands between his legs and groaned. "I blew it with Nicole."

His mother looked up at him. "It can't be that bad. What did you do?"

"From the beginning, I told her I didn't want a serious relationship and never would. So by the time I took my head out of my . . . you know . . . and told her I loved her, she didn't believe me."

Her eyes took on that sad, disappointed look he hated. "Oh, Sam."

He looked up at his mother, feeling like a naughty child about to be scolded.

"I could kill that girl for what she did to you. Jenna should have ended things way before you two got to the altar." Ella shook her head. "And afterward, I never could figure out how to make you see there was something wrong with her and not you."

He lifted his gaze toward the afternoon sun. "You know, I wish I'd gotten over myself sooner, but there was no reason. No one who affected me enough to make me want to stop —"

"Feeling sorry for yourself?" his mother asked with a gentle laugh.

His face heated with embarrassment, but she was right. "I can't change the past, but

I want to convince Nicole for the future. But she wasn't raised by warm, loving parents. She doesn't have reasons to trust or believe what I say." He shrugged. "And I took so long to come around, I don't blame her."

His mother pulled him into a quick hug. "Gone are the days when milk and cookies hold all the answers."

Sam laughed. "I figured maybe you'd have some words of wisdom."

"I'm thinking you might not need any," she said as a white Mercedes pulled up to the curb.

Nicole's white Mercedes. He knew she'd gotten the car back from the repair shop, having followed up without telling her.

At the sight, Sam's breath caught in his throat.

"Something tells me she's not here to see me." Ella rose to her feet, and Sam did the same. "I'm going to make myself scarce," his mother said.

Waving to Nicole as she climbed out of the car, Ella walked down the bluestone path to enter the house through the open garage. When she worked on her flowers, she used the mudroom entrance so she didn't track dirt inside.

Hands in his shorts pockets, heart pounding, Sam walked to the driveway, waiting for Nicole near his car.

She strode up to him, wearing a white skirt and soft yellow tank. He itched to hold her, to take her in his arms and feel her soft curves against him and know all was right in his world again.

He didn't know what she was doing here, and he didn't want to spook her by pushing too fast. Her skin was pale from the hours spent inside working; her eyes were wary. He hated that look, never wanted her to feel unsure with him.

"Hi," she said softly.

"Hi."

She bit down on her lower lip, her uncertainty showing. "You're a hard man to track down."

"Not if you know where to look. And obviously you did." He grinned, liking that she'd known how to locate him.

"Your house, the police station, Joe's . . . this was my final stop."

"Well, now that you found me, what can I do for you?"

She drew a deep breath, blowing it out again before beginning. "I wanted to tell you I'm sorry. I realize I wasn't fair to you. You stood by me, you told me you loved me, and I turned my back on you." Her eyes were bright and glassy, self-recrimination obvious in her expression.

"Nic—"

She shook her head. "I need to say these things and you need to let me. Please."

He nodded, hurting for her. "Go on."

"You never gave me mixed signals. You weren't ready for a relationship and I knew that. I was the one who changed the rules midway through. I realized I couldn't have sex without getting emotionally involved with you. I . . . I fell in love. And even when I told you, I didn't expect you to say it back. Of course I wished you had." An embarrassed smile pulled at her lips.

He was dying to end this speech with a kiss, but she needed to have her say.

"And when you finally did, I pushed you away because I was so embarrassed by the things you heard my parents say. My father was bad enough, he was cold and aloof, but my mother? She belittled me and trashed me until all I could think about was, why would you want me after hearing all that?"

His fingers curled into tight fists as he fought with himself to give her the space she'd asked for to say her piece, but he lost the battle and stepped close, pulling her hard against him. "You don't need to explain."

She relaxed, her soft curves molding and curling against him until she was in his arms where she belonged.

"I need to finish this, okay?"

"Okay." He loosened his hold and she eased back, looking up at him with bright shiny eyes.

"I told myself that since you had one foot out the door from the beginning, I should protect myself now, because it was only a matter of time until you were gone. I thought my mother's words pushed you the rest of the way." She pursed her lips at the memory.

He winced, knowing he'd given her cause to feel that way.

"I just . . . I was so devastated by my mother's words that I couldn't believe you loved me like you said you did. But you didn't give up. You picked me up for my opening, and kept visiting. You sent my favorite flowers even when I didn't let myself acknowledge what they meant. And then my father came to visit."

Sam reared back at that. "If he hurt you again —"

She shook her head. "Just the opposite, in fact. He said he refused to help Tyler's father out because of what he'd done to me. Sending the Russians after me." She drew a deep breath. "And he told me I matter. And he said it because *you* stood up to him. You essentially told him he was a shitty parent, and in doing that, you told me that *I* matter to *you*."

She sniffed, wiping at her damp eyes, and laughed at herself. "I'm a mess. But the point is, I should have believed in you way before I finally did."

"Are you finished?" he asked. "Because I have something to say."

She smiled, lighting him up inside. "Yeah, I'll be quiet now."

He grasped her hand in his. "You didn't believe in me because I didn't give you a reason before. But I swear to you, I'll never give you cause to doubt me again."

Nicole had learned a hard lesson, letting her parents and insecurities dictate her emotions. "I've been miserable without you. Even my grand opening lacked the luster it should have had."

"I missed you too. But I'm so damned proud of what you accomplished." He grinned, and all the remaining tension fled her body.

"I'm pretty proud too. I guess I had a minor glitch in my programming," she said, embarrassed at how badly her parents had gotten to her. "I'm used to not getting much from them, but having the man I love witness it?" She shuddered.

"It's over. And if they want to see you after this, they're on their best behavior or they can stay home."

She brushed her fingers over his cheek. "Because I have my very own cop . . . I mean *detective* to protect me."

"You're damned right." Taking her off guard, he swept her up and into his arms, a place she hadn't been in too long.

She squealed. "What are you doing?" She glanced around but they were still alone, nobody watching.

"Taking you home with me where you belong. We'll take this year and enjoy, but afterward? We'll reevaluate that lease on the house, because I'm not keeping separate places longer than I have to."

She laughed. "I like that you're doing long-term planning."

"Baby, with you, I'm planning on forever."

Her heartbeat thudded hard in her chest, his words giving her the comfort and security she'd always craved along with the bonus of love and passion thrown into the mix.

She just had one lingering question. "Sam? Are you sure your family will accept all of me? I mean, Victoria's locked up for the foreseeable future, but someday . . ."

His eyes took on a determined glint. "She's your twin. If she gets well and healthy and is released, she's family. Somehow we'll make it work."

She closed her eyes, wondering what she'd done to deserve this special man. She sighed with happiness and nuzzled her cheek against his. "I missed this," she whispered. "I missed you."

"I love you, Nicole." He shifted her, reaching into his pocket so he could grab his keys and unlock his truck. "And now I'm taking you home to show you how much. We'll get your car later."

She laughed as he walked around to the passenger side so she could get in. "I like how you think, Detective. You're perfect for me."

"We're perfect," he said with a grin. "Perfect together." He grinned and slid his lips over hers in a kiss that teased her with things to come.

A long, happy future of many, many wonderful things.